By

A.M .Westerling

ISBN: 978-1-77145-022-5

PUBLISHED BY:

Books We Love Ltd.
Chestermere, Alberta
Canada

http://bookswelove.net

Dedication

To my boys.

Acknowledgements

A big thank you to my fun and fabulous critique partners, Victoria Chatham and M.K. Stelmack. Also, thank you to the helpful staff at the About Bristol website.

Mary Ann,

enjoy!

astrid :)

aka

a.m. westerling

Prologue
London – 1798

The instant the Duke of Cranston staggered slack-jawed and glassy-eyed into the Eversleigh's ballroom, Lady Josceline Woodsby knew the evening would turn into utter disaster.

A disaster which would doubtless encompass her, for the obviously inebriated Duke was her father. She licked her suddenly dry lips.

Shocked silence descended as he, swaying on unsteady legs, surveyed the gathering with an unfocused gaze. His moth-eaten wig sat askew, his black evening jacket was wrinkled and stained, and his boots sorely needed polishing. In short, Lord Peter Cranston, her once distinguished, once proud father, had degenerated into a pathetic caricature of his former self.

A guffaw split the silence. Already she could see the craned necks, the bowed heads whispering behind raised fans, the callous looks cast first her way, then to her father, then back to her. The titters and whispering started.

Heat engulfed her face clear into her scalp. Surely this nightmarish scene was not happening. She glanced sideways and caught the sympathetic gaze of her dearest friend, Lady Elizabeth Watson.

"Josceline! Daughter!" bellowed the duke although the words were so slurred it came out more as "Jozzlin! Dodder!" which almost suggested he was ordering her to wobble about the dance floor. An order she might find grimly amusing another time but not here, not now.

The titters and whispers grew louder.

Her heart pounded with shame and it rattled against her ribcage like a dice in a cup. Tonight's invitation had been addressed to her alone. How had her father known she was here? Perhaps Mrs. Smeets, the housekeeper who doubled as her maid, had told him. If so, she would be sure to have a word with the woman reminding her that discretion was the time-honored trait of a lady's maid.

Josceline glanced at her friend again. "And there you have," she whispered through lips stiffened into a false smile, "the sole reason I shall never marry. After this display, I will surely be blackballed."

Elizabeth leaned over and laid a plump hand on Josceline's arm. "Don't jump to hasty conclusions," she consoled. "The high Season is still a few months away."

Then Josceline saw the portly, unkempt figure following her father; her heart subsequently plummeted to her stomach where it hammered a ferocious cadence against the creamed chicken she had consumed at dinner.

Mr. Thomas Burrows. Mr. Burrows, the wealthy merchant who, in a bid to marry into a titled family, chose to overlook Lord Cranston's sullied reputation to gain the hand of his only daughter. The same Mr. Burrows who now leered at her in far too suggestive of a manner. Her skin crawled.

From the corner of her eye, she noticed the imposing figure of Lady Eversleigh steaming towards her. Josceline groaned. She had no idea her father would show up uninvited and her hostess would likely not believe her. She braced herself for a verbal barrage.

But no, Lady Eversleigh merely gave Josceline a withering glare as she passed by to advance towards the unwelcome guests. With feathers bobbing and bosom heaving, she gestured frantically to several liveried footmen to remove the men in a desperate bid to save the evening from degenerating into mayhem.

As the guests' attention was diverted to the entertaining spectacle of burly footmen tumbling the two out the door, Josceline slumped into her seat and wiped an unsteady hand across her damp forehead. She tucked her feet beneath her chair to hide the well worn heels of her slippers and neatly pulled her skirts over her legs before smoothing clammy palms over the blue silk. She eyed the lace trimmed hem ruefully. Elizabeth had leant Josceline the gown and she could only hope no one would remember her friend wore it to the opening assembly of Almack's last year. It would fuel the gossiping tongues even more.

She lifted her head and scanned the crush of bodies in the flower bedecked room. Lady Eversleigh's intervention had been successful - the glow from candle-lit chandeliers spilled a golden aura over the whirling couples on the dance floor. Couples. All happy couples. She looked away, blinking back tears.

"This evening's events will fade soon enough." Elizabeth's calm voice penetrated Josceline's misery. "You know how fickle the ton is when it comes to scandal and tittle tattle. By next week this will all be forgotten."

"I know." Josceline sighed. "It is just so difficult to attend these events when one's father is a pariah. All I want is a decent man to love me. Me, Josceline, not Lord Cranston's daughter." She turned to Elizabeth. "It seems no men of my social standing can overlook my father's unsavory reputation and sizeable debts, not even for the chance to marry the daughter of a duke. Plus I am now three and twenty, more than a few years removed from the debutantes coming out this season."

"Shallow fools the lot of them," declared Elizabeth stoutly.

"Now my father has decided I am to marry Mr. Burrows." She shuddered at the remembrance of the man's leering gaze. "After this evening's embarrassment, the last thing I wish to do is obey my father. Particularly by marrying that odious man."

"Marriage is what is expected of us." Elizabeth tapped Josceline's arm with her fan and regarded her friend with an earnest gaze. "But it's not the only solution."

"No, it's not the only solution," Josceline agreed reluctantly. "I could be a seamstress but-," she held out her hands, displaying several pin pricked fingers. "I fear sewing is not a strength." She dropped her hands to her lap. "I could become a companion or lady's maid but no one would hire the daughter of a dishonored duke."

"You have always been clever in the school room, much more clever than I ever was. You could teach. Or become a governess." Elizabeth sat back with a satisfied expression on her round face. "A governess. That's it. That's what you could do."

"Yes, I have considered that but it still leaves me with the same problem. Who would hire me?"

"Mama mentioned to me just this morning that her cousin, Lady Oakland, is in need of a good governess." Elizabeth squeezed Josceline's hand. "I shall speak to her about it. With my mama's blessing, they shall doubtless find you more than acceptable. Besides-." She leaned over to whisper in Josceline's ear. "They live west of London, almost on the coast. Far enough away, surely, that no word of your father's scandal shall follow you."

Josceline leaned her head against the wall behind her. A governess. She quite liked the idea. Working as a governess would give her the dignity of earning her own way. And leaving London would take her far from wagging tongues and her father's desire to give her hand to the highest bidder. Yes, a governess in a country estate would do quite nicely.

She'd contemplated it before but hadn't thought it possible. But with the help of Elizabeth and her mama it could happen. Her papa would not be happy with her choice but it was her life to do with as she wished.

Mistress of her own destiny. How pleasing, and yes, how daring.

Now that would give the tongues something to wag about.

Chapter One

Clifton Hotel, Bristol, England
Two weeks later

"I believe," drawled Christopher Sharrington, "the final trick is mine." He placed his card on the ebony inlaid table with calm deliberation and raised his gaze to his opponent. "Preposterous," sputtered Lord Oliver Candel. "I accuse you of foul play." He clutched the edge of the table with soft, pudgy fists and half stood, leaning towards Christopher. Disdain lifted one corner of his full-lipped mouth; scorn glittered in his watery blue eyes.

"Foul play?" Christopher swept his arm around the dimly lit room, encompassing the small crowd gathered around watching. "These gentlemen will attest to the fact no foul play was involved." He scanned the faces around them but all evaded his gaze, one bystander even going so far as to blatantly inspect his fingernails.

Candel caught the slight motion. "You see," he taunted. "You are nothing but a commoner. None shall stand for you."

Damnation, the man was right. Well, if no one would support him, then he would continue on alone.

"The wager is won by me. Fairly." Christopher reached out to grab the parchment sheet laid on the table between them like a marker in a battlefield. However, before he could reach it, Candel snatched it up and bolted from the room.

Stunned at the man's impudence, Christopher sat for several minutes, struggling for breath against the white hot anger crushing against his chest.

Again. Yet again, he had been snubbed by the upper class. It had happened countless times as a growing lad. And now this evening too. First, by the witnesses to this evening's game and then with his opponent openly reneging on the wager placed.

Worst of all, the man had run off with the ship's deed that would have been the foundation for Christopher's future.

Only this time, he would not stand for it. This time, by whatever means necessary, he would retrieve what rightfully belonged to him.

* * *

Christopher slapped his hands together against the cold. Damnation, could Lord Candel not have chosen a less inclement night to travel? He pulled off a glove and rubbed his nose – he'd been waiting in the frigid air so long, it had lost all feeling. Had he perhaps missed the man? He shook his head. Of course not, from his vantage point on the hedge-ringed knoll and with the help of a feeble winter moon, he had a clear view of Bath Road beneath him.

Not for the first time, he strained his ears to catch sound of an approaching carriage, but there was nothing, only the metallic crunching of his favorite mount, Vesuvius, chomping the bit and an occasional equine snort spewing clouds of frosty breath about them both.

And not for the first time, he was beginning to doubt the wisdom of confronting Candel on a deserted, moonlit road. True, the man had stolen his winnings but perhaps a duel at dawn's light would have been better rather than the highwayman's gambit he was about to employ.

There was still time to back down, guide away his horse and gallop off into the night with nary anyone the wiser. But no, he admonished himself, Candel was a noted coward, well known for avoiding the dueling field at all costs. He was more likely to accede to Sharrington's demand for payment when delivered at gun point far from prying eyes. He patted the loaded pistol tucked into his waist. If need be, he had one shot.

The horse perked its ears and turned its head to the road below. After a few seconds, Christopher heard it as well: the jingle of the harness and the thud of hoof beats against the frozen ruts, the creak of a coach and the "geeup" of the coachman. He watched the coach approach, noting the slightly slumped form of the driver – drowsing, no doubt. He also noted the absence of footmen - he might have reconsidered if he had more than the driver to contend with. Luck was with him, then.

A thrill of anticipation coursed through his chest as he swung into the saddle.. At last he would receive what was due to him. He dug his heels into his horse's flanks and man and beast thundered down the hill to burst through the hedge like avenging marauders.

Heading straight towards the carriage, pistol waving in the air, great coat flapping about his thighs, he pulled up the horse at the last possible moment and leapt off.

"Halt!" His voice sliced through the crisp air. "Candel, I know you're inside. I want what is mine."

The carriage stopped within scant feet of him, the coachman pulling so hard on the reins, the front pair reared and stumbled back, almost upsetting the carriage, causing the front lantern to swing crazily. The driver wound the reins about the rail then raised his gnarled hands. "I ain't armed," he whined. "This road be patrolled regularly."

"I'm not the slightest bit interested in you and your sorry skin," Christopher snarled. "I am acquainted with your passenger and wish to speak to him. This road is patrolled, so this shan't take a moment." He held out his free hand. "Give me the lantern."

With a mutter, the coachman unhooked the lantern, swinging it down to jam it into Christopher's open hand with a surly "'ere." Christopher almost gagged at the gin fumes as the man leaned closer. A sorry excuse for a coachman – how ever did he keep his position?

Holding high the lantern, he stalked to the door of the carriage. He rapped the pistol muzzle on the scarred wood, certain the rat-a-tat-tat would echo inside with enough ferocity to scare the occupant into compliance. "Lord Candel, come out and face me like a man. I demand the note I won from you tonight."

There was no answer. With a muffled oath, Christopher jammed the pistol into his waistband and flung open the door. Leaning forward, he maneuvered the lantern so he could peer into the gloom of the carriage. He swiveled his head to the front squabs. Even in the dim lantern light, he could see the empty seat was lumpy, velvet worn bare through years of use. He frowned. The worn fabric, coupled with the shabby exterior, set off warning bells – a dandy like Candel would never deign to ride in such a decrepit vehicle.

He swiveled his head the other way to inspect the rear squabs, his eyes widening in surprise when he spied the lone passenger, a young woman.

From beneath a frippery of fur and grosgrain ribbon that could scarcely be called a bonnet, a pair of green eyes fringed with the longest black lashes he had ever seen glared at him. Her face was pale with fright and a scrape on her temple oozed blood, yet her chin was lifted, the lush lips firmly set. He admired her display of bravado - she may be apprehensive but she did not show it.

His eyes dropped to inspect the rest of her but there was naught to be seen, buried beneath a moth-eaten heavy woolen mantle as she was.

Damnation, Candel must have been delayed. Christopher clenched his teeth at the unfortunate turn of events.

He'd stopped the wrong carriage.

Chapter Two

"I haven't the faintest idea what you are talking about." A melodious female voice flowed over him. The cultured tones surprised him – they were at odds with the state of the carriage, both inside and out. Furthermore, now that he had a chance to inspect her more closely, even her bonnet had seen better days. Obviously a lady of the upper class but one who had been beset by hard times.

"I am in a hurry." She spoke again, gaze snapping impatience, voice dripping with anger. "As you can see," she pulled one slender arm free from the mantel and swept it about, "Lord Candel is not here. Now if you would be so kind as to step aside and let us on our way? My coachman found it too agreeable at the last posting inn and consequently I'm late for an important engagement. And you, sir, are merely aggravating the situation. Please step away immediately."

Christopher could not resist the challenge issued by her eyes. "And if I do not?" He deliberately made his voice lazy, wanting to see her reaction to his insolence.

"Then I shall contact the authorities and accuse you of attempted abduction," she replied crisply and with an air of authority reminding him somewhat of Mr. Smithson, his tutor. Mr. Smithson, too, had issued orders expecting full compliance at all times. An expectation he had disregarded on many occasions, much to the chagrin of his mother.

The young woman waited expectantly for his answer and he wondered at her calm demeanor over her current predicament. Most females of his acquaintance would swoon in such circumstances.

"Don't I frighten you?" He narrowed his eyes. Perhaps her anger had blinded her to the potential danger.

She leaned forward and tapped him on his chest. "No, sir, you don't. What does frighten me is the opportunity I shall lose if I do not make my engagement. Please, kindly remove yourself from this carriage or as I mentioned already, I shall report you to the proper authorities." She settled back against the squabs, ignoring him while pulling the blanket up to her chin as if that alone was sufficient to make him leave.

"Go ahead." Christopher shrugged. "You have no idea who I am." Quite frankly, he doubted many of the ton knew who he was – a situation he meant to change soon.

"Ah, but I do know of Lord Candel. I'm certain a persuasive letter should bring forth the information I need." She lifted her chin and glared at him anew, eyes gleaming with annoyance.

He stifled a smile. Aye, she had a temper to match the russet curls pulled back from her face.

A single drop of blood rolled down her temple. She swiped at it with one gloved finger and stared at it in surprise. "Oh my," she whispered then lifted her eyes to gaze at him accusingly. "This is thanks to you, I suppose. I bumped my head when you stopped us. Perhaps I should add assault to the charges." She frowned, her lips turning down in such an appealing way he had to quell the sudden urge to kiss them right side up. A wave of contrition rolled over him and he fumbled in his chest pocket for his handkerchief, handing it out to her.

"Thank you." She took it and scrunched it into her fist.

Christopher's scalp prickled at the sound of approaching hoof beats. He must be off. The young woman was right. Mistaken or not, he had unlawfully stopped her carriage during a time of night normally reserved for thieves and footpads.

"I must beg pardon." He bowed slightly and placed the lantern on the floor at her feet. "It appears I stopped the wrong carriage." He didn't really believe she could influence the authorities but he would heed her threat and tread carefully for now. Besides, it was Lord Candel he wanted, not this threadbare young woman, no matter how alluring.

She snorted. "Indeed."

He tipped his hat then slammed shut the door with such force the tipsy coachman leaned over on one arm to peer down at him with astonished eyes from his driver's perch.

"The lantern's inside," Christopher ordered. "And the lady is late for her appointment so it best behooves you to be on your way."

And with that, a disgusted Christopher Sharrington leapt on Vesuvius and galloped away. A wasted endeavor this had turned out to be – he was no closer to retrieving his winnings.

Then he remembered she had said she knew Lord Candel. If so, it was conceivable she could find him, Christopher, through Candel. Another reason to hate the man although who knew whether or not she would follow through on her threat.

He could only hope not.

* * *

Heart pounding at her audacity, a bemused Josceline sagged against the seat, clutching the handkerchief. It was still warm from where it had lain against the man's chest, and soft, made of the finest lawn and embroidered with presumably his name. It almost seemed a shame to use it but she could scarce arrive at her destination with a bloodied face. Besides, a handkerchief could be washed.

She dabbed at her temple, wincing slightly then tucked the bloodied handkerchief into her sleeve.

"Oh my. I just ordered a highwayman from my carriage," she breathed, gaze pinned to the door where he had stood scant seconds before.

The enormity of her actions dawned on her and she began to shiver, great, wrenching shivers that crawled up her back and rattled her teeth. She must be cold, that was it. She grabbed the mantle and pulled it higher, over her nose, not even caring that the edge of it was greasy and frayed and it smelled of horse.

Luck was with her that the man had heeded her words and left. No, came the rueful realization, more likely he had taken one look at her and realized she had nothing. She pressed her lips together to stop them from trembling.

"Beggin' yer pardon, milady?" The driver rapped on the door and swung it open. "I needs me lantern. It be black as Satan's heart tonight." Without waiting for her answer, he reached in and grabbed it.

"Now you have your lantern, carry on to Oakland Grange, if you please." To her ears, her voice sounded boorish and she opened her mouth to apologize. Before she could, the coachman slammed shut the door with nary a comment, apparently well used to the vagaries of his passengers.

In a few seconds, the coach tilted and creaked as he climbed aboard and then came the slap of the reins and a croaky "geeup". The clip clop of hooves resumed, the rhythmic clatter renewing her anger of moments before.

Anger warmed her, spread its welcome heat into her chest and face. The entire journey had been a disaster. The mail coach had become stuck and the better part of yesterday had been lost freeing it. Then, after an uncomfortable night at the posting inn, the coachman she had engaged this morning to take her to Oakland Grange laughed in her face at her repeated orders to depart and had instead drank away most of the day with the money she had given him for the fare.

When they were finally underway, she realized the horses were old and swaybacked and could not go faster than a walk. The coach itself was ancient and did not even boast a foot warmer so she had caught a chill.

And just when the coachman had assured her "Milady, it be just a mile or two at most", they had been stopped by the highwayman.

Who did that rogue think he was, she fumed silently, to stop her coach, scaring her witless and then offering a clearly insincere apology.

In her mind's eye, she could see him: Tall, so tall he need not stand on the step to peer inside. Dark, so dark, his hair, worn long, blended into the night sky. His eyes, although she had not been able to make out the color - brown, she thought - had inspected her with an intensity that fair scoured her skin and she felt her cheeks warm at the remembrance. Couple all that with a firm, clean shaven chin and generous mouth and under different circumstances she would certainly describe him as handsome.

He didn't fit her idea of a highwayman at all. Highwaymen were a scruffy, disreputable lot - this man had been dressed in evening clothes beneath the unbuttoned great coat. Too, his handkerchief was of the finest fabric and richly embroidered – scarcely the accoutrement of a dissolute man.

Her heart beat faster at the memory of him; that angered her too, that the man, whoever he was, had caught her attention as if she was fresh from the school room.

At the thought of the school room, she remembered why she was in the coach in the first place. Therein lay the real root of her anger. She, who prided herself on her punctuality and through no fault of her own, would be late arriving for her new posting as governess to the children of Lord and Lady Oakland.

Certainly not the most auspicious start.

Chapter Three

Josceline stepped gingerly from the coach. Much to her surprise, every window in Oakland Grange glowed with candlelight. Had they been awaiting her arrival all this time? With frozen fingers, she managed to pull out the slim, gold pocket watch from where it hung around her neck and in the muted glow of the single oil lantern standing sentinel at the top of the crushed stone drive, checked the time.

Almost midnight. She slipped the watch back into her neckline and curled her fingers into her palms to warm them. Drawing a deep breath, she willed her shoulders to relax. Finally she was here. Her stomach grumbled reminding her it had been a long time since her last meal.

Then she spied the waiting carriages. Lord and Lady Oakland were entertaining this evening. Apparently her late arrival would not go unnoticed. Her heart sank.

"Yer bag." The coachman dropped it at her feet.

"Thank you." She nodded coolly. The man was a disgrace to his trade but to reproach him now would serve no purpose. She turned to face the front porch, picking up her carpet bag and gripping the handle tightly. It was heavy and bumped against her legs as she ascended the steps.

Behind her, the hack's wheels crunched down the drive, fading into nothing until all she heard was the rattle of bare branches in the wind.

She raised the polished brass knocker and let it fall. It hit with a frosty "clank", the sound echoing off the stone driveway.

Nothing. The door remained closed.

She tried again, lifting it and banging it a number of times. From inside, she heard the thump of footsteps and then a sharp "clack" as the bolt was drawn.

The massive door swung open. Framed in the light stood a rotund man - the butler, she supposed.

She hastened to introduce herself. "Lady Josceline Woodsby. Late of London. I've come for the position of governess to the children of Lord and Lady Oakland. My carriage was delayed -." She stopped at the disinterested look on the man's face. Best to save her explanation for her new employers.

"Come in. I am Howard, butler of Oakland Grange." He stood back and gestured. "I shall tell my lord you are here." He waddled off, swaying side to side like a carriage with broken springs.

Josceline moved into the foyer and dropped her bag on the Persian carpet that stretched from the doorway to the base of a mahogany staircase winding gracefully to the second floor.

Clasping her hands at her waist in a vain attempt to stem the butterflies, she looked about to get her bearings. In the shadows beyond the staircase stood a grandfather clock, its stately tick tock tick tock soothing her. She had nothing to fear, she chided herself. Elizabeth's mama had assured Josceline the position belonged to her.

She moved forward a step or two. To her left hung a large portrait of a man dressed in forest green on a beautiful bay hunter; to her right, an arched doorway opened into a salon – she could hear laughter and the tinkle of glass. A few notes sounded from a pianoforte and someone began to sing an aria from Mozart's "The Marriage of Figaro". It was one of her favorites and she began to hum along.

Not wishing to peer in and risk appearing rude, she chose to study the portrait. A throat cleared behind her, a masculine grunt. She whirled about, nerves churning anew.

A tall, thin, blonde-haired man in black evening clothes inspected her through a tortoise shell lorgnette. "Lady Woodsby? I am Lord Oakland."

"Yes." She curtsied. "I am sorry I am late."

"The position is no longer available. It has already been filled." A disdainful Lord Oakland folded the handle of his lorgnette and tucked it into his pocket before looking down his nose at her.

"What?" Josceline's jaw dropped; gape mouthed she stared at the thin man before her.

"We expected you much earlier, yesterday, in fact."

Stunned, she finally remembered to close her mouth. This couldn't be. She opened her mouth again to question the man but he continued talking. She closed her mouth, waiting to hear the man's explanation.

"Yes, another candidate arrived this morning and Lady Oakland and I have engaged her services."

"There must be a mistake," Josceline replied crisply. This was not the time to be timid. She had not come this far to be cast off so easily. "Lady Watson informed me her good friend Lady Oakland had agreed to my posting."

"Be that as it may, the position is filled."

She pulled out her letters of reference and waved them in the air. "I have excellent references, Lord Oakland. I assure you I am tardy through no fault of my own."

The man shrugged. "I can hardly entrust the care of my precious children to someone who cannot even find her way in a timely manner."

"But how shall I return to London? My hack has left. I cannot leave."

"That, Lady Woodsby, is none of my concern. If you will excuse me, I have guests to attend to." His voice was cold; his eyes shards of ice. Clearly the man was through with her.

Josceline's head began to whirl. The long hours in the carriage, her hunger, and now the realization her position had disappeared, made her light headed.

The hawk-nosed face of Lord Oakland disappeared into a black mist.

* * *

Josceline awoke to the acrid odor of smelling salts. Struggling to remember where she was, she lay with her eyes closed while a babble of voices wafted over her. None of them were familiar. Where was she?

Memories returned in a waterfall surge. Oakland Grange. She was at Oakland Grange and Lord Oakland had just informed her she was no longer wanted as governess. Despair nibbled at her – failure had set in before she even had the chance to show her capabilities. She kept her eyes shut, certain if she opened them, tears would trickle down her cheeks.

"I say, Lord Oakland, the chit looks as if she has seen better days." A masculine voice floated from a distance.

"Indeed. Poor thing is in a dreadful state." A woman's voice. "Look at that hideous dress."

"All of you move aside if you please and let me see."

Josceline opened her eyes in time to see a well dressed mature woman kneel beside her. White feathers spilled from the woman's black hair, matching the feathers on the lace stole draped about her shoulders, which in turn matched her high waisted lace dress. In short, the very epitome of current London fashion. They may be in the country but by no means was it the backwater Josceline had supposed.

"My dear, I am Lady Oakland. And you must be Lady Josceline Woodsby." The woman picked up one of Josceline's hands and patted it. "I must apologize. When you didn't arrive as expected, we thought you had changed your mind so we employed a local woman. Pay no mind to my husband. You must stay here tonight. In the morning we shall set things to right." Lady Oakland's face showed concern; her grey eyes were sympathetic. She was not nearly the unfeeling monster her husband was.

Josceline blinked back tears at the woman's kindness. Surely it was all a misunderstanding. Surely the governess position would belong to her after all.

She nodded slowly and looked up past Lady Oakland to the circle of eight or so shadowed faces hanging over them like a strand of mismatched beads. Her gaze roamed slowly from face to face. An odd mix they were: two young women in identical dress, twins, obviously; an elderly woman dressed in mourning; several unattached men of varying ages; a middle-aged couple. She had thought perhaps she might recognize one or two from London seasons past but no, they were all strangers to her.

Only one man hung back, leaning against the doorjamb of the salon, arms crossed. It wasn't until he turned his head that she could clearly see his face.

She gasped in disbelief.

It was the highwayman.

At her gaze, he narrowed his eyes and lowered his chin, an almost imperceptible movement. Obviously, he recognized her.

"You!" She struggled to sit up, pulling at her skirts in a vain attempt to cover her ankles. "It was you!"

Her bonnet had been knocked askew when she had fallen and a ribbon dangled in her eye. One of the men offered her a helping hand and she clambered to her feet, nodding her thanks before adjusting her bonnet and pulling aside the offending ribbon.

It gave her time to think. It seemed unlikely a highwayman would travel in the Oakland's social circle. What was he doing here? Perhaps she was mistaken.

Again she looked at him. His eyes were pinned on her as if by his gaze alone he could stop her allegations. Without a doubt, it was the man who had stopped her carriage earlier tonight.

"Do you know Captain Sharrington?" Lady Oakland too had risen and now, clearly astonished, she stood beside Josceline. "He recently bought a nearby estate and this evening we are introducing him to our neighbors."

"I do not," declared Josceline. "We have met, however." She scowled, pinning her venom on him. His obstruction had caused her tardiness.

"No longer captain, I'm afraid. I've just resigned my position in the Royal Navy." Sharrington pulled away from the wall and straightened up. "And as much as I would like to claim acquaintance with the young woman, I am afraid we have not met before. I would not forget someone as enchanting as Lady Woodsby." A mocking smile hovered over his lips. Prove me wrong, he seemed to say.

Of course. He denied any knowledge of their earlier encounter. Reason fled at his sardonic manner; anger fueled her tongue.

"He is lying," she blurted. "Why, it is thanks to him I am late. He-." She stopped when she noticed the skeptical faces surrounding her. It was a case of her word against his. If anything, she had only succeeded in making herself appear deranged with her outburst. "I must beg pardon. It appears I am mistaken," she whispered, feeling the fool. Her knees shook with fatigue. "Is there somewhere I might sit?"

Lady Oakland took one look at her and waved the others back to the salon.

"Let us sit here a moment, shall we?" She took Josceline's arm and showed her to a horsehair armchair beneath the painting Josceline had examined earlier.

A grateful Josceline took the seat proffered her. "Please do not concern yourself for me. I shall be fine in a few moments. I swear, I was certain I had met Mr. Sharrington before." She clutched the arms of the chair, the stiff fabric pricking her fingers.

"An honest mistake." Lady Oakland patted Josceline's hand. "Join us in the salon when you feel ready."

At Josceline's nod, Lady Oakland turned and swept off, disappearing into the salon. Her voice drifted back to Josceline. "Agatha, oh Agatha, do sing more for us." Notes rippled again from the pianoforte, joined by a strong soprano voice. The tune was not familiar to Josceline and she listened for several moments, welcoming the distraction. The song ended, applause sounded, reminding her of her precarious situation.

The last thing she felt like was facing the party. Really, the only thing she felt like was finding a bed to fling herself upon and pulling the sheets up over her head. She had no position, she had no means to return to London and she had only succeeded in making herself look a fool with Lord and Lady Oakland with her accusation against one of their guests. They must be appalled.

Never mind that. The problem was what could she do now? The apparition of her father staggering into the Eversleigh's ballroom shimmered in her mind. To return home to London to face his ire and an unwanted marriage with Mr. Burrows did not sit well with her.

But if not that, then what?

* * *

Christopher could not believe the rotten luck.

Snagging a glass of port from the sideboard, he stalked past the twin sisters, ignoring their high pitched giggles when he inadvertently brushed against their skirts. Damnation, seeing Josceline had rattled him so much he had forgotten their names which meant he couldn't even mount a proper apology.

Instead he swept them an exaggerated bow which elicited another round of hysterical giggles. If the two were an example of the women of the upper crust, then he doubted very much the nobility would last beyond another generation or two. Which then raised the interesting question: Why was he trying so hard to ingratiate himself into that very echelon of society? He swirled the maroon liquid around in his glass, looking into it as if he could find the answer there.

He lowered himself into his seat, slouching against the high back. If he turned his head, he could see Lady Josceline Woodsby sitting beneath that dreadfully pompous portrait of his host. Her eyes were closed, her fingers pressed to her temples. Even from here, he could see her shoulders heave from time to time.

It was obvious she was distraught. That he might have something to do with it bothered him a little. She had looked to throttle him when he had denied their chance encounter but now she just looked miserable. However, what bothered him more was that he had waylaid her carriage. If anyone believed her story, his reputation would be in tatters before he even had a chance to construct a new life apart from the Navy.

No matter the cost, he could not, would not let that happen.

Chapter Four

From the relative quiet of the hall and the sanctuary of the horsehair chair, Josceline regarded Mr. Christopher Sharrington. He seemed at ease in his surroundings, seemed to enjoy his companions, chuckling heartily at the jests and even offering a few of his own. He clapped appreciatively when the musical performance ended and lavishly praised Lady Oakland on the pleasant evening. In short, a likeable guest. Almost too likeable, as if he was trying to be something he wasn't.

Her eyes narrowed. Quite simply, his likeable manner irked her. The way he lolled in the leather wingback chair irked her. The way he held his glass, the tilt of his head, the way he laughed, all of it irked her. How she longed to wipe the complacent expression from his face.

And now, after having had time to collect herself, she knew just how to do it. And, if she managed him properly, she would have a solution to her dilemma.

She rose and moved to the door of the crowded salon, waiting for a break in the conversation to catch his attention. While she waited, she glanced around the salon. It was a comfortable room, well meant for musical evenings for it was dominated by a pianoforte surrounded by a scattering of upholstered armchairs and benches. A fire flickered cheerily in the grate to her left; against one wall, a side board groaned with trays of sweets, mismatched crystal decanters filled with assorted cordials, and a large silver tea pot ringed by matching tea cups.

Josceline felt a sudden pang - it reminded her of convivial evenings at her parent's home, before Mama died. Regret fluttered through her breast – Oakland Grange would have been a lovely home in which to live and work. Apart from the icy Lord Oakland, that is.

At last Lady Oakland noticed Josceline and gestured to her; voices fell away one by one as the others saw her until only the crackle and snap of the fire filled the air. Josceline seized her opportunity.

"Mr. Sharrington? May I have a word with you?" Josceline ignored the surprised look on Lady Oakland's face, ignored the disapproving looks on the faces of the female guests, ignored the shocked silence.

Her actions were highly improper but she had no choice if she hoped to salvage something of the situation. Surely London was distant enough that word of her behavior would not find its way there. "You will all forgive me but I shan't take but a moment with him."

She folded her arms, squarely meeting his surprised gaze. One side of his mouth lifted slightly; a charcoal eyebrow quirked. As he hauled himself out of his seat, she turned and stepped away into the hall. In the surprised silence holding the salon, she heard his footsteps, unhurried yet firm. That annoyed her too – he clearly had no interest in what she had to say. Well, he would, she would see to that.

She waited for him beneath Lord Oakland's portrait, clutching the back of the horsehair chair. This time she welcomed the prickly fabric against her palms – it reminded her to keep her wits about her for certainly Mr. Christopher Sharrington would be no easy opponent.

"It was you," she hissed when he reached her. "And I have your handkerchief to prove it." She pulled it from her sleeve and waved it in front of his face. It was crumpled and splotched with dried blood. Her blood. "Now, Mr. Sharrington, you are going to help me or I shall show this to any and all of tonight's guests."

"And?" His face remained passive although a vein throbbed in one temple.

"And I will tell them you assaulted me and gave it to me to staunch the blood." She pointed to the scrape on her temple where she had hit her head. "This is fresh, anyone can see that."

"The roads are rough. You simply bumped your head when your carriage hit a rut." He pointed to her temple. "It's nothing a little plaster won't fix. I regret to inform you, Lady Woodsby, your misfortune is no concern of mine."

"I would suggest, Mr. Sharrington, it is indeed your concern." Again she held up the handkerchief. "I do believe your name is embroidered upon this."

"I am not the only man with the name of Sharrington." He crossed his arms. "You are sadly mistaken if you think I can do anything for you."

"And you are sadly mistaken if you think you can walk away and do nothing."

"It is your word against mine." A smile hovered over his lips.

The scoundrel enjoyed this. He had no right to find amusement at her peril. She scowled at him.

"Who will they believe? The Duke of Cranston's daughter who is also companion to the daughter of Lady Oakland's dear cousin? Or a commoner, a stranger newly arrived in the area?" She could see the words wounded him, for he flinched. She pressed her advantage and held up the handkerchief once more. "Are you going to help me? Or shall I announce to all and sundry that you are nothing but a highwayman masquerading as a gentleman? I am certain the local authorities would find that of the utmost interest."

A burst of laughter rolled through the salon door. The festivities had commenced again. The others apparently had so little regard for her, a genteel woman, that they had forgotten her and her predicament. The thought stung and she resolved more than ever to make Mr. Sharrington understand her situation. She would not return to London, even if it meant stooping to blackmail the man who had unwittingly stopped her carriage.

Deliberately she tucked the handkerchief back into her sleeve. It was the only proof she had of their meeting and she must take care with it.

She clasped her hands and waited for his answer.

* * *

Christopher gazed hard at Josceline. Damnation, she had a point. Her position in society gave her much more clout than he had at this moment. Furthermore, the slightest whiff of scandal would destroy any chance he had to become accepted into the local gentry.

"And supposing I agree? How do you propose I should help you?" He emphasized "help" – he really had no idea what she thought he could do for her.

"I wish to find employment as a governess." Her cool voice matched her steely eyes and he found himself admiring her boldness. A boldness which, unfortunately, involved him.

He shook his head and held up his hands. "I am newly quit from the Royal Navy. I have no knowledge of anyone in need of a governess."

She tilted her head. "No siblings? No cousins? Surely, Mr. Sharrington, you-."

"No," he interrupted her. Really, this was all too annoying. "I don't know anyone who needs a governess."

"Then, Mr. Sharrington, I suggest you concoct children of your own. Or a child. One will do. Or perhaps you would rather face the penalty? I do believe the punishment for highwaymen is to hang by the neck until dead." She flashed him a triumphant look. Top that, she seemed to say.

His mouth dropped open. Was she mad? A child. Did she have any idea what she had proposed? Not only did he despise children, being the noisy, smelly things they were, but having children implied having a wife. And a wife was something he did not want at this particular moment. Yet Lady Woodsby wanted him to invent a child. How did she think he would pull it off?

It was obvious she watched him, for she pointed to her sleeve.

Desperate, he searched his mind. What had he told his hosts? Would he be able to invent the existence of a child? He had to, he had no choice. The hangman's noose was not an appealing thought at all. Plus, it would be impossible to exact his revenge from the grave.

He nodded slowly, once, twice. "Very well."

"Your word." She demanded. "Give me your word you shall employ me as governess."

"You have my word." If he swallowed hard, he could feel the knot of the hangman's noose against his neck. Or perhaps it was the noose the very clever Lady Woodsby had placed that he could feel.

Either way, it unnerved him.

* * *

A very relieved Josceline followed Christopher into the salon. Her bluff had succeeded. He had no idea the Duke of Cranston was a laughing stock and consequently the accusations of his daughter would carry no weight. Truth be told, she had not been at all certain he would agree to her gambit but he had.

As much as she hated to admit it, she marveled at his aplomb. No doubt facing the specter of jail and most likely death had spurred him on.

It would be interesting to see the man make his explanations.

* * *

Christopher gritted his teeth and strolled over to Lady Oakland. "Perhaps I have a solution to Lady Woodsby's predicament. If it meets with your approval, of course." He turned back to look at Josceline. "I have engaged her services."

There. It was done, he couldn't back out now. Whether he wanted her or not, she was now in his employ.

"What? Er, that is, why, Mr. Sharrington, I had no idea you were in need of a governess." If Lady Oakland was surprised, she was too well bred to show it.

"Indeed I am," Christopher declared. "It would seem the misfortune of Lady Woodsby is my gain." He looked over to Josceline. "Lady Woodsby has agreed to fill the position. Immediately. If you would be so kind as to put her up for the night, I shall send my carriage for her first thing in the morning."

"Really, Mr. Sharrington? I had no idea you had children. And your wife? Will she approve?" The way Lady Oakland asked, Christopher knew she was skeptical.

Of course, gossip had accompanied his arrival in the area. His hostess knew he had no wife. And no children.

"Er, passed away some years ago. She died of consumption while I was at sea." The ease with which the fib passed his lips bolstered his confidence. “I have a young son. He lives in Bristol with my mother. I’ve been meaning to send for him once I got settled here.”

At least this was partly true. When his mother had been alive, she had indeed lived in Bristol. He could feel sweat lining his brow and he wiped it away with his fingers. He didn’t know why the untruths should bother him – they certainly weren’t the first ones he had told, nor, most likely, would they be the last.

“How very serendipitous.” Lady Oakland clasped her hands; the feathers in her hair quivered. “A happy solution all around. If you like I shall inform dear Lady Watson of the change.” She smiled warmly at Josceline who responded with a weak nod and strained smile.

The young woman’s tepid response surprised Christopher. Perhaps she was already having second thoughts on demanding a position with him. The thought reassured him for if so, it would mean she would want free of this tangle as much as he did. He wondered at her distaste of returning to London, a distaste so strong that she had forced a situation on them both.

For now, he would go along with the preposterous suggestion but only until he managed to regain his handkerchief, the only proof she had of their encounter. Then he would send the autocratic Lady Josceline Woodsby on her way.

Leaving him to happily continue with his neatly ordered, neatly planned life.

Chapter Five

Late the next morning, Josceline waited on the front steps while Christopher paid his respects to Lady Oakland. A winter sun shone through a break in the clouds. It teased Josceline, giving the illusion of warmth when, in reality, frost glittered on the shriveled branches of the trees lining the drive. She pulled up the hood on her cloak then tucked her hands into her sleeves.

Although chill, coal smoke did not foul the air as in London. Rather, the air was crisp, clean, and tinged with the faintest salt tang. She took an appreciative breath, enjoying the pinch of the cold air in her nostrils, feeling it roll all the way into her lungs. It was as if she could be cleansed from the inside out, making a new Josceline out of the old, drab Josceline.

Behind her, her new employer bid his adieu to Lady Oakland. In seconds he stood beside her, grasping her elbow.

"Come," he said and amid a flurry of goodbyes, he propelled her down the steps towards the waiting carriage. It was new, so new, in fact, that the metal spokes of the wheels gleamed and the glossy, black exterior caught the sun's weak rays. The vehicle bespoke of recent wealth and her threadbare bag, strapped to the back, was incongruously out of place.

As they walked, her arm tingled with the firmness of his grip and she glanced up at the stern profile. Her bravado disappeared in a poof.

What had possessed her to demand employment from him? The man had stopped her coach in the middle of the night. She knew naught of him, or of his background. She should run from him as fast as she could yet now she accompanied him to his home.

Because, she reminded herself, it meant she need not return to London. And surely Lady Oakland would have stepped in if she had any doubts as to the suitability of the man.

A cloud drifted over the sun and the landscape turned dull brown, matching her suddenly sinking spirits. This was no idle adventure she embarked upon. She had found herself a station in a stranger's household and now she must work to earn her living.

She pulled free her arm, massaging her elbow for she could still feel his fingers imprinted upon her skin.

Sharrington paused to pull open the door and offered her his hand. She looked at it as if it was a toad's head.

Suddenly the position in his home lacked appeal. He could do away with her and claim she'd returned to London and no one would be the wiser. Perhaps her plan lacked proper forethought. Perhaps she should throw herself upon Lady Oakland's mercy.

She glanced back but the woman had already disappeared behind the well-polished doors of Oakland

Grange. Her sudden panic must have shown on her face for Christopher dropped his hand.

"I don't bite." Humor tinged his voice.

"Of – of course not." She ignored the mocking smile and sardonic glint in his eyes and clambered unaided into the carriage, sliding onto the rear squabs, settling herself precisely in the middle. She spread her skirts out as much as she could to make it very clear to the impertinent Mr. Sharrington she did not desire his advances in any way.

She pointedly ignored him when he climbed in, averting her gaze by looking out the window. He slammed the carriage door behind him and rapped on the roof to signal the coachman before seating himself across from her.

They rolled down the driveway and turned onto the road. The way the carriage glided over the frozen ruts as if on runners confirmed her suspicions the carriage was new. Where had the man, a former naval captain, come up with the funds to buy a new carriage? Had he been involved in nefarious activities?

She peered at him out of the corner of her eye. Even his clothing was new. As she watched, he ran his finger beneath his crisp lawn cravat, the action suggesting he was not quite comfortable with the starched edges. It gave her the same feeling she had had last night when observing him in the salon at Oakland Grange - the feeling he played an unfamiliar part.

"You look as if I am going to do away with you." The humorous tone of his voice annoyed her and she deigned to turn her head and glare at him. The rogue. He had guessed her apprehensions.

"Not to worry." He laughed, a short bark. "I'm not anxious to add murder to my list of indiscretions."

"I should hope not, Mr. Sharrington."

She turned away again to gaze out the window at the passing landscape. The ground lay draped in winter, as forlorn and colorless as her life had been in the few years since her Mama's death. Just as self-pity threatened to overwhelm her, her companion spoke.

"It would seem I have engaged a governess yet have no idea of her qualifications. Do you care to enlighten me, Lady Woodsby?"

Josceline turned her head and regarded him closely. There was no hint of mockery in his eyes - the question appeared to be rooted in genuine curiosity.

Manners dictated she must answer. She had forced herself upon the man to find herself a new life therefore it would do well to focus on the future and not dwell on the past. As if in concert with her thoughts, the sun broke through again and now she could see hints of green poking here and there through the stalks of dead grass prattling in the breeze.

"The usual, I suppose." She spoke briskly. "I am proficient in French and Italian, and have rudimentary knowledge of Greek and Latin. History, of course, and mathematics and geography."

"What of the finer arts, say music, or dance? I assume you are proficient at those as well?"

She nodded. "And watercolors. I enjoy painting and sketching." She reddened, realizing she had exposed a personal side of herself he realistically would have no interest in knowing.

"I see."

He leaned forward to gaze out the window, resting one kid-gloved hand on the sill, effectively ending the conversation. Aside from the clip clop of shod hooves and the squeak of new leather as he shifted position, silence enveloped the carriage.

She studied him through lowered lashes.

Mr. Christopher Sharrington was older than she had first thought, perhaps in his early-thirties. His earlier good humor had disappeared, replaced by obvious displeasure for his jaw was taut, the dark eye brows lowered to bridge his eyes. She hoped it was not with her for it would make her time with him uncomfortable, to say the least.

Realizing the rudeness of her perusal, Josceline lowered her gaze. However, she couldn't stop herself from looking at him. Slowly her eyes lifted, drawn to him like iron shavings to a lodestone.

Beneath the self-assured shell, an air of sadness hung about him, almost as if he had lost something precious. A muscle twitched in his cheek and she longed to touch it, to feel it quiver beneath her fingers, to smooth it away. Horrified at the impropriety of the thought, she flexed her hand to stop herself from reaching out.

He must have felt the movement for he looked at her, catching her gaze squarely with his. He said nothing although one side of his mouth lifted slightly.

Blushing, she looked away. He must think her bold.

They rode in silence for an hour or so until the carriage turned into a cobblestone drive. Several minutes later, to the sound of accompanying shouts and the pounding of feet, they stopped.

"We're here. Midland House. I assure you, there is no impropriety with your position here. I have a housekeeper, maids, a butler. In short, Lady Woodsby, we are not alone."

He skewered her with his gaze, bringing another flush to her face. Drat the man, he had knocked her off kilter.

"I assure you I shall be comfortable with whatever arrangements you have made." She nodded coolly, tightening her lips, willing the heat in her cheeks to disappear.

The carriage door swung open. With the aid of a footman dressed in livery so new it shone, she stepped out, stopping abruptly when she spied the house.

It was lovely, a rectangle of mellow brick, standing three stories tall. Ivy-covered, its mullioned windows reflected the sun into a thousand shards of light. Two massive stone chimneys flanked the structure, both rising well clear of the slate roof. A central archway on which perched a pair of stone gargoyles sheltered the front entrance. Although not a large estate, Midland House spilled warmth, inviting one to step inside and rest for awhile.

"Charming, is it not?" Christopher's husky voice carried pride and he squared his shoulders. He didn't wait for her nod but continued. "I'll have Mrs. Belton, the housekeeper, show you to your room. We shall talk further when you join me for tea."

His suddenly brisk tone of voice indicated she had been dismissed. It rankled but she worked here now and must do as he bid whether she liked it or not. It was an idea she must accustom herself to. With stiff back and tight lips, she turned and followed the rotund housekeeper.

Christopher watched Josceline stumble up the stairs behind the always efficient Mrs. Belton. He knew he had stretched protocol to have the woman show Josceline to one of the second floor guestrooms rather than to the empty governess' quarters on the third floor but he had done it regardless.

She claimed to be the daughter of a duke and deserved to be treated as such. Moreover, she wasn't here to serve as governess - she was only here long enough for him to retrieve the handkerchief and forestall any accusations she might make towards him.

However, an interesting idea had occurred to him while she had been listing her skills during the carriage ride home. He had no child but perhaps as long as she was here, he could make use of her governess skills.

For himself.

* * *

Josceline stood in the doorway of the drawing room for a few seconds. She had been determined to be punctual for afternoon tea and it pleased her to see she was the first to arrive. It would give her time to get her bearings before her conversation with Mr. Sharrington.

A tray with a silver tea service had been placed on a linen covered table in front of one of the room's two windows. On one side of the table stood a leather arm chair, on the other, a carved oak chair with a tufted seat cushion. Only two cups had been laid out, suggesting there would be only her and her new employer.

She edged her way into the room and looked at the two chairs placed on either side of the table. The arm chair was much too masculine – surely she could see a man's outline in the body-shaped depression in the leather. She sat down in the oak chair, primly tucking her skirts about her knees before looking around.

As with everything else in the house, the contents of the room were new. All the wood surfaces were gleaming, polished so recently the smell of lemon oil yet hung in the air. Mrs. Belton did her work well, apparently.

Josceline knew the good fortune of having a competent woman to oversee the daily household chores. The untrustworthy Mrs. Smeets was merely the latest of a long parade of housekeepers, for the wage her father offered did not attract the best.

Before she had a chance to examine anything more closely, footsteps pounded down the hall and Mr. Sharrington stepped into the room.

"Prompt, I see," he said as he crossed the room. He sat down across from her and smiled. "That is a trait unknown to me from the females of my acquaintance."

Christopher's voice held a hint of approval and she looked at him suspiciously. He had taken the time to wash his face and tidy his hair. His jacket had been brushed, the nap of the black velvet laid down properly so the sheen was visible. He looked every inch a gentleman.

Looks can be deceiving. Only last night, the man masqueraded as a highwayman.

"Shall I pour?" She made her voice calm but her hands shook as she picked up the pot. His frank gaze made her uncomfortable. Don't be silly, she scolded herself, you've poured tea a thousand times before.

"Do." He nodded, waiting until she had finished and had picked up her cup before saying anything more. "I have a suggestion. Perhaps you could be governess to me."

"Oh no." Surprised, she put down her cup before she even had a sip. He must be joking. "You are a grown man."

"Aye." He inclined his head. "However I intend to take my place in polite society and I have a few rough edges in need of polishing."

What mad proposition was this? He wanted her to polish his rough edges? It simply wasn't proper.

"No, I think not." She shook her head. "No." She picked up her cup then put it down again. She must make him understand it just wasn't done.

"May I remind you, you yourself had me engage your services as governess. I do not have a child but I could use instruction in some of the finer arts. Dancing, for one. And perhaps water colors." Unperturbed at her reaction, he added a spoon of sugar to his cup, stirring the tea so briskly the spoon chattered against the china.

"Dance?" Wide-eyed, she stared at him. The idea was absurd. To teach him would involve touching him. She remembered how her arm had tingled when he had escorted her to his carriage – it just wouldn't do.

"Cake?" He picked up the plate of cakes and held it out to her. At the shake of her head, he shrugged and took one for himself before putting it down. "And water colors. I've always fancied trying my hand. I admire the work of Thomas Girton."

Water colors? Girton? Was he serious? Stunned, she said nothing until she realized her silence implied her compliance. She opened her mouth to voice her protest - she must knock the preposterous notion from his head.

"I shall pay you handsomely for your efforts." He named a sum, his mien sober.

She gasped at the amount. Although the entire idea of instructing him was outlandish, the generous offer tempted her. She did a quick calculation – three months employment with Mr. Sharrington would provide enough to buy her food and lodging while she looked for another position.

Josceline reconsidered. Perhaps the suggestion was not so outlandish after all. Three months was not that long a time. If no one knew of the impropriety of her actions, there should be no harm to her reputation.

"Of course, if what I ask is beyond your capabilities, you could trade me the handkerchief for the price of the fare back to London." His eyes held a devilish glint. "Plus a little extra for the inconvenience."

He thought he could intimidate her into running back to London. Her ire rose.

"I will not be bought off or bribed, Mr. Sharrington. I prefer to make my own way." She lifted her chin. "I accept the challenge."

"Challenge?" His voice was lazy but his eyes had hardened. "Do you see me as a dull study, Lady Woodsby?"

"Not at all, Mr. Sharrington. However, do not flatter yourself that what you wish to learn shall come easily. A child's mind is much more malleable than that of an adult. It could require more time than what you are expecting." She paused to take a sip of cold tea. "I am willing to take on the task for a period of three months but I do have one condition."

He raised his eye brows. "Now you are giving me conditions?"

"Yes," she snapped. She held out her left arm and pulled out the bloodied corner of his handkerchief.

Understanding flooded through his eyes. "Of course," he said, unperturbed. "What is it?"

"That you tell no one of our lessons."

"I have no one to tell." He shrugged. "Are we agreed to a term of three months?"

She carefully placed her cup on its saucer. Although the generous offer satisfied her, it wouldn't do to appear too eager. Her ploy worked for she caught his anxious gaze when she glanced at him.

"Yes, Mr. Sharrington, we are. When and where shall we begin?"

"Tomorrow, after breakfast. In the library." He relaxed visibly against the back of his chair.

She nodded. "Tomorrow morning, Mr. Sharrington."

A ray of the setting sun shone full onto his face imbuing it with an eerie, reddish hue, giving him a forbidding air.

A shiver of apprehension ran down her back. She resolutely pushed it away.

What he requested of her was simple enough although it was blatantly obvious the lessons were only a pretext. He desired to retrieve the handkerchief thereby protecting his name.

The flimsy item was the only hold she had over him and she must guard it closely until she had saved enough money to find another position.

Assuming, that is, she would be able to find another position after being at Midland House with the disconcerting Christopher Sharrington.

Chapter Six

The following morning, Josceline took her breakfast alone. Christopher's plate sat clean and unused, silverware lined up neatly and napkin folded beside it. The skinny, pock-marked maid who came in to fill the servers on the sideboard informed Josceline the master had eaten elsewhere and she was to join him when finished.

His absence rankled in that he did not wish to share his meals with her. Yet she must accustom herself to this – as a governess, she had none of the rights of a family member.

And oddly, his absence also disappointed her. She lingered over her jam-filled scone, half-filled with the wishful notion he would stride into the breakfast room but he did not appear.

As much as she enjoyed the cheerful room, with its yellow walls and crisp white lace drapes, she couldn't wait for him any longer or she would risk being tardy, a trait she recognized he abhorred as much as she.

She drained her already empty tea cup and patted the stickiness from her mouth with her napkin. There was nothing for it but to make her way to the library and see if he was there.

Two wrong turns later, Josceline found the library. The door stood slightly ajar and with firm knuckles she rapped on it with enough force for it to swing open.

"Come in."

Stomach churning in trepidation, she stepped across the threshold. The spacious room ran the entire width of the house. Mullioned windows filled one wall from floor to ceiling; the entire wall across from it was lined with a jumble of books and papers.

She spied Christopher at the far end, sitting with bent head at a massive mahogany desk. By the looks of things he worked on a book of accounts. Several ink-smeared maps were pinned on the wall behind him, mute evidence of his naval career, as was the black bicorne hanging on a peg beside the door.

Rooted to the spot, she watched him dip his quill into the pewter inkwell. The soft morning light spilled across his face, illuminating the creases lining his forehead and the laugh lines radiating from the corners of his eyes. His mouth was set in a slight moue of concentration and he scratched several figures before lifting his head to peer at her.

Her heart fluttered as he caught her gaze. Don't be silly, she scolded herself. He was her pupil, nothing more.

"I trust you found breakfast to your satisfaction?" He laid aside the quill and leaned back to stretch.

"Yes, delicious, thank you." She nodded. "The company lacked, however," she added boldly.

He caught her meaning immediately and a dull flush colored his cheeks. "My habit is to eat early. I like a brisk walk in the morning as it clears my head of the cobwebs. I had no idea I needed your permission to do so."

It was a pointed comment and now she flushed. It was not her place to criticize how he spent his mornings.

"This is quite a collection of books." She changed the subject.

"They came with the house. I don't know myself what is here. Please feel free to read them at your own pleasure."

"Oh." She swiveled her head to inspect the shelves. It was a generous offer and would help pass the evenings. She turned her head to face him again. "Thank you," she replied. "I shall enjoy it."

He regarded her in amusement. "A rather subdued response. You need not, if it does not appeal to you." He leaned forward on his elbows and looked at her, sweeping her up and down with appreciative brown eyes.

She felt his stare as surely as if he had reached out and run his fingers over her arms. Alarm crept into her at the sensation yet she refused to let it overwhelm her. It was time to throw the first dart - that should wipe the satisfied expression from his face.

"Tell me, Mr. Sharrington, how does a gentleman not know the dance?" She made her voice sarcastic.

"My father saw fit to send me to sea at an early age. As a captain's servant. I worked my way up to the captaincy of my own ship. Needless to say, it did not give me the time to engage in the more genteel aspects of life."

His voice was mild. The question had not disturbed him in the slightest, leaving her feeling foolish for her uncivil manner.

"And your time at sea was enough to give you all this?" she blurted, sweeping her arm around to encompass the library. It really was none of her concern but it was the first question that had popped into her head.

"Yes. The spoils of captured enemy ships are divided amongst the crew." He lifted an eye brow. "And you, Lady Woodsby? How come you to be governess? Particularly with your expectations." His eyes mocked her.

She flushed again, knowing he referred once more to her acerbic comment regarding his absence at the breakfast table this morning. No matter a lady's transgressions, a gentleman did not offend her, never mind twice in one conversation. He lacked much more in the way of the social graces than simply not knowing how to dance.

The task daunted her more by the minute.

And they hadn't even set foot on the dance floor.

"To avoid an unwanted marriage," she replied crisply. She would not give him the satisfaction of knowing he had rattled her. "My father wished to pawn me off to a merchant." She shuddered as a vision of the vile Mr. Thomas Burrows rose in her mind. "I decided it would be more to my liking to become a governess. This is my first posting," she added.

"Shall we begin?" His voice was suddenly brusque and he looked at her with fierce eyes. "The carpet has been removed." He jumped to his feet and strode around the desk to stand in front of her.

His reaction startled her and she took a step back. Perhaps it had been unwise to disclose this was her first posting. Well, then, she would show him she could very capably handle her duties.

"There is no pianoforte." She tipped her head back to look at him. Yes, she could teach him the steps but it would be difficult to put them all together without a musical instrument. "Do you not have a music room that would suit the purpose better?" She stammered over the last words for his looming proximity wiped all reason from her mind.

"No. I suggest you count very loudly, Lady Woodsby."

She glared up at him at his ridicule. But no, his face was mild although merriment lurked in his eyes.

"Very well, Mr. Sharrington." She lifted her hand. "Shall we begin?"

Christopher focused on her upraised hand then lifted his gaze to her expectant face. He had seen the tell tale shudder when she referred to the merchant her father had wanted her to marry. He could only assume all British aristocrats sneered down their noses at common men who made an honest living.

What would she think of him, Christopher, when she realized he intended to earn his living as a merchant captain himself? Would she snatch back her hand to look at him with the same disgust that had limned her face at the thought of the man her father had wanted her to marry?

Much to his surprise, he found he wanted her admiration. It made no sense, for within three months she would be gone so why the devil should he care what she thought of him?

But he did. Very much.

* * *

"I warned you, did I not, Mr. Sharrington? The finer arts are not so easy to master. Now once again from the beginning."

Christopher groaned. "And what is it I have done incorrectly this time?"

He ran his fingers through his hair. It was his fifth morning of lessons in the library and the lovely Lady Josceline Woodsby was proving to be a stern task master in all matters related to dance. And this was only the Contredanse. How many more were there to master? He groaned again.

He was beginning to doubt the wisdom of seeking her instruction. First, his feet hurt like the very devil. Second, he had no capabilities whatsoever of keeping any semblance of a rhythm. And third, and most disturbing, he was not entirely immune to the charms of the green-eyed, russet-haired young woman standing before him.

A young woman who would find him repugnant when she found out how he meant to earn his living and the loathsome secret forcing him to do so.

Somehow, the whole exercise had become a test of endurance.

She spoke and he, barely listening, focused his gaze on her lovely mouth, watching in fascination as sumptuous lips flickered over pearly teeth.

"You are holding your hand like a rag doll. You are the man and you must lead your partner firmly so she knows where she is going," she commanded. "Like guiding a horse."

"Enough for today," he sighed, dragging his gaze away from her delectable mouth. "Pity the poor student."

Damnation, he had reached a point that he awoke in the middle of the night counting and trying to remember the steps. Anything to coax a smile from her.

She cocked her head and gazed at him unsympathetically. "Hardly poor, I should think. It's a matter of concentration and practice. After one reaches a certain level of competence, it becomes an enjoyable pastime."

Christopher doubted that sincerely.

"Be that as it may, I've had quite enough for today." He put on his jacket. "I have several urgent matters to attend to."

Thankfully she accepted his explanation without question.

"Shall I see you at tea?" Her cheeks were flushed with exertion and she fanned herself with one hand.

With a perverse sense of satisfaction, he noted she had found today's lessons demanding as well. He assured himself the short lesson benefited Lady

Josceline only and had nothing to do with his aching feet and yes, aching loins. To put it simply, he was doing the gentlemanly thing by acceding to her lesser physical prowess.

At his nod, she inclined her chin then turned and swished away. Her dress rippled with the sway of her hips and he found he couldn't tear his gaze away, even tiptoeing to the library door to watch her step down the hall. A glimpse of a trim ankle rewarded him.

She disappeared from sight and he sagged against the door jamb. Frankly, he didn't like the way his heart beat faster when he caught her fragrance – violets and a hint of sandalwood, as far as he could tell - or when she beamed at him in approval for a figure well executed.

He needed that handkerchief and he needed it now or he was sure to turn into a raging madman.

He had inspected her sleeves every day in search of a tell tale bulge but had seen nothing. She must have hidden it somewhere. The next time she went out to take some air, he would search her room.

When he found it, he could send her on her way. Of course he wouldn't leave her destitute. He would pay her enough to assuage his guilty conscience.

Besides, the whole business had diverted him from gaining the debt owed him by that rogue Lord Candel.

Yes, the sooner he located the handkerchief, the better.

* * *

Josceline knew Christopher watched her as she walked away – his eyes burned a hole in her back. She held up her head and shoulders until she turned the corner at the far end of the hall then let her shoulders slump, dropping her chin to feel the pull against the tension in her neck and upper back. Slowly she rolled her head from side to side, circling her shoulders until the stiff ache disappeared.

It was just as well the lesson had been cut short today. If it had gone on much longer, she would have collapsed, skirts and all, into a puddled heap on the floor.

As she had feared, the dance lessons were taking their toll on her. Every brush of his hand, every graze of his shoulder, every glance caught with hers, set her gasping for breath and her heart to pounding.

To be sure, she put on a brave face, giving him encouragement and praise when it was due but it was becoming more and more difficult to instruct the man when other distractions kept arising.

Like his easy smile. And his hearty laugh. And the way his brows quirked in disbelief when she showed him a new step as if to say, "You are in jest, are you not?"

Josceline sighed. What had she agreed to? It had been, what, five days? And already she was reduced to a quivering lump inside. What state would she be in by next week? Next month? How long had she agreed to stay? Three months? It seemed forever.

"Josceline, whatever possessed you to consent to this mad scheme?" She leaned against the wall and cradled her head against the palm of her hand. "What have you done?"

No matter the toll on her, she couldn't see her way clear to leave immediately. She had no choice but to fulfill her pledge if she had any hope of acquiring the wherewithal to find another position. When she left, she would give him the handkerchief so as to have nothing to remind her of him.

A walk, she decided. A walk would be just the thing to settle her unruly thoughts. She stood there for a few moments, waiting until her knees stopped trembling then marched up to her room to get her cloak before making her way to the slatted bench she'd found several days ago. Grey with age, the bench sagged against a brick wall at the far end of the garden in a sunny, sheltered spot. When the days warmed a little and leaves began to bud it would be a lovely locale for Christopher's water color lessons. They had not begun those as the supplies had yet to arrive from London.

Josceline dropped onto the bench then tilted her face to the sky and closed her eyes. Sparrows twittered beside her and the sun warmed her cheeks. She opened her eyes and a hawk floated high above, a circling black speck. Her eyes followed its path, a path she fancied traced the letter "E". Elizabeth.

It reminded her she must write to her friend and tell her all is well. Lady Oakland had said she would inform Elizabeth's mother that Josceline had found a position but one never knew if Elizabeth had received the news.

She must write her father as well but not yet.

A single tear rolled its lonely way down her cheeks to disappear into the fur lining her cloak.

Her father. How he had loved Amelia, her mother. And when her mother died, she could understand the sorrow that had gradually consumed him, turning him into a pathetic semblance of a man. It was as if he had lost the will to live. No matter how he tried to numb his senses with drink and gambling, he was doomed to live without his true love. Amelia.

It was Josceline's middle name and as a girl she loved to recite the two together. Josceline Amelia.

Nonetheless for all his sorrow, she could not forgive him for trying to sell her to the highest bidder. He did not seem to understand she wanted the same thing he had shared with her mother. Now, as a governess no one would offer for her, putting marriage out of reach. The bitter irony was that was exactly what she had told Elizabeth she wanted.

But that wasn't the problem, not really. Something else nagged at her.

She was afraid she was falling in love with the handsome Mr. Sharrington.

An absurd notion. The man would never love her because she existed in a grey vacuum of neither family nor servant.

Another tear rolled down her cheek.

She and only she herself was responsible for the spot she found herself in. She had made a bargain and she would keep it.

Her stomach rumbled.

It was time to leave her maudlin musings in the shadow of the weathered bench and make her way inside for tea. However, first she must go and wash the tears from her face.

At the door to her room, Josceline stopped. Something was not right. Wrinkling her brow, her gaze swept her room. It had been disturbed. The bedspread hung a trifle uneven and the drawer in her night stand sat open a crack. A faint wisp of leather and citrus hung in the air.

In a flash, she knew.

"The handkerchief," she whispered.

In a panic, she flew to the mirror and pulled it away from the wall. The handkerchief was still there, neatly folded and tucked in behind the frame. She pulled it out and held it close to her nose. It carried the same scent of leather and citrus.

A sudden chill rippled down her spine. Christopher had been in her room.

Carefully, she slipped the square of cloth back in behind the frame.

She would have to take care. If he found it, he would send her on her penniless way.

Chapter Seven

From the library windows, Christopher spotted a visibly drooping Josceline walk towards the house. Sympathy flooded through him at the sight, along with the sudden urge to clasp her close and pull her head onto his shoulder. He shook his head at the unexpected reaction. Lud, but genteel life was making him soft.

So soft, in fact, that a quick search of Josceline's room for his handkerchief earlier this afternoon had yielded nothing. He, who had run a naval ship with an iron fist, was being befuddled by a mere slip of a woman. He would have to search her room again, when he could do a more thorough job of it.

The light cadence of Josceline's footsteps echoed through the hall and he had to stifle the impulse to dash to the door and see her. An odd notion struck him: Perhaps genteel life was not making him soft. Perhaps it was the allure of the lovely Lady Woodsby.

Nonsense. He shook his head. It was simply disappointment in not finding the handkerchief bewildering him.

He headed to the sitting room for tea, but not before tidying the papers on his desk. If only thoughts were that easy to arrange.

On his way, he picked up a heavy cream envelope from where it lay on the brass tray in the entry hall. The strokes were firm, splashed across the page with the panache only Lady Oakland could master. Beneath it rested a second envelope, the paper smudged and grimy, addressed to Josceline in spidery and irregular handwriting. He tucked it into the pocket of his jacket to hand to her later.

He returned his regard to Lady Oakland's note and turned it over to break the seal. He scanned the missive, then, in disbelief, scanned it again.

"Damnation." He slammed the wall with one hand. "Lady Oakland is coming to visit to give her regards to Lady Josceline and to meet my son."

All thoughts of the handkerchief fled from his mind.

This was an unforeseen bit of nasty business. When the woman realized he had no son, he and Josceline would be left in a compromising position. He needed Lady Oakland's continued approval to be included in the local social functions and Josceline needed her good name if she intended to find herself a respectable position after she left Midland House.

Frowning, he checked the date on the note. Yesterday. Lady Oakland meant to visit the day after tomorrow giving him a scant forty eight hours to devise a plan to forestall catastrophe. How, he had no idea but to begin he would seek Josceline's counsel. She had as much at stake as he did.

Christopher charged to the sitting room, bursting through the doorway with such urgency the door slammed into the wall with a shuddering bang.

A startled Josceline looked at Christopher with round eyes. The accusation she was about to make about him searching her room died on her lips.

Something had upset him. His cheeks were flushed and his hair tousled as if he had run his fingers through it not once but many times. His mouth was a taut line, his eyes bleak.

"Whatever is the matter?" she asked, dreading his answer. The man looked as if he faced the Grim Reaper.

"Lady Oakland is coming for a visit," he growled. His lips barely moved. "To see you and my son."

"Oh," she breathed, feeling the color drain from her face. "You have no son." She felt idiotic stating the obvious.

"Aye. Your reputation shall be in shreds."

"Yours too." She grasped the enormity of the situation. Her heart sank. "Could we not tell her your son is still with your mother?"
He shook his head. "You've been here for almost a week. She would find it odd he wasn't here. After all, that is why I engaged your services."

"True." An idea occurred to her and she brightened. "When Lady Oakland comes, we could tell her I have taken your son out riding on his pony."

"No. Unspeakably rude. It will be all over the county in a matter of hours that my governess and my son snubbed Lady Oakland."

She stared at him, both hands covering her mouth. "Could we not borrow a boy for a day?" she asked finally, dropping her hands to rest them on her lap. An outrageous solution but it could work.

"You mean a sham?" He gave her an incredulous stare.

"Yes." She nodded.

"Where do we find a boy?" The words came out grudgingly, as if he thought the idea splendid but did not wish to pounce on it too quickly.

"Are there no children on the estate?"

"There are." He nodded thoughtfully. "But it may be hard to keep it secret that I borrowed someone's child."

"I know." She clapped her hands. "Could we not ride into Bristol and find a child in a workhouse?"

"That seems rather cruel, does it not? To borrow a child for a day and then return it?"

"Could you not find a position for him in the stables, say? Or perhaps in the house? I've heard horrid stories about the workhouses. Anything you could provide would be better than a life of brutal poverty."

He looked at her long and hard and she imagined she could see the thoughts whirling through his mind.

His hesitation was blatant and she hastened to reassure him. "It shall work, you will see. In three months time my position here is terminated regardless. If anyone should ask, you can say I've prepared him for school and he has been sent off."

It was not an ideal plan, riddled with loopholes. Josceline knew it but it seemed the only answer to stave off imminent disaster.

Finally he nodded. "A plausible solution. Jefferson, the head groom, has been asking for a stable boy. I shall take the carriage into Bristol tomorrow." He slanted a glance at her. "Do you care to accompany me?"

"Me?" She gaped at him.

"Yes, you. I know nothing of children."

"Nor do I."

"I should imagine you have a much better idea of it than I."

She did not have any idea, not anymore than he did. The only exposure she had had to young children was in Hyde Park. At a distance.

Josceline simply looked at him, speechless. There seemed nothing to say.

"Good." Christopher gave a curt nod apparently not bothered a whit by her silence. "It's settled. Off to Bristol tomorrow."

* * *

The little clock chimed a dozen times. Midnight. Josceline groaned and flopped over onto her back.

Over and over she had reviewed in her mind the plan she and Christopher had devised to mislead Lady Oakland. First, they would find a boy of suitable age, say, six or seven years. Next, the boy would need decent clothing which they could doubtless find at a rag shop in Bristol. A scrub down, of course, but that would not be until he arrived at Midland House. Finally, the boy need only remain silent during the meeting with Lady Oakland in order to hide his rough dialect.

It seemed a sound strategy yet her mind refused to calm.

She gave up and sat upright in the bed.

The letter to Elizabeth would clear her mind. Surely her employer would have no objection to her using paper and ink from the library.

The cheerful fire warming her room earlier had collapsed into a glittering pile of coals. The red hue from them would be enough for her to find her shoes and light a taper.

"Balderdash," she whispered at the thought of creeping through the cold, dark house. But it seemed silly to lie tossing and turning when the time could be better spent accomplishing something useful. Before she could change her mind and wriggle back under the bedclothes, she slid off the bed and jammed her stockingless feet into cold slippers. Her toes curled in protest and she cast a longing glance to her still warm bed.

Resolute, she threw her winter cloak over the thin wrapper that would be no barrier to the chill air in the rest of the house. Taper in hand, she tiptoed through the silence. Shadows from her candle skipped over the wood paneled walls until she reached the library.

It was empty. With a sigh of relief, she slipped through the door, closing it behind her with a soft 'snick'.

Josceline made a beeline to Christopher's desk, putting down the candle on one corner. She knew the carved box inlaid with ivory held paper for it had been open once during one of their lessons. The location of the quills, she was not so certain – in a drawer, perhaps.

She started with the top drawer. It was locked. The drawer immediately beneath it slid open easily and she picked up the candle to peer inside. Ledger books. Not quills. She put down the candle again and bent over to try the next drawer down. It didn't slide as easily. It stuck and she pulled at the handle with both hands.

It gave with a sudden jerk. In a twinkling she landed smack on her bottom with the drawer and its contents upside down on top of her. She had found the quills. And a spare inkwell. Its contents dripped slowly onto her lap.

"Josceline, you ninnyhammer!" The words spurted out of her mouth. Her tailbone ached from the tremendous thump and dismayed, she looked at the spreading ink stain on her cloak. Ruined. Her one and only cloak was ruined.

A floorboard creaked and she froze.

She was not alone.

Slow, measured footsteps sounded across the bare floor.

The taper flickered.

Fear filled her. She could taste it rising into her throat like bile. She did not believe in ghosts, she told herself sternly. There was no use cowering behind the desk. A show of bravado would stand her better than nothing at all. In a clatter of falling quills, she grasped the edge of the desk and pulled herself up.

To look right into the amused face of Christopher Sharrington.

"Oh!" she gasped. "I assure you, Mr. Sharrington, I was not prying. I was only looking for paper and quills. I could not sleep and thought to write a letter to my friend Elizabeth. The drawer stuck and -." The words died in her throat at the predator-like glint in his eyes.

"And you have ruined your cloak." He pointed to the stain.

"The floor, too, I fear. I do so apologize."

He leaned over to look. "No. It would seem you caught the ink. That particular inkwell was almost empty. It was in the drawer awaiting a refill."

She swallowed hard, feeling foolish. "I must beg pardon," she managed to squeak.

The moon came out from behind a cloud, suddenly washing the library in silver. Christopher's face wasn't visible to her for he had his back to the windows but she could see he wasn't in night clothes. His linen shirt gaped open at the neck, his sleeves were rolled up to the elbows and he still wore his riding boots. It would seem he had had trouble sleeping as well this night.

"You have only to ask." He came around the desk to stand in front of her. "Mrs. Belton would have brought you what you needed."

"Yes, I understand. The clock chimed and I couldn't sleep and I wished to write a letter." She was babbling but Christopher stood much, much too close. So close, she could feel his breath on her cheek. So close, she could smell leather and citrus. So close, she could reach up and touch his hair if she so chose.

He tugged the ties of her cloak, pulling her towards him.

She placed her palms on his chest, trying to push herself away. He caught her wrists with a firm grip. "Your hands are cold," he whispered before placing them on his waist. "Here, warm them."

"Oh, I could not." Panic thumped through her breast. Josceline tried to pull away her hands but they had a mind of their own. Her fingers curled into the heavy fabric of his shirt, her knuckles felt the warmth pulsing from his skin.

"Oh, but you can." He cupped his hands along her jaw and lowered his head. "You can." His lips brushed hers, once, twice.

The heat crawling from him through her hands up her arms was joined by the burn in her lips where his mouth touched hers. He lifted his head to look into her eyes.

His gaze was as much a caress as his lips had been and her stomach dropped away at the intensity in it.

"Josceline," he murmured. "May I kiss you again?" He didn't pull her close but held her jaw cupped in his hands. His eyes roved over her face as if the answer was imprinted there.

She shook her head, a jerky little movement not convincing in the slightest.

Now. Push away his hands. Run. Now.

Yet a part of her didn't want to run. A part of her watched in fascination as he lowered his face over hers. His eyes were closed. How would he find her mouth with his eyes closed? Came the absurd thought. It must be the done thing, though. Her eye lids fluttered shut and she waited, focusing on the warmth of his hands against her face.

When finally his lips touched, she could scarce breathe. His firm mouth softly brushed hers and she had the oddest sensation her feet had left the ground and she floated in mid air, anchored by his lips.

Josceline tightened her hands against his waist and could feel him shudder. His lips parted and his tongue played against her lips, teasing them. She opened her mouth to gasp and his tongue darted inside, flicking against hers, challenging. A whimper escaped her throat.

He must have heard her for he pulled away his mouth. "Josceline,' he whispered. "You are so very, very beautiful."

His voice broke the spell and her feet returned to earth with a bump. Her knees were weak, and her chin sagged into his hands.

He stepped back, a pleased smile playing on his lips. "It would seem now I am the tutor and you the neophyte. Fair play, I would say."

She gaped at him, certain that the kiss had been a dream. No, her stomach churned and moisture pooled between her legs. She knew she should be outraged, appalled, screaming vile epithets at him and battering her fists against his chest.

Instead, she stood motionless trying to make sense of it.

She had enjoyed it.

She wanted more.

How very improper of her. Apparently she was as degenerate as her father, making her her father's daughter after all. The notion appalled her.

"If you will excuse me, I shall return to my room." Bitterness tinged her voice and she avoided his gaze.

"Of course." He inclined his head, as polite as if they had just finished a dance lesson.

Josceline risked a quick glance at his face. She did not inspect his features closely because she didn't want to see the censure she was certain filled his eyes.

Her instinct told her to flee and flee she did. His chuckle chased her as she pelted across the library. Left behind were her taper and the mess of quills and upended drawer but it mattered naught. Escape was a must.

With hands outstretched against the darkness, she raced up the stairs and down the hall to the sanctuary of her room. She heaved shut the door behind her and leaned against it, heart pounding and feet aching with cold.

Hadn't she told herself he lacked in the social graces? The kiss in the library proved just that.

The midnight visit to the library to write Elizabeth's letter had not gone as foreseen. Sleep wasn't going to come any easier after all. If anything, it had now become impossible.

Drat the man.

* * *

Christopher hadn't meant to kiss her.

He had heard Josceline creep down the hall and curiosity had nudged him to follow her to the library. At first he thought she meant to find a book but when she headed straight for his desk, he realized she searched for something.

Was she suspicious of him and his background? But no, the locked drawer containing his personal papers didn't interest her.

He'd had a hard time stifling his laughter when she had emptied the contents of the quill drawer over herself.

Actually, he had meant to admonish her against going through his desk, no matter her excuse. However, the appealing sight of her in her cloak with the lace of her night wrapper peeking out about the throat had snared his attention and when she turned luminous eyes to his, all good intentions had been tossed willy-nilly to the winds. Manners be damned, he wanted to kiss the source of his frustrations.

He'd enjoyed every second of it for the reality very much trumped the fantasy. Heady stuff, her lips, pliant and tasting somewhat of honey and peppermint.

A rueful thought crossed his mind: The kiss had not eradicated her hold over him at all. In fact it had strengthened it, leaving him wanting more. As if he'd opened a box of bonbons and eaten the first one and now had to peel back crumpled tissue paper to find the second one.

Rightly or wrongly, he couldn't wait to kiss her again. Soon.

Chapter Eight

Late the next morning and in the dismal confines of Bristol's workhouse, St. Peter's Hospital, Josceline found herself staring at a string of boys dutifully lined up by the mistress. An assortment of faces peered back at Josceline, some sullen, some hopeful, some bewildered, yet all etched with the unmistakable lines of hunger. She lowered her head, unsure how she could choose one when all were desperate.

The building itself sat beside the river Avon and the unmistakable odor of rotting fish, rotting garbage, and tar sifted through the workhouse making it difficult to concentrate on her task.

That and the realization Christopher stood a scant few feet behind her. She'd tried all morning not to think about last night but her traitorous lips tingled with the remembrance of it. Her very body tingled with the remembrance of it. Was it the man or the kiss disturbing her so? How could she make sense of it for of course she, a proper lady, would not, could not allow him to kiss her again.

To say her wits were addled was putting it mildly.

"Well, dearie, which will it be?" The gnarled woman with the broken front tooth leered at her. The woman's grubby dress hung shapeless about her only notched in at the waist by her equally grubby apron.

"I, ah, that is to say, I -." Josceline's voice trailed away. The task proved to be more difficult than anticipated and her heart twisted at the dreadful condition of the children. At least it took her mind off the kiss.

"Ye said ye were wanting a boy. Mrs. Wilkinson always aims to please." The woman tucked a lock of stringy hair beneath her tattered mob cap before pointing to the shortest. "That be Tom. He's only been here a month or two."

"I see." Josceline took a reluctant step towards the boy. "Hello, Tom, how old are you?"

Tom looked up at her with dull eyes, his face a mass of bruises, some fading to yellow, others still an angry purple. His too-large shirt and breeches hung from his skeletal frame and chilblains riddled his bare feet. Josceline's stomach heaved at the sight of his swollen, reddened feet and she had to look away to hide her tears.

"I reckon he's four or five. His ma took to the drink, she did."

"We were looking for someone a bit older. Someone who could be trained in the stables." Christopher moved up to stand beside Josceline.

He must have sensed Josceline's distress, for he dropped a supportive hand on her shoulder. The familiarity of the gesture gave her comfort and she tightened her lips and looked again at the ragged lot before her.

"Well, mebbe ye'd be happier with Philip." Mrs. Wilkinson pointed a black-nailed finger towards the lad standing to Tom's right. "He's Tom's older brother. Ye could have 'em both for the same price. It be difficult keeping enough food in the place to feed any of 'em." She turned calculating eyes towards Christopher.

"I have no need for two boys," Christopher replied firmly. "One is all we need."

"They both be hard workers." The woman's tone was wheedling and her gaze darted to Josceline. "What do ye say, milady? Two lovely little boys?" She shuffled over to the two and pulled them forward.

The younger one started to cry, large drops sliding through the grime of his cheeks. His brother grabbed his hand. "Don't worry, Tommy, I won't let nothin' happen to ya." The lad turned pleading eyes towards Christopher. "Please, sir, I'm the only thing 'e has."

If anything, Philip's clothing, held together with a knotted rope about his waist, was more tattered and grimy than that of his brother. However, he stood tall and faced them unafraid.

"No," Christopher interjected. "I stand firm. One boy is sufficient."

His voice shook slightly and Josceline wondered at it. She herself was afraid to speak for fear of bursting into tears at the pathetic sight.

"Stop yer sniveling." Mrs. Wilkinson slapped the little one's cheeks.

Tom continued to cry, shoulders heaving with silent sobs. Philip pulled him close and wrapped both arms about him. The two stood together with heads bowed as if together they were a stalwart force.

Revulsion at the woman's callous manner filled Josceline and she made a sudden decision.

"Agreed," she said briskly. "We shall take them both. They are brothers, Mr. Sharrington, we shan't split them. Surely you can find another spot for the second one?"

She avoided looking at any of the other boys. Yes, poverty existed here, in London, everywhere else in the world as far as she knew, but to stare it in the face was horrible.

An incredulous Christopher tapped her arm. "May I remind you we only need one?" he asked, voice strangled.

"I do not care, Mr. Sharrington. Let us take these two and be done with it." She looked back at Christopher beseechingly.

The second Josceline's eyes hit his, Christopher knew he was lost. The anguish in her face seared his heart and he now regretted bringing her along. Aye, he had witnessed much in his life but the genteel Lady Josceline would have been shielded of life's ugly realities.

He sighed. "Yes. We shall take the brothers."

What in blazes had he just agreed to? Brothers? When he supposedly only had one son? Plus the way they looked now, they would never clean up properly. The sham was sure to fail.

However, the grateful look Josceline flashed him made the whole mad attempt worthwhile.

He would do his best not to disappoint her.

* * *

Feeling somewhat like Mother Goose, Christopher shepherded Josceline, Philip and Tom to the carriage. The boys hopped inside immediately to escape the damp cobblestones but Josceline hesitated a moment to wipe tears from her cheeks before climbing in.

He waited outside while she laid a rug over the boys, tucking it securely beneath their bare feet. She settled herself beside the two and then he swung himself onto the bench to face them all. Three pairs of eyes inspected him, two blue pairs wide-eyed and astonished, and the third a moist green.

Damnation, he had no idea what in blazes to do next.

A diversion. He needed to provide a diversion to avoid feeling like a butterfly pinned to a board.

He rapped on the roof. "To the harbor if you will. I want to see the ships."

He scowled at them, immediately feeling the cad when the two boys shrank from him. Josceline, however, seemed to have regained her equilibrium.

"What a lovely suggestion, Mr. Sharrington. I am sure Tom and Philip should enjoy that immensely." She smiled down at the two although her lips quivered.

The sight reassured him – he wasn't the only one ill at ease. Placing his hands on his knees, he leaned forward to take a closer look at the two boys.

They gazed back at him solemnly, the expressions on their faces reminding him of new recruits on his former frigate "HMS Sophia Dorothea". That's it - he snapped his fingers mentally. He would consider them both as new sailors. And the first thing they would need would be uniforms.

"Shoes," Josceline said absently as if she read his thoughts. "Socks. Pantaloons. Shirts. Jackets. Mufflers." She looked at him. "Perhaps after visiting the harbor, we could find a rag shop or haberdashery."

"Aye." He inclined his head. "And a dining room or coffee house or some such. I wager the lads are hungry."

"Yes sir," Philip piped up, apparently emboldened by the thought of food. "We're hungry." A wide-eyed Tom stared at Philip, mouth an "o" at his brother's daring.

A wry grin crossed Christopher's mouth. He well remembered himself as a growing lad battling constant hunger. "Forget the harbor. Let's find somewhere to eat, shall we?"

Josceline gave him a startled look, patently surprised at his suggestion.

He shrugged. "Men who are well fed obey orders. I should imagine the same principal applies to boys."

"How thoughtful of you, Mr. Sharrington."

Mr. Sharrington. Must she continue to call him that? He would much rather she called him Christopher. Needless to say he couldn't ask that of her, but the thought enticed him.

* * *

With the help of a fish monger, the coachman managed to find the Greyhound Inn several streets over in Broadmead. They ate in a private room in the back, a hearty dish of stewed eels and potatoes which Josceline thoroughly enjoyed. Dessert came, a lovely lemon sweet, and the boys devoured it so quickly, it was as if they had inhaled it. She thought to reprove them for their lack of manners but relented at their blissful expressions. Tomorrow, perhaps, but not today. Doubtless their young lives so far had been dreary.

"I've asked the proprietor for the nearest haberdashery. We'll find one on Broad Street." Christopher laid aside his napkin and stood up. "I'll call the carriage."

Bristol was a harbor town, its streets cluttered with wagons piled high with lumber, bales of cotton and barrels of rum, along with fine carriages and farmer's carts. It made for slow going but the window shades were up and she made a game of spotting sailors with Tom and Philip. At length they turned onto Broad Street and pulled up in front of the shop. Christopher stepped out of the carriage and turned to face Josceline.

"Perhaps it would be best for you to wait here," he said. "I shall take the lads and put them in the charge of the haberdasher."

However, as soon as the three stepped inside the shop, Christopher could see a battle loomed with the proprietor for the man was none too pleased to see the boys on his premises as evidenced by his lowered eyebrows and jutting jaw.

"Excuse me, sir, those nippers are not welcome here." With a disdainful sniff, the man tried to usher them out of his shop.

"Come now, where's the harm?" A surprised Christopher stopped dead in his tracks. It hadn't occurred to him that it might prove difficult to replace the boy's clothing.

"The harm is to my other customers." The man held a scented pomade to his nose and pointed. "They, ah, smell."

"Your establishment appears to be vacant." Annoyed, Christopher swept an arm to encompass the room with its shelves of folded shirts, hats, and bolts of fabric.

"I do not deal with riff raff here, my good sir. Please take the children and leave."

Riff raff. And the man had included him, Christopher, in that statement. His hackles rose and he took a step towards the proprietor, who stood his ground and glared at Christopher through narrowed eyes.

Lud, but he was in no mood to find another shop. And he was in no mood to argue. A tidy sum should quiet the tailor's fears and he pulled out a sack of coins and tossed them onto the counter with a hearty 'clink'.

"I believe you will find more than ample to outfit the two. Make it quick and I shall double the remuneration." Out and out bribery but he had had enough of Bristol and its busyness. Time to venture home to the peace of Midland House.

At the sight of the bulging sack, greed replaced distaste on the man's face.

"Of course, my good sir, of course." With an obsequious bow, he backed away and signaled to an assistant. "You heard the gentleman, clothe these two. And shoes, if the gentleman agrees, we'll send to the cobbler for shoes."

Christopher nodded. "I have another matter to attend to. I shall return in half an hour." He stalked out. Already the boys were a bother although in fairness to them, it was the shopkeeper who was the bother.

He ducked into the adjacent shop.

Something in the window there had caught his eye and he knew just the person who would like it.

* * *

Grateful for the rest, Josceline leaned back against the squabs and pulled the rug over her knees. She half-drowsed, listening to the sounds of the street outside the carriage – the jingle of harnesses, the shouts of the hawkers and the squeal of children playing, the drifting voices of people walking past. Her hands and feet grew cold. It was chilly close to the water and the wool spencer she wore today did nothing to keep her warm.

Her cloak would have been welcome but after last night's debacle, it lay crumpled in the bottom of the wardrobe in her room.

Butterflies tumbled in her stomach. Yesterday, it had seemed plausible to find a boy in an orphanage to pass off as Christopher's son. Today, the reality was so much more complex, starting with the reality they now had two boys. Boys who reeked of urine and coal smoke, boys who needed the attention of a doctor, boys so thin, they would never be mistaken for anything other than what they were – street urchins. The task seemed insurmountable. The only comforting thought was Christopher. He had as much at stake as she did. Surely between the two of them...

"Lady Woodsby?"

Her eye lids popped open to see Christopher holding a large box and several smaller packages wrapped in brown paper and string. He tossed the packages on the floor but held the large box out to her.

"For you." A self-deprecating grin lifted the corners of his mouth and her heart lurched. "I saw it in a shop window. I thought it would match your eyes."

Her gaze dropped to the box, cheerily wrapped in red and blue striped paper and tied up with gold ribbon. A gift? For her? Whatever for?

"Open it."

"No." She shook her head. "I cannot accept this. It's not proper."

"Proper?" He laughed, his eyes crinkled shut in the manner she was beginning to adore. "It's a gift, how can that not be proper?" He stopped laughing and looked at her.

"Gentlemen do not give gifts to unmarried young ladies." Josceline made her voice severe. "So no, thank you."

She cast a longing glance towards the box. It had been ages since she'd received a present and her fingers itched to open it.

"Let us say I'm no gentleman. Does that help?" He held the box out to her again, grinning. "Take it, Lady Woodsby. Consider it as part of your wage."

The impish grin was her downfall. That and the lock of hair that had escaped the leather thong at the nape of his neck and fallen across his forehead. He looked young and carefree and for an instant she could imagine the boy he had been.

"Oh very well," she grumped. "Do you always get your way?" She took the box. It was heavy and she almost dropped it.

"Not always." He reached out a hand to ease the box onto her lap. "But yes when it's something important."

She caught her breath at that. He had bought something for her he considered important. Could that mean he cared for her a little?

The box lay across her knees. He watched her and she felt her cheeks redden. Hesitantly, she pulled off the ribbon and lifted the lid.

"Oh," she gasped.

It was a cloak. The most beautiful cloak she had ever seen, of bronze felted wool and lined with what she was sure was sable.

She lifted her head. "I cannot –." The words died on her lips at the tender expression on his face.

"You can, Josceline," he whispered. "And you will." He lifted it from the box and draped it about her shoulders. "Look in the packages."

Speechless, she unwrapped them all to discover a matching sable muff and bonnet, and a bolt of satin fabric the color of copper. For a matching dress, of course. Eyes brimming at his thoughtfulness, she raised her gaze to his.

"Thank you. They're all beautiful."

"Tom and Philip should be fitted by now." His voice was brusque but he brushed her cheek with a gentle finger before turning to walk away.

She watched his retreating back, not knowing what to think. Did he really care for her?

Or did he mean to buy another kiss?

* * *

It had cost him a pretty penny but the moment Christopher had seen the cloak in the modiste's window, he knew he had to buy it. True, the ink stain on her old cloak had not been his fault but he did feel responsible for what happened beneath his roof.

Her reaction pleased him. She had been touched, he was certain of it. Whistling a jaunty tune, he returned to the haberdashery to find the lads looking with astonished faces at each other's new clothing.

"Tom, Philip, don't you both look splendid." They yet needed a bath but they looked a little less disreputable in the new clothing. His hopes rose. Perhaps the deception for Lady Oakland tomorrow would succeed.

"Thank ye, sir. My brother thanks ye too," Philip said. "Shoes. We ain't never 'ad shoes." Beside him, Tom nodded energetically.

"You are welcome," replied Christopher. He cocked a finger. "Come."

Holding hands, they followed him without a word. The three left the shop and waited for a break in the traffic to cross the road to the waiting carriage.

"'Pon my word, Sharrington, my eyes did not deceive this morning. It was you leaving the Hospital with these motley two. Have you taken up as nursemaid, wot? And where's the pretty piece of fluff?"

The familiar, hated voice grated on Christopher's ears and he turned to see Lord Oliver Candel, tapping a brass-handled walking stick and regarding them with an insolent sneer from beneath a fashionable beaver hat.

An impotent rage rose within Christopher and he clenched his jaw. This arrogant dandy, decked out in a red and white striped vest, yellow culottes and turquoise tailed coat, was the real reason Christopher found himself in the awkward position he was in.

If the man had paid his debt like an honorable individual, Christopher would never have stopped the wrong carriage, leading to him engaging the services of Josceline as governess.

And if Josceline wasn't his governess, he would not need a boy to fill the role of his own son. Meaning he wouldn't now be shepherding two boys who weren't his to pull off the mad scheme. A scheme which now, thanks to the untimely meeting, could be exposed.

At this particular moment, not even the thought of green eyes and russet hair could soothe him.

Christopher jammed his hands into his pockets to refrain from ripping off Candel's starched shirt frills and ramming them down his throat.

Damn it all to Hades. What rotten luck.

Chapter Nine

Just a few feet more and Christopher would have had the boys safely ensconced within his carriage. He had to nip this in the bud before Candel came to any conclusions regarding the boy's parentage.

"Not that it is any concern of yours but I am doing a favor for a friend," he said haughtily. Traffic eased for a moment and he gave the boys a little nudge. "To the carriage," he ordered. "I shan't be a moment."

He gestured to the coachman to mind the two then turned back to the fop who stood and watched as Philip and Tom dodged across the street.

This wasn't the time or place he would have chosen to confront the man but he had to divert Candel's attention from the boys.

"May I remind you, you owe me a gambling debt?" Christopher kept his voice low and ignored the curious glances looking their way.

"Gambling debt? I owe you nothing."

"Yes. Gambling debt," he growled, irritated by the man's drawl. His fingers twitched - he wanted nothing more than to grab Candel's throat and throttle him.

"Why, from our set to the other night? It was just a friendly game. Consequently," he tapped

Christopher's shoe with his walking stick, "I do not have to pay you."

"We shall see." Christopher ground out the words. He glanced over his shoulder to the waiting carriage. The boys had disappeared inside. "You and I have unfinished business, Candel." He pulled out a calling card. "Saturday. Expect me on Saturday."

Rage washed over him anew as Candel took the card between pincered thumb and forefinger as if it carried the Black Death.

"I dare say I may be receiving visitors that day." Candel tossed the card to the ground and ground his heel on it. "Or not." He stood there with an expectant look on his face, an insolent smile playing on his greased lips.

The tactic was an obvious ploy for Christopher to call out the man but he would not give Candel the satisfaction of rising to the bait. Christopher's military training had taught him that in some circumstances, this being one of them, discretion was the better part of valor.

Ignoring the man, he turned on his heel and made his way to the carriage. Luckily the hubbub on the street drowned out Candel's derisive laughter and he took a few deep breaths to calm himself before opening the door and leaning in.

"I found this in my pocket just now." He handed Josceline the letter that had been tucked away in his jacket. He had felt its sharp folds when fumbling for his card. "I do apologize, it came yesterday but what with Lady Oakland's note, I forgot about it."

"Oh." Her face was horror struck when he handed it to her - obviously she recognized the hand writing.

"I'm going to sit with the coachman. Take some air." A good stiff breeze would wash away his rage. Besides, he needed to think ahead to tomorrow's impending visit from Lady Oakland.

He gestured to Tom and Philip. "You two may sit on my seat."

Obediently, the two scrambled over. Promising. At any rate, they obeyed orders. He gave them a small salute before slamming shut the door but not before casting a concerned glance towards Josceline.

Her face was drawn, white. She looked as if she had seen a ghost.

"What is it?" he asked, uneasy at her reaction.

"Not of your concern," Josceline whispered, eyes glued to the envelope. She fluttered a hand in his vague direction. "Please, do not worry for me."

Mercifully, he didn't question her further. From a distance Josceline noticed the slam of the coach door, then the creak and sway of the carriage as he swung himself up beside the coachman.

Her head spun. The letter was from her father and she had no desire to read it. He had been none too pleased when she had announced her decision to take herself from London and earn her keep. His rage and disappointment was such she had thought she was lost to him forever, which suited her for it left her free to pursue a future as a governess.

But now he had written her.

He was not done with her, then.

“What’s wrong, miss?”

Philip’s hoarse little voice broke through her whirling thoughts and she raised her gaze to him. He looked back at her with a solemn gaze. Her heart ached for him at his expression. How could one so young hold such a serious demeanor?

His expression prompted her as to where she was and why. Certainly tomorrow’s impending visit unsettled her. And certainly it all hinged on how well the boy played his part. For now she would turn her attention to the boys, and in particular Philip.

She would wait until she reached the sanctuary of her room to read the letter.

But it burned where she tucked it inside her spencer.

* * *

Disdain curled the lip of Lord Oliver Candel as he watched the Sharrington carriage disappear into the hubbub of Bristol’s streets. How crass of the man to remind him of the gaming debt and certainly not the action of one of the peerage to pick a public walkway in which to do so.

How had a man of Sharrington’s ilk even gained entry into Bristol’s finest gaming establishment? Fumed Candel. Furthermore, how presumptuous of the man to hand over his card as if he, Oliver Candel, would gladly open his doors to the scum.

He slammed his walking step into the ground. *Watch your step, Sharrington, or you shall rue the day you sought to challenge me.*

* * *

As Christopher rode home to Midland House beside the coachman, the fresh air cleared his jumbled thoughts and allowed him to consider Lady Oakland's visit tomorrow in a more relaxed frame of mind.

It really shouldn't be too difficult to convince the woman Philip was his son. Tom, the younger boy could simply be kept elsewhere during the interview.

With a light heart, he jumped off the coach and paused to admire the tranquil façade of Midland House. An odd thought swam through his mind. Midland House deserved a proper mistress. Like Josceline. And children. Like Philip and Tom.

Nonsense.

He shook his head. Marriage wasn't yet in his plans for he must first set himself up in the shipping business. No, he corrected himself. First he must convince Lady Oakland he had a son. By her good graces, his acceptance into polite society would ensure the success of his business.

The carriage door thudded open and two boyish shapes tumbled out.

"Philip? Tom? Mind you wait for me." Josceline's voice drifted from within.

"Yes, miss." They chorused as one as if they had been practicing their manners but they jumped from one foot to the other while they waited, eyes wide as saucers as they inspected the surroundings. They began to wrestle, grunting and laughing and trying to topple each other over, a far cry from the sad sight of this morning.

Lud, how resilient and full of energy young boys could be. His newly found confidence about tomorrow waned. They had less than twenty four hours before Lady Oakland arrived and at this particular moment the two reminded him of nothing less than unschooled rambunctious puppies.

A few seconds later, a slender, ivory hand grasped the doorway and his eyes were drawn to a dainty foot reaching for the top step. Chagrin cascaded through him. In his apprehension about the impending visit, he had totally forgotten his manners.

"Allow me." Christopher reached for Josceline's hand, careful to drop it once she had reached the ground. He needed all his reason and he mustn't let his attraction to her bamboozle him.

She turned limpid green eyes to him. "Mr. Sharrington, please have a footman take Philip and Tom to the stables," she said calmly. "The boys and I have had a lovely visit and I promised them if they sat still during the ride home they could see the horses."

"Splendid suggestion," agreed a dumbfounded Christopher. Apparently Josceline was prepared to take charge. Confidence welled up again. They were two adults, he reminded himself, surely they were the equal of two orphaned boys.

They waited by the carriage until the footman came and took the youngsters.

"Bring them to the kitchen when they've had their fill," ordered Christopher before turning to take

Josceline's elbow. They strolled across the drive towards the house.

"There is much to be done before tomorrow," Josceline said. "Most important, however, is a good bath. Check them for lice, that sort of thing." She slanted a glance at Christopher. "They're both very eager to please. Although Tom is shy, I found Philip to be engaging and bright. I think he would do as your son."

He nodded. "I had thought the same. Plus he is of the right age."

They began to climb the steps to the front door. On cue, it swung open to reveal the tall, spare frame of Tedham, Christopher's butler, who stepped back politely to let them pass.

In the entrance hall, Josceline paused. "I, er, have something to attend to in my chamber. Perhaps you could engage Mrs. Belton to take charge of the boys' bath?"

Take charge of their bath? How absurd. That was nanny's work. He opened his mouth to refuse but she raised a stern finger.

"I shall direct the rest, Mr. Sharrington. All I ask is for you to ensure the boys wash."

Something in her voice stilled his protestations and he peered at her sharply. Trepidation lined her face and her hands trembled.

"What is it, Josceline?"

She shook her head, lips compressed. "I shan't be long."

He watched her climb the stairs, dragging her feet as if she was on her way to her execution.

Something had upset her as soon as she had entered the house. Something requiring her attention.

But what?

* * *

Josceline trudged up the stairs. Christopher was obviously curious over her sudden change in mood but he had accepted her request graciously. For that she was grateful.

In truth, she could no longer postpone reading her father's letter even if it meant feeling remorse for putting the bath in Christopher's hands.

Finally she reached her room. It was late afternoon and the curtains were drawn against the early spring chill, the fire already lit. She pulled up a chair beside the fireplace and pried open the seal on the envelope which she then tossed into the flames. She clutched the letter in her fingers, watching the envelope as it withered into black curls before being consumed by the fire.

Enough procrastination, the letter would not go away by not reading it. She unfolded it and tilted the page toward the flickering light:

"Daughter,

Lady Oakland informs me you are now in the employ of a Mr. Christopher Sharrington. Surely being mistress of your own home is more to your liking. Mr. Burrows is predisposed to overlook your indiscretions and still wishes to take you to wife.

I await your response."

Respectfully,
Your father.

The letter was succinct. Her father was not one to mince words. How serious was he? Had he written the letter in a lucid moment or a drunken moment? She pressed trembling fingers to her temples.

As if the sham wasn't enough, now she had the specter of her father to contend with.

* * *

By the time Christopher made his way to the kitchen, the boys had arrived. They sat on stools beside the massive fireplace watching the cook turn the spit on which hung a venison haunch. A corner of his mouth lifted - he could almost see the drool pooling in the corners of their mouths.

"Good evening, Mr. Sharrington." Mrs. Belton scuttled into the room. She stopped dead in her tracks at the sight of the children in the kitchen yet her well schooled, plump face remained expressionless. Nevertheless, her eyes, full of questions, darted to his.

"Mrs. Belton, I place these two in your charge. They need a good scrub down and supper."

Christopher turned to waggle his finger at the two. "Mrs. Belton will care for you."

"Yes sir." They nodded in unison although he felt a twinge of foreboding at the impish look in Philip's. The eldest lad appeared to have settled in handsomely leading Christopher to wonder what high spirited behavior might ensue.

He turned back to the astonished housekeeper.

Wiping her hands on her apron, Mrs. Belton nodded her head. “As you wish, Mr. Sharrington. How kind of you to take in orphaned boys. Are they brothers?”

“Yes,” he answered curtly. Trust the staff to know more about his own life than he did. “Put them in the nursery for tonight.”

“The nursery? That will not do, Mr. Sharrington. The nursery is empty.”

Of course it sat empty. Refurbishing the nursery wasn’t high on his list of priorities. Actually, it wasn’t on his list of priorities at all because first he would need a wife. Come to think of it, a wife wasn’t on his list of priorities either. And not likely to be any time soon. He quashed those thoughts to attend to the problem at hand.

“Where would you suggest, Mrs. Belton?” he asked, lifting his palms skyward.

“Why, with me, of course. I’ll have one of the footmen set up a pallet on the floor beside me. That way, I can keep an eye on them if they need anything.” She clucked sympathetically. “Poor wee things, skinny as two sticks they are. They look as if they haven’t had a proper meal in days.”

His heart sank at her last pronouncement. Precisely. They looked underfed. If Mrs. Belton had spotted that within seconds of meeting them, wouldn’t Lady Oakland notice the same?

Be that as it may, he couldn’t change that now.

“Then give them a proper meal this evening, Mrs. Belton. Excuse me.” He knew he sounded abrupt but it was fast becoming apparent to him the boys were going to be more trouble than he had expected.

At the door, Christopher stopped to take a last look at Philip and Tom. A chuckle burst from him at the sight of two dubious faces watching the wash tub as it was pulled to a spot in front of the fire.

His chuckle turned to out and out laughter as the doubt on the faces turned to disgust when the boys realized the water being poured into the tub was meant for them. They eyed their escape before Mrs. Belton deftly nabbed them by the ears, one in each hand.

"Undress and get in," she ordered.

A smile lingered on his lips at the sight of two squirming boys flinging off their clothing, all the while securely fastened by the ear in Mrs. Belton's pudgy fingers. If nothing else, the two would be well clothed and clean tomorrow.

But he couldn't dispel the foreboding tickling the hairs on the back of his neck.

* * *

The foreboding didn't disappear once he found Josceline in the drawing room. She sat motionless, candle light flickering on her face, her mind a hundred miles away.

He crossed the room and dropped into the leather arm chair beside her. Odd how comfortable it felt, he in his leather chair, she in the carved oak chair just across the side table from him.

"Are you unwell?" Lud, the last thing he needed this evening was for Josceline to take a fit of the vapors or fall ill.

She started at his question and turned to him with vacant eyes. "Quite well, thank you."

"The letter?" It was the only thing he could think of that could have upset her so. Strangely, whatever troubled her at this moment troubled him also. An odd feeling. As if she meant more to him than she really did.

"I already told you, it is nothing to trouble you -."

"There you are mistaken, Josceline." Concern unleashed his foolish tongue. He shouldn't have called her by her given name, it showed a dreadful lack of manners.

"- but it is from my father, if you must know."

At the mention of her father, the color returned to her face and the life back to her eyes.

"What of your father?"

She'd only mentioned him once before, something about an arranged marriage, if he recalled correctly. Relations between father and daughter must have soured.

She ignored his question and launched immediately into her thoughts about the impending deception.

"Tomorrow." Her voice grew brisk. "Lady Oakland's visit. Tom shall be kept with Mrs. Belton in the kitchen. Philip shall be introduced as Philip?" At his nod, she continued. "I see no harm in using his proper name. He is a bright lad and if we ask him I am sure he will remain silent when brought in. Only for a minute or two then he can be taken away. I shall instruct him tomorrow morning." She stopped and looked at him as if trying to gauge his mood. "Mr. Sharrington?"

He cocked an eyebrow, silent encouragement for her to continue.

Her steady gaze matched his. "Have you thought about what to do with the boys afterward?"

The boys. He heaved a sigh and got to his feet to wander to the window. Night had fallen so naught could be seen of the garden outside. A pity, really, for perhaps if the sun shone he would have a cheerier outlook on the whole situation.

Foolishly, he had supposed they would disappear after the charade. Of course that wouldn't happen. However, if the sham with Philip proved successful thereby avoiding disaster for Christopher and Josceline, then the least he could do was care for them until they were old enough to be on their own. "Not yet, however I shall approach Jefferson tomorrow morning about working them in the stables."

Josceline nodded.

She had seen Christopher's panicked face when the two boys were rough housing outside the carriage. He had almost looked to call the whole thing off. To be sure, Josceline herself felt ill at ease with Philip and Tom but the success of the whole venture depended on self-assurance.

"They are just little children," she reassured him. "What could possibly go wrong?"

Chapter Ten

The following afternoon Josceline sat in the drawing room in what she now regarded as her chair, the carved oak one, when Tedham announced the arrival of Lady Oakland.

She scarce got to her feet before the woman swept into the room. Wearing an oversize ruffled bonnet of burgundy satin, she reminded Josceline of a barouche at full gallop, an impression made even stronger when she abruptly halted in front of Josceline as if an inattentive driver pulled up on the reins at the last second.

Lady Oakland pulled off black kid gloves and stuffed them in her beaded reticule, then adjusted her fringed shawl of matching burgundy satin before impaling Josceline with her gaze.

Her attire looked as if it came straight from the latest fashion plate, leaving Josceline feeling woefully inadequate in her serviceable brown walking dress. She had worn it so often the arm pits were stained.

To conceal this, Josceline wore her finest shawl, a finely spun wool the color of fresh churned butter. She'd pulled it tight about her and pinned it with her mama's cameo brooch. The brooch usually gave her confidence but today, in light of her guest's elegance, it just made her feel like someone's pauper cousin.

Especially seeing that, if one looked closely, there was a tiny chip missing – the reason why it hadn't been sold with the rest of her mama's jewelry.

"Welcome, Lady Oakland. How pleased we are to have you visit," Josceline said with as much poise as she could muster.

"I had a most interesting conversation with Lord Candel last night at Major Pennington's dinner party." Lady Oakland regarded Josceline closely. "It would seem he saw Mr. Sharrington leaving St. Peter's Hospital yesterday with two young boys. Was he mistaken?"

Balderdash, not only was Lady Oakland the picture of elegance, she was also direct.

Deny it. Deny all of it.

"I, ah, I do believe he is mistaken." Josceline groped for the back of the chair beside her to steady herself. Lord Candel had seen them? How was that possible? Her heart thudded against her chest so firmly, Josceline was certain the fabric of her dress jerked in rhythm. She had to wet her lips before she was able to say anything else.

"No," she finally managed to choke out, "Mr. Sharrington did not leave Midland House yesterday."

Where was Christopher? Had Tedham not announced Lady Oakland's arrival?

Desperate, she looked over the woman's shoulder to the drawing room door but the doorway and the hallway beyond were empty. She strained her ears but heard no footsteps. It would seem she was on her own to deal with Lady Oakland. She turned her gaze back to their guest and squared her shoulders.

"That is what I told Candel," replied Lady Oakland. "That one is a scoundrel who likes nothing better than meddle into matters not of his affair." She looked around. "Is Mr. Sharrington not joining us with his son?"

"I'll ring for tea," Josceline blurted. "And send one of the footmen to find Chris –er, Mr. Sharrington." Her face grew hot. Her nerves were so rattled, she'd almost called him by his given name. However, Lady Oakland didn't appear to have noticed. Josceline fumbled for the bell pull.

"There is no need," Christopher stepped into the drawing room. "My apologies, Lady Oakland." He swept a bow. "I was caught up with ledgers in the library. I lose track of all time when I'm there."

"Good afternoon, Mr. Sharrington. I just recounted to Lady Woodsby, Lord Candel has the most dreadful story. He claims to have seen you and two young boys in Bristol yesterday."

"Why, how could that be, Lady Oakland? Lord Candel is surely mistaken." He answered calmly and his face held a quizzical expression.

His response appeared to satisfy Lady Oakland and Josceline began to relax.

"I told him so," replied the woman smugly. "I told him you had a son living with your mother in Bristol."

She had a busybody's air and Josceline knew full well Lady Oakland's gossip would make or break the deception.

"Most assuredly so." Christopher nodded, apparently unperturbed by the woman's story. "I only have one son. Lady Woodsby, would you please bring him down?" He turned to Josceline and winked. He looked as if he enjoyed himself immensely.

"Of course, Mr. Sharrington. I'll fetch him immediately."

A relieved Josceline almost galloped from the drawing room. As she left, she could hear Christopher offer to seat their guest.

Scant minutes later, Josceline returned with Philip firmly clasped in one hand. Outside the drawing room, she paused.

"Remember, you're not to say a word," she admonished, gently tapping his nose with her index finger. "Children should be seen and not heard."

"Yes, miss."

She looked him up and down one last time. His hair, so dark yesterday, had turned blonde after his bath and it curled about his cheeks disarmingly. In his new clothing, he looked as fine as any young lad she had ever seen. Only his hands betrayed him – they were tanned and rough.

"Philip, you must also remember to put your hands behind you. Like this." Josceline clasped her hands behind her and turned to show him. "Pretend it's a game."

Philip nodded and did as she instructed.

"Good boy." She smiled at him then dropped her hand on his shoulder to steer him into the drawing room.

An attentive Lady Oakland watched them approach and curiosity hovered over her like a bird of prey drifting on the wind. As she stirred her tea, to Josceline's fanciful mind her fingers resembled claws.

Josceline's stomach churned as she halted and pulled Philip beside her. "May I present my charge, Tom." Balderdash, she'd used the wrong name. Would anyone notice?

"Philip." The boy looked up at Josceline. "Me name is Philip Stanford."

Not surprisingly, the boy had noticed. And now he had done the one thing she had instructed him not to – he spoke.

His rough dialect grated on Josceline's ears and she clapped her hand over his mouth. Glancing down, she could see the mutinous set of his lips beneath her fingers.

Her stomach stopped churning and leapt into her throat; she swallowed hard several times before she was able to speak. "Yes, Philip, how silly of me to call you Tom." she squeaked, wracking her brains for a plausible excuse. "Er, you remind me of my younger brother when he was young. His name is Tom. You are Philip Stanford, er – Sharrington. Yes, Philip Stanford Sharrington," she repeated.

Even to her ears, it sounded a cock and bull story and she peeked up at Lady Oakland to gauge the woman's reaction. Her dark head was tipped to one side, the perfect picture of skepticism.

Josceline's heart sank through the floor. How could this get any worse?

"Is the tea to your liking, Lady Oakland?" Christopher's voice was hearty, too hearty.

Josceline risked a quick glance to spot him motioning wildly to her to remove Philip. She turned to do so when came a clatter of running feet and Tom, blonde curls flying, burst into the room carrying a fluffy bundle of kitten. Behind him huffing as fast as her legs could carry her, came Mrs. Belton.

"Look, Philip," Tom cried. "Look, they 'ave kittens!"

"I must beg pardon, Mr. Sharrington," puffed Mrs. Belton, "the lad got away from me."

If the situation hadn't been so grave, Josceline would have laughed out loud at the housekeeper's beet red face and mortified expression. Instead, Josceline looked away to hide the smile quivering on her lips at the sight.

Philip unclasped his hands and reached for the kitten. "Cor," he breathed. "It's as white as a swan."

His hands were almost black against the fur. Beads of perspiration popped out on Josceline's forehead. First his voice, now the hands, what was Lady Oakland to think?

Lady Oakland's eyes darted from one blonde headed boy to the other than back again. Bewilderment wrinkled her brow. "Oh my," she murmured. "They could be brothers."

"Tom is the housekeeper's grandson," explained Christopher smoothly. A muscle ticked in his cheek but he carried himself with considerable composure.

Josceline took comfort in that and willed her pounding heart to slow down.

Mrs. Belton's mouth dropped open but before she had a chance to protest, both boys darted from the room. She threw a murderous glance at Christopher before stomping after them.

"I have seen quite enough," said Lady Oakland. She put down her tea cup.

Her tone was pleasant yet Josceline saw suspicion lurking in her eyes. Suspicion that again set off Josceline's rattled nerves and she had a difficult time catching her breath.

"Mr. Sharrington," Lady Oakland continued, "I do not claim to understand what is going on here at Midland House but your son appears to be very comfortable with your housekeeper's grandson. Beware the boys do not spend too much time together. Indeed, I do not see gently reared children but rather, two boys who are ill-behaved monsters." She got to her feet and pointed to Josceline. "I fear, Lady Woodsby, you have quite the challenge in front of you." She flung her shawl around her neck. "I bid you both good day."

Without a glance back, she marched out of the room, calling for her carriage.

The whole episode had lasted less than ten minutes, not even enough time for her to finish her tea, for her cup sat half full.

The room was silent as a tomb. Josceline and Christopher just stared at each other. Far in the distance, they could hear the shrieks of Philip and Tom.

"Do you think she is convinced?" Josceline tried, and failed miserably, to keep the gloom from her voice.

"Of course," Christopher replied energetically. Too energetically, for his slumped form belied the brisk tone in his voice. He slouched back against the chair, eyes dark, mouth grim, the very picture of dejection.

A dejection, Josceline was sure, mirrored on her own face.

For one insane instant, she wanted to bury her head on Christopher's shoulder, and feel his strong arms wrapped around her. Wanted him to hold her close and tell her everything would be splendid. She closed her eyes and willed the sensation to go away – he employed her, she reminded herself. Nothing more.

She opened her eyes to catch his somber gaze on her.

"This is a fine to do, is it not?" she said finally, her voice wavering.

"Time will tell."

"Yes." She nodded and gathered up the cups to place them on the tray. "Time will tell."

But it wasn't what time would tell she was worried about.

It was what Lady Oakland would tell.

Chapter Eleven

Christopher didn't speak again until a grim lipped Josceline finished tidying the cups and had carried the tray to the sideboard. Her hand shook when she reached for the bell pull. She barely had the strength to tug at it and she had to try several times before a distant bell echoed through the house.

A protective impulse surged through him at her obvious distress. It wasn't her fault Tom had run into the room. In fact, up until then, Josceline had handled the situation with pluck, even covering up her mistake with Philip's name.

Her misery pierced him through and through. At this particular moment, he didn't give a fig for what Lady Oakland thought of him - he just wanted to lighten Josceline's spirits.

He wanted to continue as if yesterday and today had never happened.

He wanted her to smile at him and tease him.

He wanted to learn more about her for she intrigued him.

"Join me for dinner this evening?" The question burst out of his mouth to hang clumsily in the air between them.

She turned startled eyes to him then shook her head. "I thank you for the invitation, Mr. Sharrington, but I prefer to take a tray in my room."

"You've done that every evening since you've come here. Please reconsider, I would enjoy your company."

"It's what's proper. Governesses do not mingle with their employers."

He snorted. "Who made that absurd rule? Join me this evening," he pleaded. "We should discuss our next step."

"I wager our next step will depend on what Lady Oakland thinks. No thank you." She dipped her chin. "I would prefer my own company this evening."

"Please, Josceline, I'll have Cook make your favorite meal," he wheedled. "Tell me what it is and you shall have it."

She fiddled with the ends of her shawl before lifting her gaze to his. "You are insufferably obstinate, Mr. Sharrington." A smile tickled the corners of her mouth. "But it is roast squab, if you must know."

"Nine o'clock in the dining room?" he asked hopefully.

"Yes, nine o'clock. Now may I be excused?" Without waiting for his nod, she turned and walked away.

Anticipation beat a quick tattoo in Christopher's breast as he watched her leave. Tonight he would treat her as the beautiful young woman she was.

Tonight he would woo her as the beautiful young woman he could love.

* * *

Josceline fretted over what to wear to dinner. Not that she had much to fret over, for besides her brown walking dress, she only had two other choices: The jade green woolen frock she had worn to Bristol yesterday. Or, the watered blue silk she had borrowed from Elizabeth, who had insisted she keep it "Because one never knows when one shall be called upon for an evening out." At least it had long fitted sleeves and a lace fichu which gave her a modicum of modesty.

She cast a regretful eye towards the bolt of copper satin draped over the wardrobe door. How lovely it would have been to have a new dress to wear.

Nerves fluttered in her stomach as she readied herself, an entirely different set of nerves than those besetting her this afternoon.

These were nerves of eagerness, the nerves of a young woman about to dine alone with a man.

Not just any man - the man she was beginning to adore.

She spent an inordinate amount of time with her hair, brushing it until it shone, then looping it back simply with a matching blue ribbon. She pulled out several tendrils to frame her face, running them through a damp comb before twisting them about her fingers so they would curl just so above her ears. Finally, she pinched her cheeks and bit her lips to give them color.

The little gold plated clock on her mantel chimed nine times. A quick pirouette in front of the mirror and she was done. Not as finely turned out as Lady Oakland, she conceded, but presentable nonetheless. A last glance to pat her hair and she left her room, determined to enjoy the evening.

Savoring the delicious aromas wafting up the stairs from the kitchen, she made her way to the main floor. Her mouth watered and she was glad she had succumbed to Christopher's pleas to join him for dinner after all. Another cold tray in her room would have been dull after today's events.

At the arched entrance to the dining room, she paused, eyes drawn to the table.

Covered with a crisp white damask tablecloth, a multitude of silver candlesticks marched down the centre of it like so many tin soldiers. Even though every candle burned, the rest of the room hung in shadows.

In the dim light, she could see the room's immense size, the walls lined with oil paintings, its floor graced with a luxurious fringed silk carpet. The room was meant for dinner parties and for an instant she imagined herself, gracious and welcoming, sitting as hostess across from Christopher. An enticing thought.

It wasn't until Christopher pulled himself away from where he leaned against the sideboard that she saw him.

His eyes were dark, admiring and he, too, had dressed for the occasion in a navy brocade high-waisted cut away coat, black satin waistcoat and black breeches.

"How lovely you are," he breathed as he bent over her hand to drop a light kiss on the back of it. Her gaze caught on the unfamiliar sight of his dark head over her hand. She blushed, a rising tide of heat starting at her décolletage and ending up in the very roots of her hair. He lifted his head, gave her an inscrutable glance then stepped away to ring for dinner.

Disconcerted at his enigmatic air, she inspected the table more closely. At the far end closest to the fire, two places had been set such that they would be sitting across from each other. Candlelight reflected in the well polished silver flanking each gold rimmed, ivory plate.

Next to one plate sat a cut crystal decanter filled with red wine. Across the other plate lay a posy of violets. Sweet violets, the first of the season. An intimate gesture and she shivered at the promise it held.

"Allow me." He pulled out her chair. Did she imagine it, or did his hand brush her shoulder as she seated herself? She picked up the posy and inhaled its fragrance before placing it on the table beside her.

Christopher sat down and nodded to Tedham, waiting by the door discreetly. At Tedham's signal, a silent footman served the first course, a clear beef broth with dumplings. She watched Christopher pour the wine, a rich burgundy ribbon glowing in the candlelight that pooled in each goblet.

"To a lovely evening." He lifted his glass to her.

"A lovely evening," she murmured and picked up her glass to return the toast. She took a sip. His contemplation of her flustered her and she took another sip to hide her unease, glancing at the painting of a naval battle above the fireplace before returning her gaze to his.

If she did not know better, she would think Christopher was intent on courting her.

She could pretend he courted her, could she not? She sipped again, regarding him over the rim of her glass.

No, she couldn't. She was his governess for only a few months and couldn't hope for anything more. She put down her glass.

"Mr. Sharrington -." She stopped at his upraised hand.

"Please, enough of the formality. Christopher, if you will."

The wine made her bold. "Only if you reciprocate and call me Josceline."

He inclined his head.

"If I may be so forward as to make a suggestion?" At his nod, she continued. "You've hired me as governess and are paying my wage. I can tutor the boys. Surely they will be of more benefit to you if they can read and write and know their ciphers?"

"Let us not talk of the boys." His bowl empty, he put down his spoon. "Let us talk about you."

The conversation was taking an entirely too familiar turn and she marshaled her thoughts while the bowls were cleared before answering.

"There is nothing to talk about. Besides, the whole pretext of this evening was to discuss Lady Oakland and the boys, was it not?"

He lifted an eyebrow, a corner of his mouth lifted. "And a pretext it was, Josceline. As you yourself pointed out, we must wait for Lady Oakland's pronouncement before we can plan our course of action."

She puzzled over this last comment. Surely he hadn't wanted her to join him for dinner just for the sake of having her company.

The silent footman returned, this time carrying smoked trout on a carved tray which he placed with a flourish on the table before them.

"Tell me again how the daughter of a duke came to be a governess." Christopher leaned over and replenished her wine then pushed the tray closer to her. "I find it a fascinating story."

"Because the Duchy of Cranston is in ruins," she replied honestly, serving them both a slice of the trout. "My mother passed away ten years ago and my father's form of grieving was to drink and gamble away what funds we had."

"That explains it," he said with a satisfied nod.

"Explains what?"

He pointed to her dress. "The dress is well worn, as are all your clothes. I don't think the daughter of a duke would dress shabbily by choice."

She blinked at his powers of observation. Embarrassed, she raked his face, searching for condemnation but could find none, only gentle interest.

"My father sought to recoup his financial stability by offering me as inducement," she continued. "However, the only offers came from merchants and the like seeking entrance into the ton. None from our social sphere were interested in making a match for my father's reputation is not the best. I am blamed by association." She took another sip of wine. "The latest suitor was a man old enough to be my grandfather. That was when I decided to become mistress of my own life." She shrugged. "Governess seemed an obvious preference." She picked up her knife and fork and began to eat.

"Agreed." Christopher nodded slowly. "Unlike a man, a woman without means doesn't have many choices." He took a bite of trout, scarce tasting it for the admiration that filled him at her resolve. He understood her desire to make her own way. "And the letter was from your father," he guessed. At her nod, he continued, "Am I correct in assuming he does not share your enthusiasm to earn a living?"

"Indeed, you are correct. According to my father, Mr. Burrows, the gentleman in question, still wishes my hand in marriage."

"You do not wish matrimony at all?" he asked, astonished.

"If I marry, it shall be for love of a man," Josceline declared firmly, the wine having made her reckless. "And I say if, for who shall marry me as I am?"

What was he thinking at her brash declaration? His head tilted slightly to one side and he had that inscrutable expression on his face again.

"If it is all the same to you, I don't wish to discuss this further." Josceline made her voice spirited. "My plans for myself differ from my father's plans for me. It is nothing more than that. What of you? What brings a man to leave a respected position in His Majesty's navy and what must have been an exciting life?"

How neatly she had turned the tables on him. Christopher's admiration for her swelled.

"Hardly exciting," he answered. "For the most part, a sailor's life is dull. Long days at sea mending sails, scrubbing decks, that sort of thing."

"But you must have engaged in battle."

"Aye." Christopher inclined his head. "And therein lies the real reason for my resignation from the navy. I didn't have the stomach anymore for the bloodshed and horror of battle. Bloodshed and horror which is far from over as long as Napoleon Bonaparte rules the Continent." Lud, the conversation wasn't going at all as he wished. He signaled to the ever discreet Tedham to have the table cleared for their next course.

"Roast squab," said Christopher, as the cook herself appeared with the main course laid out with asparagus and peas on an oval platter. "Your favorite. May I ask you to serve again?"

He loved watching her stylish mannerisms, loved how her elegance graced his dining table and, by extension, him. Not giving her the chance to refuse, he handed her his plate.

"What will you do now?" She placed a squab in the centre of each plate before arranging the vegetables in neat piles. "Enough?"

At his nod, Josceline pushed the plate over to him. He shifted as he adjusted his plate and his foot brushed hers, sending a jolt up her leg. She jerked away as if prodded by a hot poker then glanced down at her own plate to avoid his gaze. She wasn't sure her face wouldn't reveal her unseemly awareness of him.

She picked up her utensils and tried to slice off a piece of meat. The bird flipped over and a few peas squirted off her plate to roll across the tablecloth. Heat rose in her cheeks - the man had the knack of unsettling her and she had no idea how to counter it. She peeped at him from beneath her lashes, expecting to see amusement on his face but his visage was earnest as he answered her question.

"What will I do now? I mean to earn my living as a merchant captain. That is why I've chosen Bristol. The harbor here provides the closest route for trade to the Colonies."Working for one's living was not the fashionable thing but Christopher had no choice if he didn't want to starve. He scoured her face, searching for revulsion at his declaration but her features were composed. A brief surge of hope rose within him until he realized a duke's daughter would be polite enough to hide her true feelings.

"An admirable goal," she replied graciously. She patted her mouth with her napkin and leaned back against the chair. "The cook has quite outdone herself. I swear, I am fair to bursting. Although a lady should never admit that." She giggled. Oh la, the wine had really gone to her head.

"Share the joke," demanded Christopher. "If you do not, I shall fear you're laughing at me." He pretended to glare at her before joining in with her laughter.

"Laughing at you, good sir?" She giggled again. "That I would never, never do. No, I am laughing for the sheer pleasure of having eaten a good meal. There is nothing finer, is there not, than fine food, fine wine. And fine company," she added. She hoped he would not find her forward for having said it but the audacious statement conveyed her sentiment for indeed, his company made the meal memorable.

And happily, there was more to come, for the footman laid out dessert: baked custard and berry compote, meringues, a chocolate crème, fresh fruit, cheese and walnuts. Clean wine glasses were brought for the bottle of champagne that now replaced the empty wine decanter.

"Oh." She eyed the laden table dubiously. "It was no jest when I said I was fair to burst with all I have eaten."

He chuckled. "One does not need to be hungry to eat dessert. Besides, we have an entire evening to while away. I request, nay, I demand the pleasure of your company until at least midnight." And he proceeded to fill the fresh glasses with champagne.

Josceline looked at him, then her glass with its spiraling bubbles, then back to him. Naked admiration shone in his eyes, a gentle smile curved his lips. A potent combination and one she couldn't refuse.

"I accept," she said gaily, lifting her glass to him. Just for tonight she would pretend she was not his governess.

Just for tonight.

* * *

It wasn't until the massive grandfather clock in the front hall struck two that Josceline pushed back her chair. She stood, teetering a moment before finding her balance. How had it become so late? It seemed only short minutes ago they had their desserts. In fact, it was nigh on four hours.

Christopher rose to his feet as well.

"I must bid you good night," Josceline said. "Thank you for a lovely evening." All of a sudden, she felt awkward, shy.

"And I must thank you for the lovely company."

Giving him a weak smile, she started towards the door. She kept her gaze firmly at her feet, afraid if she looked at him, her eyes would betray her desire to stay with him longer.

Head down, she wobbled to the door to spy a pair of polished black boots. She looked up.

Christopher leaned against the doorway, blocking her way. He straightened and held out an elbow to her. "It's not a carriage, but it should get you home."

"There's no need." She shook her head emphatically. "I'm perfectly capable of finding my room."

"I would be sorely amiss if I didn't ensure the well-being of my guests." Again he held out his arm.

"Bully," she muttered but she gave him a saucy grin as she took his arm.

A delicious thrill ran through her at the strong arm beneath her fingers. She tightened her grip, taking delight in the close contact and the last few precious minutes with him.

Most of the staff had long retired for the night and although Midland House was silent, their way was well lit. Candles flickered everywhere and as they walked through the dark hallways and stairs, dancing shadows surrounded them.

At her door, Christopher paused. She tried to tug her hand away but he refused, clasping it firmly to his elbow with his free hand.

Christopher hadn't thought the chance to kiss her another time would arrive so soon but he meant to take full advantage of the opportunity. He glanced about. The hall was empty, the occasion ideal.

"Josceline," he whispered, looking down at her questioning face. He couldn't wait to taste her lips once more.

He's going to kiss me again.

The frantic thought pummeled Josceline's mind. A kiss she desperately wanted but a kiss which would only draw her deeper into hopeless dreams.

The world dropped away as she stared at the lips slanted tantalizingly close to hers. Her pulse raced then gradually slowed as desire for him trickled through her veins, thickening her blood, slowing her heart until she became stillness itself.

Desire and good sense waged a silent battle within her.

Desire won.

Just for tonight. And tonight was not yet over.

She tipped her head upwards and lost herself in his dark gaze. A kiss to end a perfect evening. His arms tightened around her, his head lowered.

A screech sounded down the hallway behind them. A mewling fluffy white bundle scrabbled around the corner followed by two child-like wraiths.

At the sight of Josceline and Christopher, Philip and Tom skidded to a panting halt, eyes wide with apprehension. The kitten skittered past them and bounded away down the hall.

Beneath her chest she could feel Christopher's groan. He dropped his arms and stepped back.

Josceline moved away, not knowing whether to laugh with relief that she had been rescued from her emotions, or cry with frustration over the lost opportunity.

"Boys, off to bed with you," Christopher commanded.

His voice held annoyance, and dare she believe, a hint of regret?

"Yes sir, we're sorry, sir." Philip took charge. "Come, Tom, we'll play with the kitten tomorrow." Arm in arm, the two shuffled off and disappeared back the way they came.

Josceline took advantage of the interruption, letting good sense win this battle.

"Good night," she squeaked, squeezing past Christopher's shoulder to push open the door to her room and step inside. It swung shut behind her but she could still hear his throaty chuckle.

"Good night, Josceline. I vow, next time you shan't escape so easily."

Josceline plucked the handkerchief from its hiding spot behind the frame and stumbled to the bed. Plopping down, she held it close to her nose to inhale the scent of citrus and leather.

She couldn't remember ever having enjoyed a meal so much. And it hadn't been only the repast.

No, how she enjoyed his appreciative gaze on her, his questions as if he really wanted to know the answer, his way of making her feel as if she was an intelligent human being.

That night she slept with the handkerchief tucked under her pillow.

* * *

Christopher's erection throbbed mercilessly as he stood outside Josceline's room. How he wanted to follow her to her bed. But she was the daughter of a duke and merited his respect. She would make a fine wife for someone.

Why not him?

The idea took root. Josceline as his wife. Would she accept him as her husband? She would if he could make her love him. For that was what she had said earlier – she wished to marry for love.

A sobering reality hit him. If he took her to wife, he would have to disclose his terrible secret. Then there was the awkward notion of her birth. He wasn't of her class.

But if he married her, he would be. Perhaps not actually, but technically he would move in her social circles. Lady Oakland and her ilk would no longer prove a barrier to him.

The more he thought on it, the more he liked the idea of Josceline as his wife. And the more he liked the idea, the more outlandish it seemed.

And the more outlandish it seemed, the more impossible it became to attain. Prudence would dictate he not follow the path of an unattainable fantasy.

Perhaps it would be best to keep his distance from her. If he could.

Chapter Twelve

Josceline spent Saturday in her room mending. Two days had passed since the wonderful dinner with Christopher.

Two days where she'd dreamed of him constantly.

Two days where he'd been distant and preoccupied.

Two days where she'd gone out of her way to catch a glimpse of him.

Two days where he'd blatantly avoided her, so much so, he'd cancelled his dance lessons.

What troubled him? Had she been too forward that evening? She hadn't thought so but to be sure, her memories of it were misty and overlaid with a golden haze of pleasure.

The needle slipped, pricking her finger. A drop of blood welled and she popped the finger in her mouth. Balderdash. That was the fourth time today and if she were to have any fingers left, she had better keep her mind on her task.

With a rueful moue, she held up a pair of already much mended stockings to inspect them – the thin silk of the heels made it difficult to sew. She bent her head and carefully began to stitch, grateful to the obliging Mrs. Belton who had provided her with needle, thread and scissors.

From where she sat she could see the sweep of the front drive. The dull pewter sky spewed a fine rain that silvered the cobblestones and washed away winter's dust. A week or two more and cheery jonquils would poke their heads through to signal the start of spring, Josceline's favorite season. A little smile played on her lips at the thought. Spring lasted about three months and then she and her foolish heart could be on her way.

At the sound of reckless hoof beats, she lifted her head to see Christopher on horseback pelting up the driveway. He leapt off his mount, throwing the reins to the footman before storming up the front steps.

Even from this distance, she noticed the murderous set of his face and the deep scowl on his jaw. A few seconds later, she heard him bellow for Tedham then the ferocious slam of a door shook the floor.

What could have happened to provoke this display of temper? It did not correspond with what she had learned of him during their dance lessons together. Even during those moments of frustration, his self-control – due, no doubt, to his naval background - was in evidence as he never raised his voice or grumbled.

She put aside her sewing. Mindlessly she stared at the spatters of rain pricking the window panes and tried to make sense of his behavior. It was none of her concern yet she couldn't stop puzzling over it and what had happened to provoke it.

The little mantel clock chimed four times, a rapid ding ding ding ding disturbing her reverie as surely as if someone had rapped her on the head four times with a sharp knuckle. Time for tea. Pausing only to smooth her hair, she made her way to the sitting room, expecting to find it empty.

To her surprise, a brooding Christopher had already arrived. He sat in the leather chair, elbows propped on the arms, chin resting on his fist. One booted foot dangled over his knee, the other tapped the floor. His eyes were bleak as he watched her approach.

"What happened? You look troubled." Uncertain, Josceline lowered herself into her chair. It wasn't her place to question his mood but she had to know what had beset him so. She regarded him with steady eyes and composed face although inside her heart beat a happy cadence at the sight of him.

He looked for a moment as if he wouldn't answer then he ground out the words, forcing them out as if they were as distasteful as sour berries.

"I paid a call to that idiot Lord Candel today." He avoided her gaze.

"And what of Lord Candel?" She made her voice light. "He comes from a fine family."

"The man is a scurrilous rogue," he growled, "with the manners of an oaf. The butler denied me entrance. As I stood on the front porch, Candel gave me the cut direct. He walked past me as if I did not exist." He glanced at her. "Do you know of him?"

"Everyone knows of the Candel family. They forged an illustrious military career on the Continent, garnering the undying gratitude of King George. Lord and Lady Thaddeus Candel are favorites at court and at all the assemblies for they are a gracious couple. The son, however, is a different matter. Oliver is a feckless rake and has been dunned out of London."

"Oliver." Christopher slammed his fist on the arm of his chair. "I followed him as he walked to his carriage to call him on his manners. It gets worse." He stopped and looked her fully in the face. "He promised he would spread the tale of the two lads unless I stop harassing him."

"A tale which tattling tongues will spread far and wide," Josceline concluded. "Odd how two little boys can cause such hullabaloo."

She meant it as a jest and was rewarded with a wry snort and a momentary lightening of his expression.

"The tale may have no bearing if Lady Oakland does not support it," she added hopefully.

"We do not know what Lady Oakland believes." The scowl returned.

Josceline sat for a moment, head spinning. "What is he to you?" she asked at length. "You spoke of him the night you stopped my carriage."

Christopher hesitated. "The man owes me a gambling debt. And I mean to have it."

"What is this debt you are so determined to recover that you are willing to face social ruin?"

With hooded eyes, he scoured her face long and hard. His reluctance to confide in her was palpable; she leaned towards him as if to tease the words out of him.

"A ship," he answered finally. "A cargo ship, to be precise. The fool lost heavily at the gaming tables throughout that evening and at the end had only the ship's deed to wager with. Wiser heads counseled him to withdraw but he refused, bragging that a single ship meant nothing to him."

"There you may be mistaken," she said thoughtfully. "The Candel family dabbles in shipping and owns ships that ply out of Bristol. Hence Oliver being here. How odd he would risk losing it. He is well aware of its value."

He sank his jaw onto his fists and closed his eyes for a second. "When I bested him he accused me of cheating and refused to surrender the deed."

Her ire rose at the unfairness of it all. "Certainly there were other gentlemen who saw the entire episode," she exclaimed.

"Aye." Christopher nodded morosely. "But none stood up for me for I am unknown here. I need that ship, Josceline." He got to his feet and began to pace. "I simply don't have the means to buy a vessel of my own. Needless to say, a captain without a ship is nothing."

"You mean to become a merchant captain yet you don't own a ship?" Josceline tried, and failed, to keep astonishment from her voice.

He nodded again, his lips twisted. "My original idea involved striking an arrangement with one of the local merchants here to earn a share in a ship in exchange for my services. I couldn't believe my good luck when Candel wagered the "Bessie". I know of her for since arriving in Bristol, I've investigated the local ship yards. She's a sturdy vessel and well suited for the transatlantic trade. It seemed my prayers were answered."

"Until Candel reneged. Well, knowing his reputation, I cannot say I'm surprised to hear of his duplicity."

"If it were only the ship, I would hound Candel and be done with it. However, I need social standing if I mean to join the Society of Merchant Venturers. That will give me assured success for members are given the choicest berths and docks." He rubbed his temples. "What rotten luck for him to have seen us leaving St. Peter's."

"Would it be too difficult for you to proceed with your original plan?" As soon as she said it, she wished she could take back the words for his face became a stone mask.

"No man dupes me of what is mine," he spat. Without a second glance, he stalked from the room.

A silent Josceline watched him go, heart aching at his defeated demeanor.

There was more between Lord Oliver Candel and Mr. Christopher Sharrington than a mere gambling debt. It was written in the anguish in Christopher's voice, in the taut creases of his face, the haunted look in his eyes.

Josceline determined to find out. She much preferred his eyes filled with laughter, not the bitterness sullying them now.

* * *

Christopher didn't know why he had gone to the sitting room first. By rights, he should have gone directly to the library, where he was now.

He tossed back a glass of the fine cognac he had acquired on his final crossing to the Continent and poured himself another. The searing liquid helped clarify his thoughts.

The past two days avoiding Josceline had been sheer torture. Day and night his mind had been filled with thoughts of her.

Simply put, he had gone to the sitting room because he wanted to see her, to share what had happened, to have her tease him and make it right again.

Instead, he had only succeeded in making himself look like a useless fool, duped and tossed aside like so much rubbish.

There was the rub. He didn't want to look the fool to Josceline, he wanted her esteem.

Again he drained his glass.

Not only have I been snubbed and threatened by Oliver Candel, I am haunted at night by snapping green eyes and peach hued lips.

Snapping green eyes and peach hued lips that could send him to prison with the flash of a handkerchief.

He hurled the empty glass into the fireplace taking grim satisfaction at the jagged pieces glittering amongst the ashes. He dropped into the chair behind his desk, leaning forward on his elbows to cradle his head in his palms.

His life had become a complicated mess.

How much simpler the sea faring life, with a sturdy deck heaving beneath his feet and the clean wind across his cheeks, the salt spray in his hair and his hands firm on the wheel. That night when he had won the "Bessie", his sea faring dream began to crystallize.

The dream had been in his grasp for an ephemeral instant before it had been snatched away by a liar and a cheat. Somehow Christopher had to take it back.

Chapter Thirteen

Christopher lifted his head to gaze outside. It rained harder now, a perfect complement to his mood. He barely heard the hesitant tap over the spattering of the rain drops against the library windows.

"Christopher? I heard a crash." Josceline's neat head poked around the door. "May I come in?"

"As you please." Arms crossed, he watched her step smoothly across the waxed hardwood floor towards him.

"I have an idea. Such a simple idea, I do not know how we didn't come upon it before." A russet curl had worked itself loose to curve around her jaw and she shoved it back behind her ear impatiently.

"Yes?" He knew his voice sounded harsh but he couldn't help it.

"Let us talk to Mrs. Wilkinson, the mistress at St. Peter's Hospital. Perhaps she will take our part." Her green eyes were darkened to jade in the dim light filtering through the windows yet he could see the earnestness shining in them.

Our part. He liked the sound of that. He leaned back in his chair, hope rising as Josceline continued to talk.

"We could ask her, could we not? Or rather, you could ask her. I don't think we should risk being seen together there a second time."

Still he said nothing but thoughts began to churn through his head. Mrs. Wilkinson was the only person who could corroborate Candel's story. If she didn't back his story, then it wouldn't carry any credibility. With Candel lacking credibility, Lady Oakland would have no reason to suspect anything.

However, Candel spoke the truth, meaning Mrs. Wilkinson would have to bend the truth. Would she do so?

She would if he paid her.

As much as he hated stooping to such tactics, it appeared a plausible solution.

Of course, there was also the haberdasher but a threat from Christopher to take his business elsewhere should be sufficient for that man's discretion.

With renewed optimism, he surveyed Josceline. Clever and sharp witted, she had a head on her shoulders. He liked that. Simpering women bored him to tears.

She colored under his frank perusal. "Perhaps it isn't such a good idea after all. I must beg pardon for interrupting you. I thought-." Her voice trailed away and she clasped and unclasped her hands.

"Josceline, it is a splendid idea." He sprang to his feet and came around to take her cold hands in his very warm ones. "First thing on Monday I shall ride into Bristol and speak with Mrs. Wilkinson." He grinned at her, willing her to smile back. "We have a plan. We can begin to fight."

He dropped her hands to move away. *Keep your distance. The daughter of a duke can never be anything to you.*

The scent of violets and sandalwood lingered in his nostrils and he inhaled deeply, sure that by doing so he could capture some essence of her.

Josceline welcomed his new found buoyant air. She returned his grin, knowing hers stretched ear to ear just like his.

"You shall soon have Mrs. Wilkinson in agreement," she declared with utmost confidence. "Oliver Candel will have no proof."

"Aye," he agreed with a vigorous nod.

Relief washed over Josceline as his features lost that pinched look to be replaced with open confidence. They had a plan. She exhaled slowly, unaware she had been holding her breath. Dragging her gaze away from his face, she contemplated the rain while marshaling her thoughts.

With Candel's threat rendered impotent, Lady Oakland must be convinced once and for all that Philip was truly Christopher's son.

The discussion with Lady Oakland required a deft touch and who better than Josceline herself. If successful, her position as governess would be solidified and she could safely finish her three month term. Here, at Midland House. With Christopher.

And if unsuccessful?

She wouldn't allow herself to think upon that possibility.

She, Josceline, would deal with Lady Oakland. How, she wasn't sure, but she would find a way.

* * *

As soon as Christopher stepped inside St. Peter's Hospital early Monday afternoon, he remembered the smell: The odor of unwashed bodies mingling with the stench of the river and the pungent stab of despair.

Before scooting off, the unkempt boy who had let him in pointed wordlessly towards the bell pull. Christopher gave it a firm tug. He couldn't hear anything but presumably it rang somewhere within the recesses of the house.

While he waited, he inspected the carved wall paneling depicting biblical scenes. Incongruous and depressing, it clearly signified the building had been intended for another use.

Footsteps sounded behind him and he turned around to see the matron, garbed in the same grubby dress, shuffling towards him.

"I 'ad a feeling you'd come looking for me." She leered at him knowingly.

"Oh?"

"Aye." She nodded her head, setting the dirty mobcap to flapping. "I 'ad a visitor. A dandy. Looking for the boys. I told 'im nothing but he may come back. Determined sort, he was."

"I believe I know of whom you speak." He drew himself up to full height and looked down his nose at the woman. "The man seeks to do me harm. Could we come to an agreement, Mrs., ah -."

Damnation, he could not for the life of him remember the woman's name. The knowledge Candel had already been by to check the veracity of the boys' heritage rattled him. He sucked in a lungful of air to steady himself, ignoring as best he could the foul smell.

"Wilkinson," she interjected helpfully. "And to what would we be agreeing to?"

"Ah, yes, Mrs. Wilkinson." He pulled back his coat and patted his bulging vest pocket. "If you could forget we were here."

Her greedy eyes devoured the bulge in his vest. "For the right price, I'll even forget the boys were 'ere."

As he had expected, she sought money for her silence. Excellent.

He pulled out his sack of coins. "Say, five guineas?" He counted out five coins and held them out.

She swiped them off his palm so quickly her hand was a blur.

"Thank ye." She tucked the coins into her pocket. "I ain't seen nothing. Not you, not Philip, not Tom."

"Tell me, Mrs. Wilkinson, how do I know you'll not double cross me?" He placed his fists on his hips and leaned towards her.

His threatening stance left her unfazed.

"I knew their ma," she answered glibly. "She were a good girl who made a bad choice. Some lord took 'er to mistress but cast 'er off when he tired of 'er. She took 'er solace in a bottle which didn't leave nothin' for the boys." She swiped her hand across her dripping nose. "I'm fond of those two. The way I see it, they deserve a chance for a better life."

"Agreed." Christopher inclined his head.

"Ye can count on me, Mr. Sharrington. I won't say a word about ye and yer missus being here." She held out her hand. It glistened where she had wiped her nose.

Grimacing inwardly, he shook it. They needed her and to insult her now only had the potential to cause harm.

"She is not my wife." And yearning would not make it so, came the peculiar thought.

"As ye wish." She shrugged but her eyes held a shrewd glint. "I'm a busy woman, if ye can show yerself out."

* * *

Josceline paced restlessly.

Christopher had left early this morning to visit the mistress of St. Peter's. She'd tried to while away the time by sewing, even going so far as to lay out the precious copper satin on her bed before bundling it up and draping it once again over her wardrobe door.

Then she had gone to the library and tried to find a book but the titled spines turned to jelly beneath her eyes and became so much gibberish.

She had even looked for Philip and Tom only to be told by Mrs. Belton they were visiting Jefferson in the stable.

Thus she had resorted to walking the floors of Midland House, nerves churning, thoughts jumbled. Could the woman be persuaded to keep their secret? If so, could she be trusted?

Tedham caught up to her on her third pass of the hallway outside the dining room.

"Lady Woodsby, you have visitors."

"For me? Are you certain?" A puzzled Josceline stopped dead in her tracks.

"Yes, my lady, they await you in the drawing room."

"You've already shown them in? Could you not have asked me first?" She wasn't in the mood for idle chatter. Other matters preoccupied her mind.

Tedham flushed. "Of course, my lady, how wrong of me. However, the gentleman insists he is your father."

"What?" she exclaimed. Faintness overtook her. Swaying, she put her hand on the wall to steady herself. "You said visitors. Who else is with him?"

"The other man claims to be betrothed to you."

The butler's answer sounded as if it came from a great distance and she could scarce make sense of the words.

Her father and Mr. Burrows.

Here.

Now.

And she was alone in the house.

"I must beg pardon, my lady. I thought I was doing the right thing." Voice apologetic, he bowed.

Josceline shook her head and drew in several shuddering breaths before responding. "It is not of your doing. The last thing I expected was a visit from my father or I would have given you proper instructions."

"Shall I send them away, my lady?"

She stared at him for a full moment, trying to comprehend what he had just said. The thunder pounding in her ears made his words unintelligible.

He shuffled uncomfortably and coughed behind his hand. His faded blue eyes were anxious as he looked at her. “Er, my lady, shall I send them away?”

“No.” She shook her head. “No, I shall speak to them.” The opportunity to deal with her father and his expectations of her had arisen. All she had to do was walk to the drawing room and state her case.

However, her feet refused to cooperate. It was as if they were mired in the mud of her jumbled thoughts. She had enough worries over the boys that she couldn’t even begin to muster her arguments to her father.

She didn’t know what to do.

Christopher. She would tell Christopher. He would make it right.

“Yes.” The shake became a nod. “Yes. Yes, send them away.”

* * *

Christopher returned in a much better frame of mind. Whistling a jaunty tune, he bounded up the front steps, swinging open the door to catch Tedham shambling past with a tray of silver flatware.

At the sight of Christopher, the butler’s brows shot skyward. He pulled his face into its customary bland expression before turning to face Christopher fully.

"Lady Woodsby had visitors," he pronounced, holding the tray in front of him like a jumbled barricade of silver. "After much persuasion I managed to send them away but I fear they shall return. Most angry, they were, at not being received by her ladyship." Uneasiness limned his features; he fidgeted from foot to foot.

Foreboding rolled through Christopher. Clearly the visitors had caused trouble.

"Visitors? Who would visit Lady Woodsby here? Is she all right?" He grabbed Tedham's arm and shook it. "Tell me, man, speak."

"Perhaps the young lady should tell you herself. If you will excuse me, sir, I must be on my way." Tedham wobbled away as fast as the heavy tray would let him.

A bemused Christopher watched him scuttle off. Lud, the man was a trembling mass of nerves. What had happened? Who had come by to fluster the butler so?

Josceline. He had to find Josceline. She would tell him what the devil had happened.

He bolted down the hallway towards the drawing room, slowing down enough to see she wasn't there before continuing to the kitchen to find Mrs. Belton. The housekeeper would know Josceline's whereabouts.

Mrs. Belton wheeled around to face him when he burst into the room.

"I've been expecting you, Mr. Sharrington," she declared cheerily. "Quite a set to, there was, but Tedham and our two stoutest footmen managed to get rid of those horrid men."

"Where's Lady Josceline?" he barked.

"Taking a bit of fresh air in the garden, Mr. Sharrington. I think you should talk to her."

* * *

Christopher found her slumped on the stone bench. Without invitation, he plopped himself down unceremoniously beside her and turned his head to look at her. Delight shot through him when he saw she wore the cloak he had given her. One corner of his mouth lifted - it suited her as much as he had thought it would when he had seen it in the shop window.

However, she wore it much like armour, for the sable trim encircled her throat tightly and the bronze folds were wrapped about her as if she could hide herself away in it. His gaze darted to her face - it was white, filled with distress. The visitors, whoever they were, had upset her.

He lifted a questioning eye brow and waited for her to speak. Her lips trembled for a few seconds then "Father was here," she whispered. "And Mr. Burrows."

"You are unharmed?"

Josceline nodded.

"Would you please tell me what happened?" He half-twisted towards her, planting one booted heel on the ground to balance himself on the edge of the bench.

She appeared not to heed the exasperation in his voice yet it seemed she took comfort in his presence for she pulled herself up and lifted her chin before squarely meeting his gaze.

"They came by unannounced." Her voice was steady, matter of fact. "I did not see them although I heard raised voices. Tedham sent them away. Nothing more than that."

"It is more than that for it is plain to see you are disturbed," he muttered.

Josceline kept her eyes on Christopher. From beneath furrowed brows, his gaze swept Josceline's face so thoroughly it was almost as if he brushed her with gossamer strokes. Genuine concern filled his voice and eyes.

For her.

Joy coursed through Josceline at the realization. It was as she had thought, hoped, wished - Christopher would make things right. Her anxiety disappeared in a poof.

"Father wishes me to marry Mr. Burrows. I had no idea he would pursue me to make it so." She eyed him unabashedly. "I should like your help for now they have found me, I expect they shall return."

"One dragon has been slain and now another has reared its scaled head," he groaned, crossing his arms to lean his shoulder against the weathered brick wall behind them.

Josceline gave him an anxious glance. "A dragon has been slain?"

"In a manner of speaking. Mrs. Wilkinson took the payment I offered and has agreed to hold her silence. I feel we can trust her for she seems to care for Philip and Tom."

"That is welcome news." She shifted and her cloak fell open. She caught his glance as he looked to where her bosom swelled above her neckline. A familiar tide of heat surged across her cheeks at his frank inspection and her scalp prickled with it. A half chuckle escaped his lips. Balderdash. The rogue knew full well he had flustered her.

Tugging the edges of the cloak firmly together, she watched two sparrows swoop past them, welcoming the distraction while she tried to regain her decorum. The birds landed in a berry bush a short distance away and fluttered from branch to branch, merrily chirping all the while. They, too, felt the coming spring.

She watched them for a few minutes, waiting for her cheeks to cool before she turned back to Christopher and the matter at hand.

"Now we have your father to contend with," he stated when he saw he had her full attention again. "He will force you to accept Mr. Burrows."

"Can he force me if I am gainfully employed? I think not."

"What are you suggesting?"

"Let me call on Lady Oakland. She'll receive me," she said with a bravado she was far from feeling. "As long as she is satisfied nothing untoward is happening beneath your roof, we have nothing to fear."

"Your father has followed you here. Are you certain he'll be dissuaded by the fact you have a position here?" Christopher's voice was dubious.

"Yes." She injected as much confidence into her reply as she could muster.

"I don't agree." He shook his head. The familiar unruly lock of hair fell across his forehead and he raked it back. "As I understand it, he has much to gain with your marriage to Mr. Burrows. He shall not easily walk away from that."

"Then what do you suggest we do?"

Her question appeared to take him off guard for a range of emotions flickered across his features – resentment, desperation, indecision, and finally, calm. He slid off the bench to drop to his knees in front of her then laid a hand on her knee.

"Marry me instead," he blurted.

Chapter Fourteen

The world spun crazily for a few seconds then dropped away leaving her in a silent void. Josceline clutched the edge of the bench, not caring that her cloak had dropped open again.

"Marry you?" she croaked. Is that truly what she had heard?

Christopher pulled away his hand and rocked back on his heels before giving her an uncertain nod.

Gradually the world righted itself, the sparrows resumed chirping, and a faint breeze rattled bare branches against the brick wall.

Wordless, she stared at him.

The longer she remained silent, the more unfathomable his expression became until finally, he stood up. He jammed his hands in his pockets and waited for her response.

She tried to make sense of his question. Had Christopher just proposed marriage to her? Was he daft? He, who was looking for social acceptance, would saddle himself with the daughter of the disreputable Duke of Cranston? Had he been serious?

She played with the thought of marrying him for a moment or two, savoring it while she looked away from him to gaze into the garden. How easy it would be to acquiesce, to accept his proposal, to lay all her problems on his shoulders. Then she could be with him forever.

While the thought of marriage to Christopher tempted her, she could not accept his proposal. She would hinder him in his quest for recognition, not help him. Would he understand?

Josceline grew cold and at first she thought it was with despair until she saw her cloak had fallen open. With shaking hands, she closed it, this time ensuring she tied it securely.

"I cannot accept your proposal." Her voice broke as she said it. "I cannot, Christopher. Because-."

"Forgive me, I spoke in jest," Christopher interrupted smoothly. "Nothing more." A dull flush colored his cheeks.

"A jest," she echoed stupidly. How could he jest about something so important? Did he think her a fool?

"It is a solution, is it not?" he drawled.

His flippant tone sliced her to the core. So it had merely been a jest. To him, perhaps, but not to her and her heart ached with the cruelty of it.

In any case, she wouldn't give him the satisfaction of seeing how much he had wounded her. She sucked in a big breath of air, letting her chest rise until she sat rod straight.

"Of course," she responded briskly. "A jest." She got to her feet. "Send one of the footmen to Oakland Grange with my card. I shall call on Lady Oakland this week if possible if you would be so kind as to lend me the use of your carriage?"

He nodded.

"Oh, and Mr. Sharrington?" She wondered if he would notice her use of his surname. "I shall take on Philip and Tom immediately. You no longer make use of my services and I should like to feel useful."

"As you wish." He gave her a curt nod.

"Thank you." She deliberately avoided his gaze as she said it. "I intend to start tomorrow."

Christopher watched her walk away, shells crunching beneath her feet as she trod the path. A gust of wind caused the hood of her cloak to slip off, revealing a mad tangle of russet curls. His palms tingled with desire to caress them and he balled his fists to stifle the temptation.

It hadn't been a jest, he thought morosely as she finally disappeared from view behind a gnarled plum tree. He truly wanted to take Josceline to wife. Only the second the words had fled his mouth, he realized the error he had made. She had called him Mr. Sharrington meaning his crass comment had only served to widen the gulf between them, not draw them closer.

Of course she wouldn't marry him, a nobody, a commoner and worse, a would-be merchant. Wasn't it clear her distaste with Mr. Burrows was because he was a merchant? Why would she change her mind about that? She hadn't, as proven by her negative answer.

In truth, Christopher should be relieved because his secret would remain secure. Instead, self loathing filled him.

Slowly he followed her from the garden.

* * *

Almost a week passed before Josceline called on Lady Oakland. A week which, if perhaps not uncomfortable, no longer held the easy camaraderie she had shared with Christopher.

She found herself alone much of the time. At breakfast, his empty plate stood as evidence he had eaten long before her before going about his daily business.

If he wasn't closeted in the library for the day with the door shut, then he was out on his favorite mount doing whatever it was needed tending by him.

After his ridiculous proposal, she reverted to a cold tray in her room in the evenings which must have suited him for he didn't take her to task on it.

Thankfully, she had Philip and Tom to help while away the hours or it would be a bleak and lonely existence. Every night when she readied herself for bed, she reminded herself she was another day closer to finishing her three month assignment at Midland House.

And every night, she slept with his handkerchief under her pillow before tucking it back into its hiding place behind the mirror the following morning.

Christopher's carriage turned a corner and Josceline leaned forward to peek out the window as it clattered up the crushed stones leading towards Oakland Grange. A sparse blanket of fresh green lined both sides of the driveway and the buds on the trees had thickened noticeably.

A new season beckoned, a far cry from the lifeless landscape of several weeks ago when she had knowingly placed herself in the company of a handsome stranger.

However, he was a stranger to her no longer. Rather, each and every one of her dreams centered on him and inexplicably she couldn't force her wayward thoughts to behave.

But what if, for a moment, he had been serious about the proposal of marriage?

Nonsense, he had made it perfectly clear there was nothing behind it.

That being so and in order to clear both their names, she must confront Lady Oakland and convince her of the validity of her position as Christopher's governess.

She forced herself to step out of the carriage to a meeting she dreaded when she would have much rather have turned tail to return to the sanctuary of Midland House. Her knees trembled as she climbed the steps. The door swung open beneath her upraised fist to reveal the taciturn butler. Apparently, she had been expected.

With clammy palms and knotted stomach, Josceline followed him into the salon. She recognized the room, where Christopher had announced he would hire her.

Today the pianoforte stood as lonely sentinel for the room was empty save for Lady Oakland, seated in the armchair closest to the window. The sun broke through at that instant. The harsh light was unkind to the woman for it shadowed her wrinkles and highlighted the silver sprinkling the dark locks.

"Lady Woodsby, what is it you wished to see me about?" Lady Oakland's tone was petulant and two deep lines fell from the corners of her mouth to score her chin.

"I have come to dispel any doubts you may have about the legitimacy of my position as governess to Mr. Sharrington."

Josceline moved to stand in front of Lady Oakland for she hadn't been invited to sit – an obvious ploy on the part of the woman to put Josceline at a disadvantage. She dug her nails in her palms to keep her wits about her.

"Lord Candel insists otherwise. That you are no governess for Sharrington has no son," sniffed the woman.

"Lady Oakland, Oliver Candel is a disgrace to his family and hardly one to be believed."

Cold from the chill floor seeped through the thin soles of Josceline's slippers. The cold in her feet echoed the cold of Lady Oakland's manner, making the interview not at all comfortable.

Josceline shifted from one foot to the other, trying to warm them a little, focusing intently on Lady Oakland's next words.

"He claims to have proof." The woman's gaze narrowed. "He spoke to the matron at St. Peter's."

Josceline drew herself up. "If I may remind you, I am the daughter of the Duke of Cranston. My word should mean more than that of a mere viscount. Philip is indeed Mr. Sharrington's son."

Lady Oakland tilted her head to one side. "I have heard stories of your father, the Duke," she said slyly.

The blood drained from Josceline's face and her features felt as if they had turned to stone. Stories of her disgraced father had spread even here. She must steer the conversation back to the matter of the supposed son.

She shrugged. "My father has nothing to do with this. I choose to work as governess for I wish to make my own way."

"An admirable undertaking. Tell me, Lady Woodsby, do you subscribe to the musings of Mary Wollstonecroft?"

"Only in that I feel education is of benefit to everyone. Being a governess allows me to do that."

"But why not embrace marriage? As you yourself pointed out, you are the daughter of a duke." Lady Oakland crossed her arms before gazing again at Josceline.

"As I said, I choose to make my own way. The indiscretions of my father are no reflection on me."

"Yet you so boldly claim to be his daughter."

"I'm not here to talk about my choice in life," she snapped. The woman needled her deliberately. "I am here to assure you Mr. Sharrington has a son."

"So say you."

"You yourself have seen Philip." Josceline hoped desperation did not color her words.

"I have only seen a young boy who you declare to be Philip Sharrington."

"If you don't believe me, why not visit the orphanage yourself?" Josceline lifted her chin. "They should tell you the truth for they have nothing to gain and nothing to lose."

Lady Oakland stared at her long and hard. "Very well," she replied at length. "For I admit we could banter on this endlessly and still find no resolution."

"Thank you," Josceline replied as graciously as she could. "I am certain a timely visit to St. Peter's will give you the answers you need."

Her feet were numb with cold, toes cramping in protest. It was time to end the conversation.

"I must take my leave."

"As you wish." Lady Oakland waved a dismissive hand.

Weak-kneed, Josceline returned to the waiting carriage, scarce noticing the fresh faced footman who helped her in. She collapsed onto the squabs, grateful for the coal brazier to warm her feet and the robe to pull over her lap.

The carriage jerked and rocked and they were off. The gentle sway and rhythmic clip clop soothed her nerves and she relaxed against the back cushions.

This meeting merely confirmed her changed impressions of Lady Oakland. The evening they had met here at Oakland Grange, the woman had exuded false sympathy. In reality she was merely a gossip monger, filled with self-importance, and in the face of Josceline's insistence, harmless enough. Or so she hoped.

However, Lady Oakland's comment about marriage disturbed Josceline. The only offer made for her so far that she would have seriously considered had been an admitted jest.

It stung.

In truth, Josceline would quite happily settle on marriage. But only to the right man. An image of Christopher slid through her thoughts before she hastily thrust it away.

* * *

Josceline went to her room and hung up her cloak before returning to the drawing room. Christopher must have heard her return for he waited for her there. He rang the bell and fussed over the cushions of her chair before allowing her to sit.

Almost as if he had been waiting for her. As if he cared about her.

Josceline threw him a curious glance and thought she caught a flash of affection in the otherwise unperturbed brown eyes. He turned away as if to hide his expression before seating himself.

It wasn't until Mrs. Belton had deposited the tea tray on the little table between them before bustling off again that he spoke.

"Was Lady Oakland agreeable?" he asked. His words were mild but his tone was urgent. Clearly he had spent an anxious afternoon waiting for her.

"She has agreed to speak to the matron at St. Peter's." Josceline nodded. "As long as Mrs. Wilkinson keeps her part of the bargain, the sham will become reality."

She pointed to the cups with an enquiring glance and at his nod, poured the tea. Its exotic fragrance swirled about her and she took an appreciative sniff. Her mama had always said there was nothing a good cup of tea couldn't fix. Lately Josceline had tested that theory often, judging by how many times in the past few days she'd shared a cup in the cozy kitchen with Mrs. Belton in a futile effort to forget Christopher's proposal.

"Splendid." A smile crossed his lips. "Jolly good show, Josceline. You've done it. You've saved us from the sharp tongues."

He leaned over to grab her hand, lifting it to his mouth to brush it with tender lips before dropping it. Reluctantly, she thought. Or perhaps that was wishful thinking on her part.

"We can only hope Oliver Candel hasn't convinced the woman to change her mind."

"Nay, he shall not." Christopher shook his head. "I sincerely believe Mrs. Wilkinson has the best interests of the boys at heart. As should we, for they've served our purpose well. I suppose to maintain the charade, we must be sure Philip is seen out and about. How go the lessons with them?"

"Very well. They are both bright. Christopher?" She twisted her fingers, hesitant to broach the subject. "What do we do with them now?"

"Now that Lady Oakland has passed approval on us?"

"She hasn't passed approval yet. Remember, Mrs. Wilkinson must corroborate our story," Josceline cautioned.

"Which she will," he rejoined heartily. "The boys must stay in Midland House for now, continuing with their lessons for undoubtedly any son of mine will be well-mannered and educated. I don't see the harm in including Tom. It's reasonable to assume an only son would find amenable companionship with the grandson of the housekeeper."

"How kind of you. They are not of your blood."

"Kind?" He snorted. "Not kind at all. I wager that the root of all kindness stems from an ulterior motive on the part of the giver. In our case," he quirked an eyebrow at her, "I am ensuring our reputations remain intact."

"But still kind," she protested. "Other men would send them to the stables or the fields."

"They are someone's sons and have nothing, not even the love of a parent. I am an only child, Josceline. I know something of loneliness, be it for a parent or a sibling. I would think both would encompass the same feeling of loss." A sorrowful air hung over him briefly before his manner became purposeful. "Now that Philip is safely ensconced as my son, we must tackle Lord Oliver Candel. I mean to claim my ship. I mean to get the "Bessie" and put her to the use for which she was intended."

He drained his cup and replaced it on the saucer so firmly Josceline was sure it would crack. Sympathy welled up within her at the brief glimpse of the sorrow within him, a sorrow he took great pains to conceal.

A sorrow somehow entwined with his reprisal against Lord Oliver Candel.

A sorrow one day she would like to discover.

Chapter Fifteen

The envelope lay on the brass tray. Christopher stared at it for a moment, incredulous. It carried Lady Oakland's handwriting. Nay, it could not be – it had only been three days since Josceline's visit to the woman. It must have been delivered to Midland House by mistake.

He grabbed it and turned it over to inspect the wax seal. It was indeed the "O" of Oakland. He ripped it open to read the brief message:

Lord and Lady Oakland request the presence of Mr. Christopher Sharrington and Lady Josceline Woodsby for an evening of dinner and dance at Oakland Grange on Friday, March 16, in the year of our lord 1798, at the hour of eight o'clock in the evening.

Respondez s'il vous plait

The invitation could only signify Josceline's visit had been successful. Lady Oakland must have accepted Philip as his son, otherwise, they wouldn't be invited to Oakland Grange.

He whooped as he read it again. Excitement coursed through him and his first thought was to tell Josceline. It was mid-morning and she would be in the nursery with Philip and Tom. By rights he shouldn't interrupt the lessons but exhilaration propelled his feet – the invitation was too important not to share immediately.

He didn't knock but pushed open the nursery door. Up until several days ago, the room had been bare but somehow Josceline had managed to find a chair and two stools. A primer lay open on her lap; a slate sat on a makeshift easel in front of her and she held a piece of chalk in her hand.

The spear of jealousy at the sight of her russet head bent over the blonde heads of Philip and Tom surprised him. You're a grown man, he told himself firmly, and hardly one to be resentful over two young boys.

He stepped into the room and three heads swiveled as one.

"Mr. Sharrington!" Josceline exclaimed. Philip's and Tom's eyes grew round, so round it was as if he was being inspected by four blue saucers.

Obviously, his entrance had been an abrupt one.

"I must beg pardon for the rude interruption," he hurried to explain, "but I have important news."

Puzzled, her gaze raked his face before she turned to the boys. "Philip, Tom, we are finished for the day. You may be excused."

The two scrambled to their feet and darted away. Their footsteps rattled down the hallway, accompanied by howls of joy. He shook his head at the sound; one corner of his mouth lifted. Evidently the two did not yet understand their good fortune at being taught to read and write.

The room fell silent before Josceline finally closed the primer with a soft “snap” to place it on one of the stools, balancing the chalk on top. She stood and turned to face him, dusting off her hands on her skirt. “Well? What’s so important it couldn’t wait? I just had them settled in and paying attention.” Her indignation was palpable.

“It’s about my dance lessons,” he began.

“What of your lessons?” she interrupted, eyes flashing. “You yourself canceled them. If I recall, the reason you gave was that you were otherwise engaged and did not have the inclination to continue.”

“We still have an agreement, Lady Woodsby. I mean to hold you to it. Besides, we have an invitation to an evening at Oakland Grange.” Triumphant, he held it up. “I shall need more practice.”

Josceline’s mouth dropped open. “Oakland Grange? Lady Oakland has invited us to Oakland Grange?”

“Read it yourself.” He thrust the paper in front of her nose.

She scanned it then raised incredulous eyes to his. “It is done. By virtue of Lady Oakland’s invitation, she has accepted Philip as your son.

“I’m anxious to continue the dance lessons and suggest we meet this evening.”

“This evening?”

“Yes, this evening,” he stated emphatically. “We’ve several dances still for me to learn, do we not?” He wasn’t certain that was actually the case but the prospect of attending the Oakland’s evening of dinner and dance gave urgency to his words.

She nodded.

"Then let's not waste any more time. I shall be waiting for you in the library at seven o'clock. Until then." He inclined his head and took his leave.

As he strode down the hallway, he counted to the rhythm of his footsteps: one two three four; one two three four. A grin stretched across his face. He couldn't wait to start the dance lessons again - to feel Josceline's soft hand in his, to smell the fragrance of violets and sandalwood so distinctively hers, to hear her breathless count as he whirled her about.

Satisfaction filled him. He had received another invitation to Oakland Grange and his acceptance into local gentry was all but guaranteed. Even better, he would share the event with Josceline.

Whistling jauntily, he headed to the stables. A brisk gallop on Vesuvius would help pass the time until seven o'clock.

Josceline stared at the door, imagining she could still see Christopher's shadow. It was done. Her position here as governess, and hence her reputation, was secure.

Nonetheless, she wasn't sure how she felt about continuing with Christopher's lessons. True, part of her was ecstatic at the prospect of being alone with him but part of her dreaded it for she was certain her disobedient heart wouldn't behave.

She sighed and shook her head. She had agreed to teach him how to dance so she must keep her part of the arrangement. If she lost her heart in the bargain, then so be it. Doubtless she would find it again when her time at Midland House came to an end.

The stately chimes of the grandfather clock echoed up the stairs. Two o'clock.

A joyous grin lifted the corners of her mouth and happiness propelled her towards her room. The intervening hours until Christopher's lesson would be well spent scrutinizing the length of copper satin draped over her wardrobe door.

It would make a perfect dress for the evening at Oakland Grange.

* * *

An unfamiliar glow spilled from the library door, illuminating the hall as Josceline approached. The light was so bright she worried for a second or two that perhaps the room had erupted in flames. Nonsense, quiet ruled the house; it couldn't possibly be on fire.

But when she entered the room she saw it was, in a manner of speaking, for an assortment of lit candles filled every available ledge. Several branched candelabra, a number of single tapers, wall sconces and even the fireplace flickered with life. An inviting sight and slowly she advanced into the room, eyes darting to and fro in an attempt to take it all in. She scarce heard the click clack of the door as it swung shut and caught the latch.

Christopher lounged against his desk, hands tucked into his pockets. As she came closer, he took a sip from the snifter of brandy beside him before he stood up.

"Mrs. Belton is appalled at the wastage but I reminded her that the room should be well lit if we don't wish to harm ourselves." He chuckled. "I daresay the last thing we want is to find ourselves in splints and plasters."

"That is the hazard of doing things in the evening. It does tend to get dark." Josceline could have kicked herself at her inane comment – it made her look foolish, which was the last thing she wanted Christopher to think of her.

"We could wish for moonlight," he said, voice husky. He advanced on her, eyes shadowed, mouth curved in a welcoming smile. His hair was damp, the unruly lock for once neatly tucked into a leather thong, his shirt clean, and boots freshly polished.

Her heart jerked at the sight. He'd made an effort to clean himself up. Her eyes strayed down to her brown walking dress. Why hadn't she bothered to change into at least the jade green frock?

Because she was here to do her duty, to instruct Christopher on the finer points of the Contredanse. And after that, the quadrille, the minuet and, if time permitted between now and their evening at Oakland Grange, the cotillion.

She gritted her teeth and ignored the fluttering in her stomach as she placed her hand in Christopher's outstretched one. He grinned at her obvious discomfort and she felt her cheeks flush.

"Shall we begin?" She made her voice stern which merely served to draw another grin from him. "We were learning the Contredanse."

"Spoken like a true governess," he teased.

"Which I am," she retorted. She compressed her lips, aware she must appear prudish but determined to keep her composure.

"You are."

He agreed so pleasantly she wanted to smack him.

"But I am the pupil," he continued, a devilish glint lurking in his eyes, "and your employer, which I think gives me the right to request the subject."

"What subject would that be?" she asked primly.

"I request the waltz."

"The waltz?" Her screech echoed off the ceiling and bounced off the floor, eliciting a hearty chuckle from him.

"By that response do I take it to mean you're unfamiliar with it?"

"No. Yes. That is." She stopped, trying to collect her thoughts. She had waltzed with Elizabeth in the privacy of her bedroom but even then they weren't certain they had been doing it properly. It wasn't yet common and all they really knew was that it required a three beat.

And a very close proximity to one's partner.

She blanched at the thought. "No, I don't know how to waltz," she squeaked.

"Perhaps I could teach you."

"You?" She gaped at him. "You don't know how to dance. That is why you engaged my services, remember?"

"Yes, me," he said smoothly, drawing her into his arms. "I spent a little time on the Continent. It's very popular over there. So it's true I don't know any other dances but I do know that one."

"It's not considered appropriate." She clenched her fists and held herself away from him stiffly.

"No?" He pulled her close, grabbing one balled fist in his left hand and placing her other balled fist on his right shoulder. "I disagree. I think it very appropriate. It is simply an Austrian folk dance therefore what is the harm?"

"Stop." Josceline pulled free her fists and placed them on his shoulders to push. "It's hardly likely the Oaklands shall present the waltz at a country ball."

He curved his arms around her waist, not letting her go and she bent backwards away from him, her knuckles against his shirt white with the strain.

"And being in the country implies what exactly?" He winked.

"That we are in a boorish backwater," she snapped. Now she sounded shrewish but she was past caring. She simply couldn't think straight wrapped up in his arms.

"Boorish backwater." He laughed outright. "But it is the latest thing on the Continent and I suggest we bring it here. To bring the boorish backwater, as you call it, up to the latest mode."

Speechless she stared at him. Bring the waltz to Oakland Grange? It was sure to draw unwanted attention – the one thing they must avoid.

She shook her head. "I don't think we want to bring undue attention to ourselves. Or have you forgotten Philip and the lengths we went to ensure all believe he is truly your son?"

Shocked, she looked at her hands. Of their own volition, they had uncurled and now her fingers lay long against his chest. Through them she could feel him heave a sigh.

A log in the fire cracked, tumbling onto the hearth, and sending a shower of sparks up the chimney. Reluctantly he let her go.

"I must tend to the fire. And you're right, of course."

She turned away, putting her hands onto fevered cheeks and sucking in a great breath of air as she gazed through the window.

The moonlight Christopher had wished for earlier hadn't materialized. Not even a star pricked the pitch black outside. The darkness bespoke of danger – like the danger of the forbidden wants tumbling through her mind.

She wanted him to hold her. She wanted to feel his strength against her softness. She wanted him to kiss her again.

"Josceline?" He tapped her on the shoulder.

She started at his touch and dropped her hands to twine them in her skirts.

"The Contredanse it is." He made a great show of stepping back and holding up a hand. "But don't think I mean to give up on the waltz."

"Of course." She hastened to correct herself when she realized he could construe the wrong meaning. "The Contredanse, that is. I am afraid, Mr. Sharrington, if you wish to waltz you must find yourself another partner."

She emphasized his name to remind him of her station as his employee.

Clearly he caught her meaning, for he cocked an eyebrow and one corner of his mouth lifted for a second. Amusement bubbled in his eyes and at the sight she had the urge to smack him again. He was having great fun at her expense, she fumed silently.

"One two three four." Glaring at him, she began to count and move through the figures.

Her glare appeared not to bother him a whit. With a bland smile, he moved along with her, winking whenever she caught his glance.

She's not going to get off so easily next time, Christopher chuckled to himself. A waltz with her is what he wanted and a waltz with her is what he would get. At the thought, he inadvertently applied a little too much pressure to her hand and she stumbled.

Two green eyes spit fire at him and she tossed her head so vehemently that a curl shook free to frame her face. With a forceful swipe, she tucked it behind her ear.

"I must beg pardon," he murmured.

She accepted his apology with a grudging nod then twirled away, counting all the while. He was rewarded with a whiff of violets and sandalwood which just made him want to crush her to him all the more so he could inhale more deeply.

He didn't, though. He kept his face blank so she couldn't read his thoughts, allowing him to dwell on the pleasing dream of her in his arms, sweeping her around the dance floor to the strains of a Viennese waltz.

She was right, of course. To put themselves on display at the Oakland's dinner party would negate the accomplishment of successfully portraying Philip as his son to Lady Oakland. He consoled himself with the thought that a waltz with her would be all the sweeter when it finally came to pass.

Josceline stopped counting and came to a stop, moving away a fraction before she spoke. "You have a splendid grasp of the Contredanse. Now on to the minuet."

Her cheeks were flushed, and a slight sheen of perspiration coated her forehead. The unruly curl had fallen across her cheek again and he reached out with a finger to tuck it behind her cheek. His finger grazed her skin and she gave him a wary look that reminded him of a startled wild doe.

Lud, never mind dancing. He needed to kiss her. Now.

Chapter Sixteen

Josceline saw the intent in Christopher's eyes, saw him lean in towards her, felt the pressure of his hand tugging her closer. Candlelight gilded his face, throwing his features into sharp relief.

His very handsome features, she thought boldly before his lips swooped down to hers to obliterate all reason.

He tasted of brandy and oddly, chocolate. Chocolate? When had he eaten chocolate?

All thoughts of chocolate and brandy disappeared when his mouth teased open hers. It was as if her lips were glued to his because her mouth opened as well. His tongue flicked against hers and shocked, she tried to pull away only to find she couldn't escape his embrace for her hands had somehow become tangled in his hair. He probed her mouth with his tongue, playing with hers such that her knees turned to jelly. She sagged into his bulk.

He must have pulled away for she heard him whisper. "You shall fall."

And he picked her up to seat her on the desk, pushing apart her knees to stand between her legs. Gazing at her with heavy-lidded eyes, he pulled the pins from her hair and it fell in a disordered mass about her shoulders. He kissed her again, harder this time, raking his hands through her hair and sliding them down her back to land on her hips. Gently, so gently she could barely feel it, he adjusted his hands to massage her thighs then grabbed her knees to pull her closer. Through her skirts she could feel his male hardness as he rubbed against her.

Josceline's thoughts scattered like seed pods on the wind.

Wrong, oh so wrong.

She didn't care.

She kissed him back, following the flow of her feelings, wondering, nay, craving to know where he was leading her. Her heart pounded and her breath came in short little gasps, for she was afraid if she took a deep breath, she would lose the tantalizing sensations he aroused in her.

Cold air wafted on her skin. Without her noticing, he had lifted her skirts. His fingers traced her legs to the apex of her thighs and he rubbed gently the little nub hidden there amongst the crisp curls.

"Please," she whimpered, writhing against his fingers.

"Please what," he demanded, his voice a growl. "Please stop?"

"Yes. No. I don't know." What had he just asked her? To stop? How could she stop? It was he who had to stop whatever it was he was doing to her, it was he who had to stop bewitching her.

His scent enveloped her, drugging her senses. Citrus. Leather. Her thoughts were incoherent fragments now for the pressure and movement of his fingers drove her mad.

"No, don't stop," she moaned.

More. Faster. Harder. Don't stop, don't stop with your fingers there.

"I won't stop, Josceline. Not unless you want me to."

She shook her head, and he chuckled low in his throat, spearing her with a possessive gaze before raising his hands to cup her breasts.

Her head spun as the warmth of his palms penetrated the fabric of her dress. He tweaked her nipples through the fabric. They pebbled, pushing against the fabric of her shift and he tugged the dress down off her shoulders to take first one nipple, then the other, in his mouth.

Her head lolled back and shocks of pleasure rocketed from her breasts to her woman's place. Her legs spread wider and dimly she could feel the edge of the desk against the backs of her thighs. That sharp edge was her last link to reality and it snapped as he slipped his hands under her legs to pull himself even closer, grinding his pelvis against hers before pulling back to slip his fingers in between them again. The outside world faded away and all she could feel was the sweet pressure there, between her legs.

"Please," she whimpered again.

Please? What was it she was pleading for?

But her body knew for she began to rock against his hand, rocking, straining, pushing, searching.

And then she knew.

The first wisps of pleasure, a pleasure she had never known before, solidified and it was as if she had crested a mountain peak only to fall spiraling, spiraling, down, down.

Shuddering, she collapsed and fell back on her elbows, sated with contentment. Eyes closed, she relished the sensation as long as she could until nothing remained, only a warm glow throughout her body.

Christopher watched her climax, saw her flush, smelled the seductive odor of her woman scent mixed in with violets and sandalwood. He knew he would hate himself later but he couldn't control himself. He had to take her.

He had to take her now.

Unfastening his breeches, his penis sprang free, throbbing with life, already crowned with a drop of white, heavy cream. Maneuvering carefully, he positioned the sensitive tip at the apex of her thighs, prodding, nudging, searching for the hidden place he knew would give him the release he sought.

She was slick, ready for him.

"Hold me," he whispered. And she complied, shifting forward to wrap her arms around his neck. Her gaze was mysterious yet knowing and an unsteady smile trembled on her lips.

"Forgive me," he breathed, knowing he was likely to hurt her as he broke through the barrier of her virginity.

He locked his mouth on hers and thrust. Beneath him, he could feel her body stiffen but she didn't make a sound. Her muscles squeezed tight around his member and he groaned with the sweetness of it, of her.

He held still for a moment to let her become accustomed to the feel of him inside her. Then she shifted slightly to wrap her legs around his waist, beginning a cascade of sensations he couldn't stop. He thrust once, twice, three times and exploded, shouting his climax to the heavens.

The force of his ejaculation stunned him and he had to lean against the desk, bracing himself with one arm, holding Josceline in the other. His knees shook and his nose filled with the heady combination of her scent of her woven with his. A primeval surge of conquest steadied his legs. He didn't want to pull free, not yet and instead he leaned back a little to drop a tender kiss on her lips.

She was dazed, flushed, mouth swollen. "Someone shall find us here, like this."

Another surge of conquest passed through him at her breathless words. She, too, had felt the searing passion between them.

"They shan't disturb us, the door is latched," he reassured her then dropped another light kiss on her lips. He could quite happily remain in her embrace forever.

A sobering thought. One which he should examine more closely when in the sanctuary of his own room.

Limp as a rag doll, Josceline glanced away and glimpsed her reflection in the darkened window. Her skirts were tangled around her waist, her shoulders and limbs white, hair a riotous mess. How appalling. If someone had passed by in the garden, they could see through the windows. She looked a proper whore. Or what she imagined a proper whore would look like.

Worse, like a proper whore, she had enjoyed it, every spine tingling second. Even now, her legs still circled Christopher's waist.

Tiny fingers of shame poked her. She was as weak as her gaming drunkard of a father. He, too, succumbed to flimsy pleasures and the ton scorned him because of it. Now they would scorn her on her own actions if it ever came to light.

Was losing herself to Christopher worth the potential recrimination? Truly, she didn't know for she didn't know his intentions toward her.

And sadly, it was too late. Gripped by the sensations he had aroused in her, she had given herself to him with nary a thought to the consequences.

Her thighs started to cramp and she dropped her legs to the ground, looking away in embarrassment as she struggled to rearrange her clothing. He took a step back, and adjusted his breeches.

"If that is the minuet, then I should look forward indeed to learning it further," he quipped weakly.

Incredulous, she gazed at him. He tried to make light of the situation and appeared untroubled.

At her accusing stare, guilt flashed though his eyes. Again she looked away, trying to make sense of his mood.

"Do you regret this?" he asked gently, reaching out to take her chin in his fingers, turning her face so she looked at him full on.

He had read her thoughts. How did he know her so well he could see what lay behind her eyes?

"No." She lowered her gaze then raised it to look unflinching into his eyes. "It's nothing more than what people already thought," she announced defiantly.

"By people, I assume you refer to Lady Oakland," he said, lips twisting derisively. "We've conquered that battle already, or do I need to remind you of our upcoming invitation?"

"As you say." She nodded, biting her lips. She would never, ever admit to him she had enjoyed it. Proper ladies did not enjoy the attentions of their husbands, or so she had been told by Elizabeth who had it, she claimed, on good authority from her mother.

"I promise you, this shan't happen again," he said hastily. Too hastily. As if self-reproach consumed him. "I will not speak of it."

"Nor shall I," she whispered.

Yes, she wouldn't speak of it but that didn't mean she wouldn't think of it. Silent, and without another glance in his direction, she walked away.

* * *

She threw herself across her bed, his final words echoing in her ears: "This shan't happen again. I will not speak of it."

Shaking hands pulled at the bed cover, balling it in her fists. She had disappointed him and that was why he didn't want it to happen again. She had given him her virtue and he hadn't enjoyed it.

What did that say about her, for she had enjoyed it, very much. Not just the strangely exquisite physical sensations, but the feeling of closeness with

Christopher. Now she knew why Maggie Mary, the upstairs maid, simpered whenever Horace, the eldest footman, came by. Now she understood the knowing glances they tossed at each other when they thought no one saw.

And now that he had ruined her, he could send her on her way and there wasn't a thing she could do about it.

True, she still had his handkerchief but perhaps it wouldn't be enough of a deterrent for him anymore. She had threatened to unmask Christopher as a highwayman, holding as proof the blood stained handkerchief but in truth, it had been a ruse, and a successful one at that.

Christopher had believed her assertion that as the daughter of a duke, his word would not hold against hers but now, he didn't need her anymore. With Philip established in his home, Christopher had gained the confidence of Lady Oakland and with it, his entrance into local society. It would be easy enough for him to engage another governess.

The thought hurt more than she cared to admit for she had come to care about the orphaned brothers.

If he sent her on her way, would he provide her with a proper reference or would she be left penniless once again? And then? Home to London and marriage to Mr. Burrows? The irony didn't escape her. Without her virginity, she no longer had value for her father and the wealthy merchant.

Fool, to think she was beginning to love the handsome Captain Christopher Sharrington when all he had wanted was to use her.

Fool, she had fallen to his charms, had not even offered the slightest bit of resistance.

Fool, to hope that perhaps he cared for her, even a little.

Fool.

Her frame shuddered with great wracking sobs.

* * *

Filled with self-loathing, Christopher poured himself a brandy. Tossing it back, he poured himself another then slammed down the snifter on his desk so hard the ledger on it jumped.

Damnation, what had he just done? He had taken her, the daughter of a duke, like a common strumpet. Here, on his desk in the library, where anyone could have walked in on them.

The only thing was, she was no common strumpet. She was the woman he loved.

The notion hit him like a free swinging boom on a mizzenmast.

The woman he loved.

And he had treated her with a lack of respect. He'd lost his self control then tried to make a jest of it.

He gave a ferocious kick to the desk chair, sending it crashing to the floor.

Idiot.

He wouldn't blame her if she hated him. If, deservedly so, she hated him, could he yet win her love?

For that's what he wanted more than anything, more than the "Bessie", more than the chance to build a sea faring enterprise, more than acknowledgement from Bristol's aristocratic society.

He wanted Lady Josceline Woodsby's love. Could he win it now? Or had he thrown away his chance with her over a stupid lapse in judgment?

At the memory, his loins started to throb, making him even more disgusted with himself. Making love to her had been wonderful, even better than he could have imagined.

And would be even better the next time, for now her body knew how to respond.

"If there is a next time," he groaned aloud to the wall of books silently watching his anguish.

He would have to make it up to her somehow. She had put on a brave face but he had seen her face crumple as she'd turned to walk away.

Her scent still clung to him. Violets and sandalwood. It was, he decided, his favorite scent. A scent he could easily wake up to the rest of his living days. Well, there was one way that could happen.

He would do right by her and marry her.

True, unlike the men of her class, he had to earn a living but there was honor in that. He wouldn't take no for an answer. He would marry her and let the devil take the consequences.

Even the consequences of her disgust when she discovered who he really was.

Chapter Seventeen

Christopher waited for Josceline most of the following day: first in the breakfast room where he sat until the sausages congealed in a greasy mass in the bottom of the chafing dish, then in the library where he left the door open so he could hear her step, and finally in the drawing room, eliciting a startled response from Anna, the downstairs maid when she brought in the tray with the cups and saucers and a plate of plum cake all covered with a linen cloth.

When by actual tea time Josceline still hadn't appeared, he rang for Mrs. Belton.

"She's kept to her room all day. Poor dear must be famished," the housekeeper said. "And the boys have missed their lessons. I wonder what is amiss?"

He shook his head, suspecting the worst. Josceline didn't want to see him because of what had passed between them last night in the library. Naturally, he couldn't share that with Mrs. Belton so instead he said in the blandest voice possible, "Perhaps you could send her to me and I shall see if I can find out what ails her."

"As you wish," Mrs. Belton bobbed a curtsey then trotted off, keys jingling, mob cap bouncing.

An apprehensive Christopher waited. Two maids scampered by in the hall, giggling. The happy sound irked him. Of course they didn't know he had just committed the biggest blunder of his life, he thought sourly.

He moved to the window, tapping his fingers on the sill, staring outside mindlessly and not seeing the flocks of starlings high in the sky and the tender buds swelling with spring's arrival.

The grandfather clock chimed the half hour. Half past four. It chimed again to signal another quarter hour. He began to pace.

Her absence spoke volumes. She didn't want to see him. If so, it left him no choice but to accost her in her room. A very improper action and one which would set the servants to chattering but he would take it if he had to.

He continued to pace, past the chairs and table where they always took their tea, to the fireplace, to the window, then past the chairs and table again.

It wasn't until the grandfather clock chimed five times that Josceline appeared.

"You sent for me, Mr. Sharrington?" She paused in the doorway of the drawing room, face wan, eyes circled with black shadows. She had slept as little as he had last night.

He flinched at the use of his surname. Her voice was cold, distant and she avoided his gaze.

"I am sorry for what happened last night." He approached her slowly. His arms burned with the desire to hold her and coax the sad expression from her face. "Forgive me."

And much to his shame, he felt himself harden at the thought of feeling her against him again, even if only in comfort. He shuffled sideways to stand behind a chair to hide the evidence of his desire for her.

"There's no need to apologize," she shrugged. "What is past is past."

"I cannot undo what happened but I can make it right. I should like to take you to wife."

If nothing else he now had her full attention for she flicked him with a scornful look.

"Another one of your jests?" she asked disdainfully. "And even if it is not, the answer is no. I have decided it would be best for me to leave Midland House."

His heart lurched at the thought.

"I can't allow you to do that," he answered swiftly. "What of Philip and Tom?" *What of us?*

"Engage another governess," she said flatly. "Although perhaps you should make it clear other – ah, duties are involved."

The barb embedded itself firmly in his chest, dislodging a sliver of desperation. "I am sincere in my offer of marriage, Lady Woodsby."

Her eyes widened at his usage of her title. At least she still listened.

"And I am sincere in my response." She drew herself up with all the grace given her by generations of breeding. Haughtily she continued, "Your misguided attempt at restitution is of no interest to me."

Christopher didn't let himself be cowed at the thought of the differences in their birth, so obvious by her current demeanor. Think. He must say something to make her change her mind, to convince her to accept.

"As my wife, you could help me. You claimed you want to make your own way." He took her hand and clasped it in both of his. "Marry me. Become my partner in shipping. Together let us build the next East India Company."

Josceline pulled free her hand, not believing the audacity of the man.

So that was it. It was all about his cursed ship and his plan to build a shipping enterprise. Feelings for her had nothing to do with it, making amends had nothing to do with it.

"Let me see if I understand you. You wish me to become your partner in shipping," she said icily. The idea was too ludicrous for words.

"Yes." He nodded.

"A shipping enterprise which has no ship."

He reddened. "I can understand your reticence, but I do have a ship."

"But you do not really have possession of the ship. Lord Oliver Candel has it."

"Not for long. I shall gain possession of it," he replied confidently.

"So say you," she scoffed. "I may not be an expert in the world of trade and commerce but even I can see the fallacy of becoming a helpmeet in a shipping company which has no ship. No, I have no interest in your enterprise. And no, I shan't marry you. My answer is final." She turned on her heel and moved away.

"Josceline, there could be a child." His calm voice sliced through the air.

She stopped dead in her tracks.

A child.

A consequence she hadn't considered. The only daughter of the disgraced Duke of Cranston could not possibly bear a bastard child. How much more dishonor could the family take? How would she care for it? The baby would have no future.

However, her being with child was not certain. She could wait for her monthly flux if she wanted to take that chance.

He pounced on her silence. "Any child of mine will not be born a bastard."

Slowly she turned to face him.

"Who said the child would be a bastard?" she asked coolly. "My father wishes me to marry Mr. Burrows. No one would be the wiser."

"You do not wish to marry Mr. Burrows," he drawled, apparently unworried by her words. "If I recall, you said he was old enough to be your grandfather. It would be a shame to waste your youth on a man with one foot in the grave."

"I would much rather marry Mr. Burrows than you, Mr. Sharrington, for at least he respects me and the institution of marriage."

Josceline couldn't believe how easily the untruth slipped from her lips. The only respect Mr. Thomas Burrows had for her was the opportunity she gave him to enter the rarified strata of upper British nobility. Furthermore, her father would receive money, making her little more than an item of barter.

It pained her to admit it, but Christopher's proposal did interest her.

But not this way, not the way it had unfolded.

"He only respects the entry into the ton that marriage to you will give him. And your father gains, of course," he shrugged, "as I assume he will end up with quite a nice dowry in his pocket."

His reply echoed her thoughts perfectly, making her angry that yet again he read her mind.

"And isn't that what you wish as well?" she spat.

"Yes, I won't deny it. But I'm giving you the chance to be something, to be more than a pretty frippery on your husband's arm." Now he took both of her hands in his, squeezing tightly to make sure she couldn't pull them free. "All I ask, Josceline, is to give serious consideration to what I am saying. If, after twenty-four hours, you still wish to be on your way, you are free to do so. If nothing else, consider this – let me claim the child – if there is a child - as mine."

"Is that so important to you, Mr. Sharrington?"

Somber, he nodded. "A child should know his own father."

She scoured his face with perplexed eyes, surprised at his adamant assertion. What did he know of fatherless children? More to the point, why would he care? He'd never professed to love her so why would he care what happened to her and a child she may or may not be carrying.

The seconds ticked by and still she struggled to control her thoughts.

Finally she tugged her hands free. Twenty four hours. What could it hurt for her to stay another twenty four hours. If nothing else, it gave her more time to plan an alternative course of action if she decided not to accept his proposal.

"Very well. I shall consider it. But you must promise me that if I choose to go, you will relinquish all contact with me and the child, if there is one. You will also pay me my full wage as agreed upon. Or I shall go to the local authorities and inform them of your nefarious midnight activities."

He reeled back as if she had struck him.

"As you wish," he grated, nostrils flaring. "If you choose to leave, there shall be no further contact between us. Therefore I should like the return of my handkerchief upon payment of your wage. To ensure that is the case, you understand."

"It is as I wish. And do not flatter yourself that I wish to keep any item of yours." She made a show of side stepping past him then fled, seeking the sanctuary of her room to think.

Twenty four hours was not such a very long time to make a decision affecting the rest of her life.

* * *

Another sleepless night and sunrise hadn't come too soon. Wide-eyed, Josceline lay on her back, watching the rays of light creep across the carved plaster ceiling and trying to ignore her aching body.

Her head ached from fatigue, her heart ached for the decision facing her, her buttocks ached where she had been pressed against the desk and most telling of all, she ached between her legs.

A decision had not come to her.

Indeed, her thoughts had bounced around her mind so much, she had become dizzy and nauseous with uncertainty.

She sat up. If she didn't share her doubts, she was sure to go mad. Mrs. Belton would listen. She wouldn't have to know everything but Josceline could air her thoughts. Perhaps hearing them would help her clarify her choice.

Quickly she threw on her clothing before splashing a bit of cold water on her face from the painted porcelain basin on her dresser. Her skin stung with the chill liquid and it steadied her. After swiping a comb through her hair, she tied it back with a ribbon. It hung loose down her back but at least it would be out of her face. Yanking her shawl from the hook beside her door, she left her room.

The house barely stirred yet she encountered Maggie Mary, whisk broom and bucket of ash in one hand, bucket of kindling in the other, on her early morning rounds to lay the fires.

"Is Mrs. Belton available?" Josceline asked, hoping her voice did not betray her anxiety.

"Good morning, miss." The maid curtsied. "Yes, miss, she's in the scullery counting the eggs. Cook says someone's been stealing them."

"Thank you." With barely a nod, Josceline hurried off.

"Lady Josceline!" Mrs. Belton exclaimed when Josceline burst into the scullery. "This is hardly the place for you."

"May I have a word with you?" Josceline tried, and failed, to keep desperation from her voice.

Mrs. Belton took one look at Josceline's face and grabbed her arm. "Come into the kitchen, the milk has just been delivered. Fresh from this morning, my dear, and it will give you a little energy to tackle the day."

She nattered on as she dipped a heavy cracked mug into the bucket of frothy milk, wiping the drips on her apron. "We'll go to my room so we can chat in private. There's nothing the servants like better than to overhear the troubles of a member of the household. I suspect what you want to discuss is nobody's business." Then she grabbed a scone from the rack cooling on the table, wrapping it in a clean napkin. "Come," she said, crooking a pudgy finger, leaving Josceline no choice but to follow.

Mrs. Belton's cozy room immediately put Josceline at ease, with its iron bedstead covered by a pretty pink patchwork quilt, the windows looking into the mews behind the main house, and the little desk placed to catch the daylight. On top of the whitewashed dresser sat a little stone pot filled with pussy willows.

Mrs. Belton pointed to the pink cushioned rocking chair, and obedient, Josceline sat, pushing off with one foot to set the chair in motion.

The housekeeper placed the mug and scone on the shelf beside Josceline then pulled out her desk chair, turning it around before she sat down on it with a satisfying "Ooof."

"My knees hurt sometimes," she explained. She pointed to the mug. "Drink. And when you have finished, eat the scone, it's still warm from the oven."

Josceline did as she was told. The frothy, fresh milk reminded her of being a little girl sitting in the kitchen with the nanny, causing a surge of homesickness that threatened to set off the tears pressing so closely against her eyes. She blinked them away then started on the scone, laying it aside after she choked down a few bites.

Mrs. Belton gave an understanding nod. “Not hungry? At least finish the milk, my dear.”

Patient, she sat while Josceline drained the mug.

“Now tell me what ails you,” she prompted gently.

Josceline clasped and unclasped her hands. All the arguments she had marshaled during the long night fled and her mind was blank.

“He has asked me to marry him,” she blurted at last.

“Mr. Sharrington?” At Josceline’s nod, she continued, “And is that so terrible? They way you look, I thought perhaps the sky had fallen.” The kindly woman chuckled.

“It’s not what I wanted.” Josceline shook her head. “I wanted to make my own way. I wanted to find a man I could love, and who could love me.”

“Make your own way? Hogswaddle,” snorted Mrs. Belton. “As much as I think you are an engaging young lady, your talents are wasted as governess. You are meant to be mistress of your own grand estate.”

“I am?” Josceline stared at the plump woman sitting not two feet away from her. The idea of being mistress of her own domain pleased her but she had written that off long ago - when no one had come forward to offer for her. That was when she had entertained the idea of marrying for love. Like a fairy tale.

"But what of love?" She had to ask, had to know what the housekeeper thought of that notion.

"Love can grow," mused the housekeeper. "It is like a rose bush at the end of winter. Cut off the dead parts and water it and nurture it with garden scraps and the like. Over time, it will turn from brown, dead branches into something green and beautiful, with handsome flowers full of color and fragrance."

"A rose bush," Josceline repeated, confused. Why did Mrs. Belton talk about matters of the garden?

"Lady Josceline, what I am trying to say is, cut off the bad and throw it aside. Nurture the good and see what grows. Look." Mrs. Belton pointed outside.

Josceline followed her gaze to see Christopher walking from the stable with Philip and Tom gamboling around him like puppies. Life at Midland House was good to them - their cheeks had filled out and their skin had lost its unhealthy pallor. And something unexpected - utter joy shone from their cornflower blue eyes. The two had healed quickly from their ordeal in St. Peter's.

He had only taken the boys to save his own reputation, she reminded herself, not as a favor to them.

And to save hers as well.

Even so, the boys benefited – he treated them as his own.

"I find it odd a grown man can spend so much time with children," she remarked as Christopher and the boys disappeared from view behind the corner of the stables.

"I suspect he's lonely and working on his ledgers can only fill so many hours in a day. He's gone from the confines and hubbub of a ship to an estate house where no one can be his friend because he is the master. He has no family and he has no friends so what is the man to do?"

Christopher lonely? Before she could comment, Mrs. Belton continued.

"But he is too a kind man. He kept all of us on, he did, after the old master died. The house had fallen into disrepair and he's brought it back to life. It's a house in need of a mistress and a family." She fixed Josceline with a piercing stare. "He has asked you to be mistress here."

"Yes." Josceline nodded grudgingly, unwilling to picture the goodness inherent in Christopher. Whether the world knew it or not, the wretch had taken her virginity and she wasn't willing to gloss over the fact as yet.

"As far as making your own way, would it be so terrible to find your place at Midland House? It's good for you here too, Lady Josceline. You've lost the angry, miserable look you had the day you arrived."

"Me!" Josceline exclaimed.

"Yes, you." The housekeeper leaned over and patted Josceline's knee. "You, the two lads, and even the master himself have benefited from Midland House."

"The master?"

"Aye. The master arrived here as well with demons of his own to conquer. I wager they're still there but I believe the urgency to do so has left him. Especially since you've come here."

"I see." Josceline pondered this new bit of information.

"It isn't for me to make the choice for you but you could do worse, a lot worse than accept his proposal. Make of it what you can." Abruptly she stood up. "Cook must be wondering where I've disappeared to. Sit as long as you like, my dear, but I warn you-."

"Warn me of what?"

"A rocking chair is a lot like worry. It keeps you busy but gets you nowhere." She chuckled at her own joke. "It is soothing, though, I finish every day rocking for a few minutes in the evening." She turned serious. "Think on it carefully, Lady Josceline. Mr. Sharrington is a fine man. And Midland House could use a lovely mistress like yourself."

A bemused Josceline watched Mrs. Belton hurry off. The woman had nothing but high praise for Christopher. And high praise for her as well. According to the woman, Josceline had her place.

Here, at Midland House.

She pushed off again with one toe, setting the chair to rock, letting the motion ease her.

The housekeeper was right in one thing. Midland House was lovely, and though clean and in good repair, apparently thanks to the good graces of Christopher, it did lack the feminine touches which would turn it into a family home. She could bring in the winter greens and the Yule log and make sure fresh flowers from the garden graced every room the rest of the year. She could entertain. There would be children – perhaps one nestled in her womb already – riding fat ponies and hosting tea parties on the lawn. The question she now faced was whether or not it was the family home she wanted.

The chair slowed and eventually stopped. Josceline got up. The conversation with Mrs. Belton hadn't helped her in her decision at all.

If anything, it had made it more difficult.

* * *

Josceline's little mantel clock struck four, awakening her. She must have dozed off.

This was it, twenty four hours had passed. Almost passed, she corrected herself, she still had an hour but she doubted waiting the extra time would make her decision any clearer.

In actual fact, she was still undecided.

She meandered towards the drawing room, changing her mind with every step.

Yes, she would stay and become Christopher Sharrington's wife. However it would be a marriage of convenience and not the love match she had yearned for.

No, she would leave and continue as mistress of her own destiny. With possibly a child to care for as well.

Yes, she would marry Christopher and become the lady and chatelaine of Midland House.

No, she would retain her independence and be no man's chattel. An image of the disgusting Mr. Burrows rose in her mind.

Yes. No. Yes. No.

"Josceline!" Christopher stood as she entered the room. His expression was anxious, his hair loose and mussed as if he had run his hands through it many times.

She stopped in the door and looked at him hard. Perhaps seeing him would push her one way or the other.

"Twenty-four hours has passed," she stammered, hating herself for her seeming lack of confidence.

He schooled his features as she approached although his eyes darted to and fro across her face and his knuckles were white where they were clenched around the back of his leather chair.

As she walked across the room, she realized she still had no idea whether or not she would accept his proposal.

Chapter Eighteen

Christopher didn't say a word as Josceline drew near. His obvious dread pierced her conscience and suddenly she knew how to answer.

"Yes," she whispered. Her stomach flip flopped. She had agreed.

He smiled and closed his eyes, tipping his head back as if to thank the heavens for her answer. When he opened his eyes again, tears pooled in the corners. Visibly overcome with emotion, he nodded, grasping one of her hands gently to lift it to his lips. "You shan't regret it, Josceline. I promise you," he said huskily.

She tilted her head to one side. "You needn't promise."

"No?" He was clearly astonished at her statement.

"No." She shook her head. "A promise is not a promise unless it is kept. I should not expect it of you. For now, let us agree this will be a marriage of benefit to us both. Regret need not enter into it."

"Very well," he replied. "And now that we have decided, I see no reason to wait. If you have no objections, I shall call on the vicar this evening and arrange for special dispensation to waive the bans. What say you for a wedding Sunday following the regular service?"

"So soon?" she squeaked. At the very least she would like to sew herself a new frock from the copper satin Christopher had given her. She would be pressed to finish it in time but perhaps she could prevail on Mrs. Belton to help her.

"There is no reason to wait. Furthermore, that would allow us to announce it at Lord and Lady Oakland's dinner."

"Yes." She nodded thoughtfully. "The evening at Oakland Grange would serve as the perfect opportunity."

"Splendid. We are agreed then."

"We are. I should like to clarify two things, however."

He cocked an inquiring eyebrow at her bold statement.

"I should like to complete my three month term as governess and continue with the lessons for Philip and Tom." She may not be pursuing the self-sufficient path she had set out on when she left London but at least she could finish what she started. "With payment of the wage due to me."

"As you wish." He steepled his fingers and regarded her closely. "And the second?"

"You offered me the chance to become your partner. To help you, you said, in building your shipping company." At his nod, she continued. "Then what is it you think I can help you with?"

"We shall need investors and for that, you shall be the key. To grace my table. To entertain."

"I see." It wasn't quite what she had in mind when she thought to make her own way but working with Christopher to build his enterprise was a goal she could take pride in. She nodded. “I can do that.”

“I vow you shall do it very well,” he said gallantly, swooping an elegant bow.

She looked down at him, at his bent head and sinewy body folded over one leg. So she had done it. She had agreed to become Mr. Christopher Sharrington’s wife. By marrying him, not only would her reputation be rescued, but he offered her the chance to help him with his shipping enterprise. An enterprise which, if successful, would foster a feeling of independence in her own right.

Josceline fervently hoped he wasn’t under the mistaken impression her family name and connections would help him. She dreaded his reaction when that truth came to light.

* * *

“You look lovely,” said an admiring Mrs. Belton as Josceline pirouetted in her new dress in front of the mirror in her room Sunday morning.

“Thanks to you.” Josceline dropped an impulsive kiss on the woman’s wrinkled cheek. “I should never have finished it if you hadn’t helped me.”

“It was nothing,” Mrs. Belton said modestly. “I’ve sewed a frock or two in my time.”

“Look, the lace matches perfectly.” Josceline stopped twirling to inspect herself carefully.

Elizabeth’s hand me down watered blue silk had been carefully picked apart to serve as the pattern for the new dress. Josceline hated to lose the blue silk when she had so few frocks to begin with, however she consoled herself with the thought it had always been too tight. Too, she could use the pieces elsewhere so it would not go to waste.

She'd also painstakingly removed the lace trim from the hem of the blue silk and dyed it in a basin of tea so it turned from white to a lovely ivory shade.

Her new dress had a snug, high-waisted bodice, long fitted sleeves with ruffles around the wrists, and a scooped neckline trimmed with the dyed lace. She half turned to see the pert bow tied at the back, its long ends almost reaching her hem. The beautiful copper satin flowed over her hips to drape elegantly to the floor.

With the leftover bits of fabric, she'd had enough for a matching hair ribbon, now looped stylishly through her curls, and she'd fashioned two satin roses to be tacked to her slippers.

"I've just the thing, Lady Josceline. Wait for me." Mrs. Belton hurried off to return a few moments later, huffing and puffing and holding aloft triumphantly a tortoise shell comb. She tucked it high into Josceline's hair and stepped back to admire her handiwork.

"I vow you are as fine as any of the London ladies during the Season." The housekeeper wiped away a few tears. "The master will be speechless when he sees how beautiful you look."

Suddenly shy, Josceline looked away. She hoped so. She hoped admiration would fill Christopher's eyes. What if he thought her plain? Angrily she pushed the misgiving away. Why should she care what he thought? Today was her wedding day and all brides were beautiful, even brides of convenience.

How surprised Elizabeth would be when Josceline wrote her the news of her nuptials. A pang of guilt passed through her at the thought her dear friend wouldn't be there to share her special day but there just hadn't been time to invite her. Moreover, the day wasn't that special for she entered into a contract with Christopher, nothing else.

She turned back to the housekeeper, flashing what she hoped was a gay smile. "Shall we? I do believe the carriage is ready for us."

"Oh dear, yes of course, it won't do to keep the master waiting. Such an honor it is, for Tedham and I to be standing up for you."

The remainder of the day passed in a collage of images, one swimming into the next: The ride in the shiny ebony carriage and the feeble spring sunshine which barely took the winter chill from the air; the church, ivy clambering over its mellow golden stone walls; the few villagers still lingering after the morning service giving her inquiring glances as she alit from the carriage; Mrs. Belton handing her a small nosegay of daffodils; Christopher in his finest black wearing an inscrutable expression as he slid a ring on her finger; the vicar, absentminded and with kind grey eyes beneath a shock of unkempt white hair droning on and on until at last all she heard was:

"By the power vested within me, I now pronounce you man and wife."

Christopher leaned over to peck her cheek. They signed the register, and as they left the church, she tossed the nosegay to a little girl playing on the front steps.

Just like that, it was over. She was now Christopher's wife.

For better.

Or for worse.

* * *

It already was worse, fumed Josceline later that afternoon. Without her knowledge or permission, her things had been moved into the room adjoining Christopher's. Entirely reasonable, of course, for it was intended for the mistress of the house but that meant her bedroom now adjoined his directly.

She glared at the door separating them - only the thickness of it kept him from her – then inspected the rest of the room. As was the case with the rest of Midland House, it was spotless, and ready for her.

An enormous brick fireplace filled one wall, its marble mantel bare save for two heavy silver candlesticks. The lovely, carved oak wardrobe, waxed to a warm golden glow, had a matching carved dresser. The sleigh style bed beckoned, overflowing with pretty lace cushions and a lovely lace counterpane. A glass hurricane lamp sat guard on the lace draped bed stand.

But Josceline loved most the floor to ceiling windows overlooking the garden and framed by royal blue velvet drapes. Through them, sunlight suffused the room including the single wingback armchair, cheerfully upholstered in blue and yellow checkered fabric. The chair, positioned perfectly, sat close enough to the fire for warmth yet still close enough to the windows to look out. Someone, Mrs. Belton no doubt, had placed a small crystal bowl filled with violets on the little strapped chest beside it and her nose filled with the sweet fragrance.

Her anger dissipated.

This was a room she could spend time in, a room she could write letters in, and read, and do her needlework. A room providing a peaceful refuge and a room she could love.

She glanced again to the adjoining door. Even now, she could hear Christopher moving about.

She tensed, waiting for him to knock or try turning the doorknob, but he didn't. A few moments later, she heard his footsteps again then the snap of the latch as the door closed.

A frisson of relief surged through her and she made her way to the chair to sit down, inspecting closely for the first time the emerald ring he had given her. Circled by diamonds, the gently worn, gold band had a series of hearts linked together. It had been his mother's, he told her in the carriage on the way home.

She leaned back her head to rest. Only her mind wouldn't obey her and thoughts tumbled one after the other. When could she expect Christopher to call on her in her room? Or would he respect her privacy until they settled more firmly in their role as husband and wife? When did he want to start the search for investors? Did he need her help in obtaining the "Bessie" from Lord Oliver Candel as well? Would Christopher be happy if she found herself with child? Or happier if she did not?

And later, when she sat across from him at dinner, only one thought rolled repeatedly through her mind – if he expected to exert his marital rights this night.

But no, after a delicious supper of lamb, duck comfit, spring greens, potatoes and fruit custard, he merely walked her, silent and brooding, to her door.

He bowed low over her hand and breathed a kiss across the backs of her fingers. "I bid you good night." He straightened and his teeth gleamed in the dim light of the hallway as he flashed a smile. "In the morning we shall talk about your role in our enterprise."

Our enterprise.

His choice of words delighted her, as did his reassuring smile. It made her feel truly his partner.

Strangely, his dream had now become hers. And just as strange, she too, wanted to see its success.

* * *

Christopher put aside the morning paper when Josceline walked into the breakfast room the next morning.

"I trust you slept well?"

An inane question yet it pleased Josceline immensely. It was just the sort of thing a husband would ask of a wife.

"I did, thank you." She helped herself to scrambled eggs, ham, a wedge of cheese and a slice of bread from the sideboard and sat down. She had only taken a mouthful before Christopher spoke.

"I look forward to announcing our marriage at Oakland Grange. I also intend to announce the establishment of our business venture."

"Indeed?" Josceline paused, a fork of scrambled eggs halfway to her mouth.

"Yes. It makes us a force to be reckoned with. You, with your background and breeding and me with my sea faring experience. What better occasion to look for investors." He patted his mouth with his napkin.

"No." Josceline put down her fork and clasped her hands beneath her bosom. "If you wish to be accepted into proper society, you must realize some things are not discussed during genteel gatherings. Men of the upper classes do not work in commerce and business discussions are better left for occasions where women are not present."

"I see." Christopher scowled and gestured to the footman to pour him another cup of tea. "What do you propose, then?"

"We inform Lady Oakland of our marriage when we arrive. As hostess, she can make the formal announcement. That is more than enough for one evening. Although we've been invited, we're not well known here and we must cultivate acquaintances."

"It seems a waste of an opportunity," he growled.

"You shall still take advantage of the opportunity. Wait until after dinner when the men retire to their port and cigars. Don't jump into the conversation, take your cue from the others and see if you can steer the conversation towards shipping. Gauge the general mood. Ask questions. Who are the prominent merchants in Bristol? Where does one meet them? That sort of thing."

He looked at her and she felt her cheeks heat up at the approval in his eyes. Flustered, she looked down to her lap and toyed with her napkin.

"Nicely put," he praised. "What you suggest makes perfect sense." He buttered a piece of bread before slathering it with berry jam. He cut it in two and placed one half on her plate. "The compote is delicious. Last year's berries, I expect."

A surprised Josceline looked down at the jam covered bread then raised her gaze to catch his.

"Do you suppose Lord Candel shall be present at the festivities at Oakland House?" Thoughtfully Christopher took a bite of the bread and jam. "Because it would be an ideal time to remind him he reneged on his gambling debt."

Josceline shook her head emphatically. "Only if you catch him in a discreet situation. The "Bessie" is a matter pertaining only to the two of you. Your grievance with him shouldn't be aired in public."

"I hate to think the rogue believes he has bested me." A muscle twitched in his jaw.

"All in due time," reassured Josceline. "Let us first make the acquaintance of our neighbors."

"I have an idea. Once we have a few acquaintances, we shall hold a house party of our own. I surmise you have friends in London who could join us here in the country."

It was as she feared. Christopher thought she had a wide circle of friends from whom she could draw.

How disappointed he would be when he discovered her only friends and allies were Elizabeth and her mother.

"Ah, of course," she stammered.

Twenty-four hours had not yet passed and already she was doomed to disappoint Christopher.

Best to deal with the evening at the Oakland's first. Then she would worry about pulling together guests for the house party Christopher wanted.

* * *

Christopher couldn't believe the lovely creature sitting across from him this morning at the breakfast table was his wife. Her hair was neatly pulled back although a few small curls wisped about her neck. Her eyes matched perfectly the emerald on her finger and the stone caught the sun's rays as she moved her hands about.

His mother's ring. How surprised he had been to discover it fit Josceline's finger perfectly when he slipped it on her finger during the ceremony. The stone flashed green again as Josceline lifted her cup and it made him think of his mother.

Proud until the bitter end, she refused to sell the ring keeping it on her finger though poverty knocked continually at her door.

After he went to sea, he regularly sent her his monthly wage but even so, her life had been meager. She could easily have sold it at any time, yet she didn't. When one day he finally asked her why, she had just smiled at him with sad eyes and said, "Love does not always allow one to think or act rationally."

At the end, dropsy took her but she had hung on until she could give him the ring in person.

"For you and the wife you shall have one day," she murmured. And just like that, she slipped away.

Josceline peeped at him over the rim of her tea cup, eyes crinkling in a smile. It sent a rush of joy pouring through him to pool in his gut.

She had once admitted to him she wanted a love match. In an impulsive silent vow to make it so, Christopher raised his cup to her. His mother's words on love echoed in his ears and he had the feeling soon he would understand more fully what she meant.

He could only hope one day Josceline would feel the same.

Chapter Nineteen

The evening of Lord and Lady Oakland's fete finally arrived - an evening which, for the first time in years, Josceline looked forward to with great anticipation.

And it was all because she accompanied the man sitting across from her on the front squabs. She glanced at him and he rewarded her with a quick grin.

"Have I told you how lovely you look?" Christopher teased, eyeing appreciatively the copper satin dress peeking out from beneath her cloak.

"You have," she replied gaily, "but it shouldn't hurt to remind me again. And I should return the favor. You cut a particularly fine figure tonight in your velvet waistcoat and evening tails."

"Saucy minx." He laughed aloud and leaned over to pat her hand but she could see her compliment pleased him for a slight smile hung on his lips.

The carriage rocked to a stop in front of Oakland Grange. With the help of several footmen who converged on them like ants to a honey pot, the two disembarked and were guided inside to a side room where more footmen were stationed to help guests with their coats.

They joined the queue waiting to be announced. Other than a few curious glances from fellow guests, they shuffled forward unnoticed.

It wasn't until Howard, the Oakland's butler, gestured to Christopher and pulled him aside that Josceline felt the first stirrings of unease.

"Is something amiss?" Josceline asked when Christopher returned to her side.

"Lord Oakland has requested my immediate presence in his library." Christopher was clearly puzzled. "How odd."

"Go see what he wants." She gave him a little nudge. "We can step back into line when you return."

She moved closer to the wall to wait, pretending to study the portraits and furniture lining the entrance way, recognizing the horsehair chair she had sat in the night she arrived from London.

She felt a tap on her shoulder and she turned to see the butler.

"There is a gentleman here who wishes to see you in private, my lady." Howard bowed. "Will you come with me?"

"A gentleman for me?" she exclaimed. How peculiar, who knew she would be here?

"Yes, he says he is your father." Her father? At Oakland Grange? Her heart leapt into her throat, constricting the flow of air and she had to make a conscience effort to breathe.

No, it couldn't be. He must have received the curt letter she had sent several days ago announcing her marriage. Furthermore, if it truly was her father, she knew him well enough to realize he wouldn't be happy she had married against his wishes.

Frantic, she scanned the crowd in search of Christopher but he hadn't returned.

She had no desire to face the duke. However, if Howard spoke the truth and her father was here, she could share her news in person and make him understand his plans for her and Mr. Burrows would not come to fruition. Her joyous anticipation of the evening crumbled at the looming confrontation.

Josceline scanned the crowd one last time - still no sign of Christopher. It shouldn't take long to talk to her father; she could return before Christopher noticed her absence.

"I shall deal with him," she replied. "Where is he?"

"Lord Oakland's office. This way, my lady." The butler pointed and let her precede him.

Reluctantly, she made her way, tasting ash in her mouth. Every step closer became more difficult as if she waded through sludge.

"Through here, my lady." The butler swung open the door.

She paused in the doorway, leaning one trembling hand against the jamb for support. Two figures turned to her: the slight, stooped figure of her father, and the burly form of Thomas Burrows.

They couldn't hurt her here, in this public gathering, she told herself. She sucked in a deep breath and stepped into the room. The door closed behind her with an ominous "clack".

Burrows hung behind, a smirk on his bulbous lips as her father advanced towards her. The duke spoke first.

"Lady Oakland has done her duty to me as your father and reported your circumstance to me. I've come to restore your honor." His voice was querulous.

"There is no problem with my honor." She clenched her fists in the folds of her skirt. "The truth is-."

He interrupted her before she could explain. "That's not what Lady Oakland has suggested to me. According to that fine lady, you are compromised."

"I beg to differ." She stood her ground.

"Mr. Burrows is willing to take you to wife. I command it to be so." He glowered at her from beneath bristling brows.

"I cannot marry Mr. Burrows."

"I am your father, the Duke of Cranston, and you shall do as I say." He moved closer and made as if to grab for her.

She took a step back.

Her father came for her, clawed hands flapping and face becoming more mottled with red as he advanced. She took another step back, then another and another until she backed into the wall.

She held her tongue with the perverse desire to see how ugly and twisted his face could become. Defiant, she crossed her arms, pressing her body into the wall tightly.

"You can't run from me, daughter." He grabbed her wrist with one bony hand and yanked at it. "Come, we return to London this night. I've spoken to our parish priest and he awaits our return."

Her father had made arrangements without her acquiescence. Anger spurted through her and her skin crawled where her father held her wrist. She tried to tug free but no matter how hard she tried, she couldn't loose herself from his grasp.

Mr. Burrows lumbered over, eyes filled with vicious intent. His rank smell filled her nostrils as he grabbed the other wrist. "Deny me, will ye? Ye think yer so much better than me?"

"No! I am wed already!" She screamed and dug in her heels but was no match against the strength of two men. The heels of her slippers scraped against the bare boards of the floor as they dragged her across the floor. She struggled and a fat hand clamped over her mouth, restricting her breath. A black mist clouded the room, lowering over her eyes until she could see nothing but blackness.

Help me! Christopher, help me!

* * *

Christopher left the company of Lord Oakland, mulling over their brief meeting as he made his way back to the entrance hall. He searched for Josceline amongst the few remaining guests milling about. How curious, she was nowhere to be seen. All thoughts of the meeting fled his mind.

She had disappeared.

He waited a minute or two thinking she had perhaps gone to refresh herself before accosting one of the footmen.

"Have you seen my wife," he barked with such force the footman shrank back.

"Yes, Mr. Sharrington, Howard took her to Lord Oakland's office."

What the devil? First Christopher himself was called away and now her? A chill surged down his spine.

"Where is this office," he demanded, leaning his face into that of the young footman who, obviously intimidated by Christopher's manner, raised a shaky arm to point.

Christopher charged down the hallway and saw the sliver of light beneath a closed door. Without bothering to knock, he flung it open with such force it slammed against the wall and rebounded, quivering.

Barging into the room, he took in the situation with a sweeping glance. Josceline was held fast on one side by a corpulent gentleman, who covered her mouth with a burly hand, while a frail, elderly man clutched her other arm.

Her eye lids fluttered open at the sound of his footsteps and she looked his way. The frightened expression in her eyes told the story.

The two must be the Duke of Cranston and the man to whom he had promised her. Mr. Burrows, if memory served him correctly. Christopher's face grew hot and he was blinded momentarily by scorching anger at the sight of Josceline held against her will.

"I'll thank you to take your hands off my wife," he snarled, advancing on them with clenched fists.

The duke dropped his hands and sidled away but Burrows jutted out his lip and adjusted his grip on Josceline.

"Never," he sneered, trying to pull Josceline towards the door. "The girl is betrothed to me. And if it hadn't been for the kind assistance of Lady Oakland, we should never have found her."

With blinding clarity Christopher understood the motive behind Lady Oakland's invitation.

It hadn't been for their benefit at all. It had been for the Duke to be able to catch his daughter and force her into marriage with the detestable merchant.

Another wave of anger surged through him and he grabbed Burrows' neck, shaking it ferociously.

"Release her." He squeezed tighter until he could feel the ribbed cords pop in the fleshy throat. Eyes bulging, the man dropped his hands from Josceline and fell to his knees, gasping for breath.

"Who are you?" From behind him came the querulous voice of Josceline's father.

Christopher became aware of the feeble blows raining on his back from the duke and whirled about to shove the man, sending him sprawling to the floor.

"Christopher Sharrington," he growled, reaching to tug Josceline to him. "This is my wife."

"Christopher, they tried to abduct me," Josceline exclaimed. She stumbled and he pulled her close, half-carrying her as they backed off in the direction of the door.

"If either of you ever touch her again, I shall kill you both, do you understand?"

Burrows, still on his knees, looked daggers at him. Lord Cranston hauled himself up and sat cross-legged on the floor, head in his hands.

"I shall kill you both, do you understand?" Christopher repeated when neither man deigned to respond.

"Understood," scowled Burrows. "You're welcome to the chit. She's more trouble than she's worth."

Josceline's father said nothing but raised his head and, with tears in his rheumy blue eyes, nodded once. Misery limned his features and for an instant he seemed to Christopher nothing more than an old, sad man.

Christopher softened his voice at the sight. "I shall have the butler escort you out immediately."

And with that, Christopher pushed Josceline through the door and closed it firmly behind them.

The force of his anger when he had seen her held by Burrows stunned him. Equally stunning was the abject fear for her safety. Even now, blood pounded hot and hard through his veins at the thought she might have been injured or worse, abducted without his knowledge.

"Did they harm you?" He grasped her shoulders so he could look her full in the face. The well lit hall, with every wall sconce burning, clearly showed her features. She was shaken but she returned his gaze firmly.

"No." Josceline shook her head. "But why were they here?"

"I believe it was at the instigation of Lady Oakland. I suspect we were invited so your father would find you here."

"I see." Josceline began to shiver. "So the invitation wasn't issued for our benefit at all."

"I don't believe so." He slammed his fist into the wall. "How could the woman behave in such an atrocious manner?" He slanted a sideways glance in her direction. "Are you cold?" he asked abruptly. "You're trembling."

She shook her head. "I'm not cold. I assure you, if I tremble, it is from anger. How could she play us for fools?"

"I am certain she had her reasons." He sighed and, slouching, jammed his hands in his pockets. "What do we do now?"

"Leave," Josceline said firmly. "It's the sensible thing to do."

Her only desire at this moment was to escape Oakland Grange. The situation disgusted her. Her fists clenched. If she saw either her father or Lady Oakland, she would pummel them black and blue. Then she would set their ears to burning with a tirade the likes of which neither would forget.

He gave her an incredulous look. "Leave? I say no. I say we stand firm." Abruptly he straightened up. "We are here. Let us attend as if nothing has happened. Let us meet our neighbors. What say you, Josceline, are you up for the challenge?"

"Are you serious?" Her eyes were round. "There may not be a place set for us."

"Which shall only reflect badly on Lady Oakland, don't you think? A hostess who cannot properly count the number of her guests?" He took her elbow and gave it a reassuring squeeze. "Shall we? I grant you the expression on Lady Oakland's face will be worth it when she sees us."

"Indeed." Josceline gave him a thoughtful look. Perhaps Christopher was right – running off was the coward's way out. If there was one thing she knew about Lady Oakland, it was that the woman kept up appearances. The last thing she would want would be for her fete to be ruined.

As for her father, all she could think of right now was the distress on his face when Christopher threatened him. Her father had grown old and she hadn't even seen it.

"Josceline? Are you in agreement?"

Christopher's concerned voice interrupted her thoughts and she forced herself back to the matter at hand – the come-uppance of Lady Oakland.

And she realized with a sudden start, with Christopher at her side, she could face anything. The remembrance of his anger when he found her with her father and Burrows warmed her - it meant he cared for her a little.

"Absolutely," Josceline declared, lifting her chin. "She's likely to fall over with surprise when we are announced after all."

Together they marched down the hall. The queue had disappeared and a hubbub of voices drifted through the doorway of the salon punctuated by the occasional raucous shout.

"Announce us," Christopher demanded to the single footman who remained.

"Of course." The footman bowed slightly. "You are - ?"

"Mr. Christopher Sharrington and his wife, Lady Josceline Woodsby," interjected Josceline arrogantly, playing her part.

Enough of Lady Oakland's meddling, she seethed silently. Doubtless, the woman had written to the duke to check the veracity of Josceline's identity. When her father had discovered her whereabouts, the woman had become her father's ally and for some unknown reason had provided him the opportunity to retrieve Josceline.

Lady Oakland had shown incredible gall. First, having the audacity to demand an introduction to Christopher's supposed son, then by inviting them to her fete under false pretences. She had sent both of them tumbling through hoops of insecurity and trepidation.

The opportunity had presented itself to take the woman to task.

Chapter Twenty

It gave Josceline grim satisfaction to see Lady Oakland's face turn ashen when they were announced. She hurried over to greet them, pretending great pleasure but also obviously puzzled as she looked behind them in the direction of Lord Oakland's office.

Apparently seeing nothing, she recovered with aplomb, inclining her head in welcome which set the ends of the string of pearls woven through her hair to swinging. A picture of elegance in sapphire blue silk, she held out a velvet gloved hand for Christopher to kiss.

"Why, Mr. Sharrington, Lady Woodsby," she cooed. "How lovely. You've arrived just in time, we're about to sit down to dinner." She pulled them into the salon.

Josceline choked back bile at the woman's artificial manner then glanced about. Perhaps thirty people were crammed in the room, no small feat considering the amount of space taken by the pianoforte and the massive sideboard. All were involved in animated conversation and no one paid attention to the recent arrivals. The heated room, bordering on oppressive, released a miasma of odors - perfumes, wine, perspiration, and burning bees wax candles. For an instant, Josceline felt light headed. She swayed and Christopher caught her.

"No longer Lady Woodsby, I am afraid." Christopher looked down at Josceline then back at Lady Oakland. "I'm pleased to introduce you to Mrs. Sharrington. We were wed this past Sunday."

Lady Oakland's jaw dropped. "My, that was rather sudden, was it not?"

"When the heart is smitten, it cares not to wait."

He said it so smoothly, Josceline almost believed it to be true. Almost. She must remember theirs was a marriage of convenience. She firmly squashed the hope bubbling up within her at his words.

"Mr. Sharrington, that is too romantic for words," simpered their hostess. "Do let me have the honor of announcing your recent nuptials."

The smile she gave them didn't reach her eyes and for a crazy instant, Josceline fancied her much like a cat ready to pounce on a mouse. She compressed her lips, tilting her head to give the woman a calculating stare. Two could play that game.

"As you wish." Christopher inclined his head, turning it slightly to give Josceline a surreptitious wink meant to bolster her courage. Wits tuned, Josceline lifted her chin.

"Everyone, everyone, do pay attention." Lady Oakland tapped her ivory satin fan against a convenient glass. The cheerful tinkle cut through the noise and gradually the room fell silent.

Every head in the room swiveled to look at the late arrivals; Josceline's armpits grew damp and a bead of perspiration trickled down her temple. She wiped it away and focused on Lady Oakland.

"I should like to announce that our dear friend and neighbor, Mr. Christopher Sharrington, wed Lady Josceline Woodsby just this past week." She turned to face them. "In the parish church here?" At their nod, she turned back to the gathering. "Yes, in the parish church here." She began to clap, dropping her fan to dangle from a cord around her wrist.

To Josceline, it almost looked like a whip. Not one with which to whip horses but one with which to whip her guests. The notion reminded her to beware of the woman.

A ripple of applause circled the room, accompanied by nods and smiles. Josceline started to relax at the heartening sound. Nonetheless, she must keep her fanciful thoughts under control or she would be outmaneuvered.

"Lady Josceline Woodsby? Here? The last I heard, she was in London, sequestered in that mausoleum that passes for Cranston Hall and refusing to see visitors." A woman's shrill voice oozed through the applause.

The voice was familiar to Josceline but she couldn't quite place who it was. She poked her head around Christopher and peered through the crowd to find the speaker. Her heart sank clear to the toes of her slippers when she noticed the heavy-set, blonde, full lipped woman with two spots of rouge high on her cheeks, push through the guests to stand in front of the three.

It was that wicked gossip, Lady Annabelle Swinton, known not only for her sharp tongue but her propensity to ferret out the most hidden secrets.

Balderdash, why was the woman here and not in London attending the newly begun Season? The woman must be forestalled or more secrets would spill about Josceline's family.

Secrets which would disappoint Christopher if he were to find out.

Secrets which, of necessity, Josceline would have to share eventually but only when the time was right.

She could hang back no longer. She must take the first stab.

"Why Lady Oakland," Josceline said sweetly, turning to her hostess with an innocent gaze. "However did you coax Lady Swinton from her lair?"

A few sniggers circled the room. Lady Oakland scowled and Lady Swinton gasped in anger. Unruffled, Josceline continued – she had ammunition of her own.

"I vow, dear Lady Swinton, was it not you who claimed she would never set foot outside of the city? What was that term you used? Country hicks? Do tell us, what brings you to a country house party on the outskirts of Bristol? Has Lord Swinton finally thrown you over for that actress he has been dallying with?"

"Josceline," hissed Christopher, chagrin imprinted on his face.

She glanced at him. Lady Oakland, he mouthed in a blatant attempt to remind Josceline of their purpose. She nodded slightly to indicate her awareness of what she was doing. He gave her an appraising look before forcing a smile and turning back to face the room.

"How dare you sully my husband's name," Lady Swinton snapped, eyes narrowing in contempt. "That is none of your concern."

"Nor should it be," interrupted their hostess, quite rightly sensing impending disaster. "I fear hunger is impinging on our manners," she soothed, casting a frantic glance to her husband. "Darling," she waved to Lord Oakland on the far side of the salon, "would you lead the way into the dining room, if you please?"

"I'm afraid I couldn't swallow a morsel knowing Lady Woodsby is at the table," Lady Swinton said maliciously.

"What a fine observation. It would surely be to your benefit if you swallowed a few morsels less." A tight smile formed across Josceline's mouth.

Lady Oakland opened her mouth to intervene but Lady Swinton held up a chubby hand.

"I simply cannot stay here in this company," she announced haughtily. "I must beg pardon but I really do feel faint and wish to retire." The woman picked up her skirts and stepped towards the doorway.

Another round of sniggers circled the room. Several guests moved closer to have a better view of the proceedings.

"You should beware," Josceline taunted. "You may come across my father in the hallway."

"The Duke of Cranston? Here, at Oakland Grange?" Lady Swinton stopped and turned to Lady Oakland. "Penelope, is this true? Do you have any idea of that man's reputation?"

"Why, er-." Lady Oakland's face blanched and she licked her lips. "He is a duke. I thought him of the highest quality," she added lamely.

"My dear Penelope, I do wish you had mentioned this to me beforehand. I've no desire to visit more disaster on this evening but I'm appalled you would have the unsavory Duke of Cranston in your house."

Shocked silence greeted her words. A horrified Lady Oakland stared at her, lips twisting as if she searched for words.

"Lady Oakland was unaware we had wed." Christopher jumped in, taking advantage of the hush. "She invited the duke here to collect his daughter. The duke brought with him his choice for son-in-law, a choice not shared by my wife."

"I only had Lady Woodsby's best interests at heart," responded Lady Oakland, voice strident. She looked around the room desperately, searching for support. "When I contacted him with knowledge of her whereabouts, her father was most worried about her, as any father would be about his only daughter. You must agree, Mr. Sharrington, her position with you was arranged in an unusual manner."

"Be that as it may, it was of no concern to you. Tell me, Lady Oakland, do you picture yourself as the doyen for the local gentry?" Christopher's tones were icy and his face hardened.

"Jolly good!"

"Well said!"

Exclamations filled the air. Someone, a man, laughed out loud but was quickly shushed. Josceline tore her gaze from the two women standing before them and scanned the room. All faces were turned their way, some amused, some wondering. Her palms grew clammy, her stomach balled.

London. It was just like being in London. People didn't even know her here and still they regarded her with amusement and surprise. No, she corrected herself, *they* were being regarded with amusement and surprise. A wave of disdain rolled through her at the assembled guests. So quick to judge.

"Why, why-," gasped Lady Oakland, lost for words. A tide of red surged across her décolletage and upwards to the very roots of her hair.

Whispers began to fly and more guests pressed in to witness the tableau unfolding in the salon.

"Lady Oakland invited us here under false pretences," Christopher said, giving their hostess a withering stare. "We were led to believe it was our opportunity to become acquainted with our neighbors and fellow countrymen. Imagine our surprise to find it was not the case. She conspired with the duke without our knowledge. Lady Oakland, I should think that is akin to kidnapping."

He took Josceline's hand and placed it on his arm. "Lady Woodsby has done me the honor of becoming my wife. I look forward to our life together and my inclusion in her circle of family and friends."

"You think she is going to give you access to the peerage?" Lady Swinton shrieked with laughter. "She is the Duke of Cranston's daughter. That shall never happen. Oh my, your blunder is too delicious for words."

Here it comes, thought Josceline grimly, she is going to tell all. Mentally she girded herself.

Lord Oakland pushed his way to the front. “This scene has gone on long enough. Cease the attacks on my wife and our good name. I would thank you two to leave.” He hauled out his lorgnette to look down at them, hawk nose tilted high.

One or two couples drifted to the door and slipped away. Lady Oakland hurried after them in an obvious bid to keep the party together.

“With pleasure,” retorted Christopher. “Come, we shan’t waste any more of our time here.”

He laid his hand over Josceline’s where it still rested on his elbow and they turned.

“I say, Sharrington, do not say you mean to leave so early. We have yet to make our hellos.”

A man’s sneering tones grated on Josceline’s ears.

Beneath her fingers, Josceline felt Christopher tense. She peeped up at him. His face was flushed, eyes narrowed, a vein throbbed in his temple. He froze then slowly pulled her around so they again faced the crowded salon.

Josceline immediately recognized the man who spoke. A dandy, dressed in scarlet breeches and a peacock blue cutaway jacket, regarding them both with an insolent grin.

A man she knew to be of ill reputation.

Lord Oliver Candel.

Christopher sucked in his breath as if to speak but he remained silent. Waves of animosity radiated from him; Josceline could feel them as surely as if a feather brushed her arm.

"Where are your henchmen? The two urchins?" Candel's voice was droll.

"My son," grated Christopher, "is home in his bed where he belongs."

"As you say, Sharrington." Candel sketched an insolent salute. "Have you played at the gaming tables recently? Mind you, if I had such a pretty piece waiting for me at home, I would be of a mind to forego that pleasure." His mouth made a moue as he raked Josceline head to toe with an insulting gaze.

"Do not speak to me of gaming. You bilked me of my winnings in a match won cleanly by me. I want the ship." Christopher's menacing tones rolled through the suddenly silent salon. He dropped Josceline's hand and took a step forward.

"My, are you still on about that?" Candel tilted his head and foppishly laid his hand against his jaw. "I don't recall such a thing happening."

"You kept what rightfully belongs to me, Candel, and I shan't rest until I have it."

Christopher turned on his heel and held out his hand to Josceline. She put her hand in his and together they walked away.

A sudden uproar followed them out the door. Interspersed between Lady Oakland's cajoles to her guests to go in for dinner, were snickers and cruel words.

"This is too comical," said an unknown woman, "Lord Cranston trying to abduct his daughter to marry her off to a man not of her choosing."

"And she already married to a commoner," said another.

"And the commoner accusing Lord Candel of theft," laughed a third.

"It shall be the *on dits* of the Season," tittered a fourth.

The comments filled Josceline's ears. Word of this would spread to London. They were a laughingstock.

Worse, she would have to immediately tell Christopher the truth about her father. Her heart sank at the thought of the bewildered look she was sure to see in her husband's eyes when he found out.

* * *

Silence reigned over their carriage ride home.

"Would you join me in the library?" asked Christopher when they rolled to a stop at Midland House. "I daresay we need to review this evening's events."

Josceline nodded. He gestured to her to precede him and they made their way indoors.

Hesitantly, she entered the library, face flushing with the memories of the night he had made love to her: His hands hot on her breasts; cool air wafting over her bare skin; the pressure of him inside her. Her woman's nub started to throb and her nipples tingled with longing.

She hadn't been here since that night, in fact, had gone out of her way to avoid it. For an instant, she had the bizarre sensation the books regarded her with reproach. She shook her head to clear away the idea and ignored the wetness gathering between her legs. There were other matters to be dealt with.

Christopher pointed to the lone arm chair. He set a match to the neatly laid fire then pulled out his desk chair to sit backwards on it to face her. He leaned his elbows on the back of it, propping his chin on his fists.

"I am sorry," Josceline whispered. The fire had yet to banish the chill from the air and she threw her cloak over her as a blanket.

"For?"

"This evening did not pass as fruitfully as hoped."

"Didn't it? Didn't we spoil the Oakland's fete? I should wager tongues will wag for months." He smiled. "Did you see Lady Oakland's face when Lady Swinton attacked her over inviting your father? And Lady Oakland's screeches when she realized the evening had fallen into disaster?"

Josceline smiled too, a weak attempt barely lifting the corners of her mouth. "But we didn't have the opportunity to meet anyone. All I remember is a room full of shadowed faces. You didn't have the occasion to discuss shipping and Bristol harbor. Then there was the business with that horrid Lord Candel." She shuddered.

"No matter," he continued heartily, "we shall host our own house party. And we shall not invite him." He winked in an obvious attempt to lighten her mood.

This was it. She had to admit no one would come. She looked away as she spoke, not wanting to see the censure sure to appear when she told him the absolute truth about the disgraced Duke of Cranston.

"I am afraid that would just be wasting our time." She forced out the words. "I have no one to invite and if I did, no one would come."

"Because of your father being a drunkard and a gambler?"

"Yes." She nodded. She clung briefly to the faint hope she could leave it at that. Then she shook her head. "No, there is more." She paused for an instant to draw in a steadying breath before continuing. "My father was accused of treason."

"Treason." He barked with laughter. "Since when is being a drunkard and a gambler akin to treason?"

"No, it's true. He discovered military documents while visiting a good friend who is particularly close to mad King George. The documents disappeared. Although there was never proof of it, he was accused of stealing them and selling them to the French thereby betraying not only our country but his friend. It is not good to cross a man who counts the king as his ally."

"Agreed." He nodded and cocked his head, waiting for her to continue.

"This man made it his duty to ensure all knew of my father's duplicity. I suppose I shouldn't make excuses for him, particularly since he tried to force me into a marriage I didn't want, but he just hasn't been the same since the death of my mother. Without her, he lost his compass in life. Anyway, it was the tipping point for him, for us as a family. We are well and truly social pariahs."

"I see." His face wore compassion, his eyes were gentle.

There was not a drop of censure to be seen; calm trickled through her. She had told him and he didn't hate her for it.

"Do we really need investors?" She twisted her fingers in the fabric of her dress. Her beautiful copper satin dress which now would probably always remind her of the disastrous evening they had just dealt with.

His face fell. "Yes," he sighed, nodding morosely. "To acquire the cargo to fill the hold. To hire the crew, to buy supplies. I would go it alone but I'm close to facing financial ruin. This?" He swept his arm around. "This is the biggest gamble of my life. When one games, you up the stakes for greater reward. The higher the risk, the higher the reward. I was sure if I played the part of wealthy landowner wishing to diversify into shipping, partners would flock to me." He looked at her. "I'm sorry I dragged you into this."

Suddenly she remembered all the times she had passed the library to see him working on his ledgers, running ink stained fingers down the columns, tallying numbers for endless hours. Even Mrs. Belton had remarked on it the day they had talked in her room. He must be telling the truth. His funds must be limited.

By rights, upon discovering they were close to ruin, she should collapse with her smelling salts at hand. Instead, the idea only strengthened her resolve.

Poverty did not scare her. Her life in recent years had been full of financial hardship. What did scare her was the thought of losing Christopher and the chance to build a life with him.

She had agreed to marry him on his promise to use her abilities in his shipping venture. Their shipping venture. A shipping venture from which she stood to gain as much as he.

"Are we close to ruin?" she faltered. "How much time do we have here at Midland House?"

He shrugged. "I have enough for us to live here for the better part of a year. I just don't have the wherewithal to equip a cargo ship. The sad truth, Josceline, we are soon to be paupers."

She regarded his bleak face. There must be a solution and together they would find it. How to make him believe she supported the endeavor?

"Wait here." She threw off the cloak and scampered off only to return with her reticule, turning it over to give it a shake. Three coins dropped from it – a shilling and two ha'pennies.

"Keep your coins," he said brusquely.

"Oh, I shall." She waved the empty reticule at him. "I brought this to show you I have as much at stake as do you."

"More so after tonight's debacle," he snorted.

"As you said," she continued briskly, "we set out to embarrass Lady Oakland and we succeeded. Of course, we weren't expecting we would get swept up in the situation. However, what has passed has passed." She gave him a rueful grin.

He responded with one of his own.

"Let us retrace our steps," she suggested.

"Retrace our steps?" He raised an eyebrow.

"Forget finding other investors for now. Let us target Lord Oliver Candel. You need your ship for as I pointed out to you, what is a shipping enterprise without a ship?"

"You're right," he nodded. A smile of grudging admiration crossed his face. "Once we have the "Bessie", we can decide how to fill her. Let us focus our attention on Lord Candel and how to retrieve her."

Chapter Twenty One

The next morning dawned clear, the sun's rays shining bright as if to banish the foul events of the disastrous evening at Oakland Grange. Josceline sat at her dressing table, brushing her hair. It should be the task of her maid but after Christopher's revelation of impending poverty, she didn't want to ask him for one.

Stroke by stroke, she tamed the curls until they shone.

And stroke by stroke she replayed the events of the previous evening: Christopher being called away to meet with Lord Oakland; Howard leading her to the library to discover her father there with Burrows; Lady Swinton and her accusations; Lord Candel stepping forward to needle Christopher resulting in Christopher's verbal attack on Candel.

The stories were sure to fly for weeks.

Shaking her head, she put down the brush and picked up a ribbon to tie back her hair, scowling at herself in the mirror. Questions churned in her mind. How could the evening have resulted in such disaster? How was Christopher this morning? What had happened between Christopher and Lord Oakland? In all the tumult of last evening, she had forgotten to ask him.

At least it was easy enough to find answers to the last two questions. She got up and went in search of her husband.

* * *

Christopher spurred Vesuvius mercilessly. He leaned low over the beast's neck. Its wind whipped mane stung his face, its tail streamed behind as the animal's powerful muscles carried them forward. Pounding hooves sprayed up clods of turf.

The sun shone yet the crisp breeze stung his cheeks and he scarce felt his fingers grasping the reins, so cold were they.

Together, man and horse raced towards the distant hazy horizon.

Only he couldn't outrace his thoughts.

Damnation. Lord Candel would ever be the scourge of his life. In her innocence, Josceline had made a simple suggestion yet she had no idea of whom they truly faced.

Retrieve your ship, she had said.

And he had agreed. How simple. Retrieve the ship.

The sad fact was, he had no idea how to go about it.

When Christopher had won, Candel snatched the deed from the table to ram it into his pocket and who knew where the deed would be now. True, others had witnessed the incident between them but none had come forward for him then and certainly none would come forward weeks after the fact.

To confront the man would serve no purpose. He had tried that and had been refused audience.

What to do now?

Retrieve the ship. How?

* * *

Upon being informed by Tedham that Christopher had taken his horse for a ride, Josceline opted to spend some time with Philip and Tom in an attempt to forget about the events of the previous evening.

They sat outside on the sheltered garden bench she favored, the boys on the ground at her feet. In one hand, she carried the chalk and slate, in the other, the primer.

"Look! Daffodils." She pointed to the yellow buds set to unfurl. Primula and grape hyacinth also poked through the jumble of dead leaves and grasses. "Spring is here."

"I like spring," Philip said importantly. "It means it's going to get warm again." Beside him, Tom nodded energetically.

"Shall we count how many daffodils we can find? The yellow ones," she added at the confusion on the boys' faces. Their expressions brightened and they jumped to their feet.

"One! Two! Three!" They ran off, fingers pointing, blonde hair flying, cheeks pink with exertion. "Four! Five!"

"Philip, Tom, stay close, we have yet to begin." She waved and was rewarded with an answering wave from Tom. Philip had disappeared behind the gnarled plum tree although she could still hear his voice. “Six! Seven!”

Best to let them run off some energy before they sat down to tackle today’s lessons. She tilted her face to the warmth of the sun, waiting for the fresh air and cheery light to cast out the remembrance of last night.

It very nearly worked except for one thing.

She couldn’t rid her mind of the memory of the look on her father’s face and the misery in his eyes when Christopher had rescued her.

Bah, it made no sense to concern herself over the well being of her father. He had never concerned himself over her well being, indeed, had let his greed for Mr. Burrows financial resources overrule his sensibilities for his daughter.

Through the budding branches, Josceline caught sight of Philip and Tom. A rush of tenderness filled her breast. Even though she wasn’t their mother, Josceline had developed love for the two and it would require something of horrendous proportions for her to ever hurt them.

Therefore for her father to wound her only revealed the desperation to which he had sunk. She finally saw him for what he was – a broken hulk of a man burying his pain. For that she could feel sympathy.

A thrush alighted on a branch beside her, chirruping its pleasure at the sun. The joyous notes pushed the load from her shoulders and she felt as if she had pulled her feet out of dank, smelly muck to run free through a meadow of buttercups and daisies.

She had Christopher. Her father could hurt her no more.

* * *

Christopher leapt off Vesuvius, throwing the reins to the stable boy. "He's had quite a gallop, make sure he has a good rub down and a fresh bag of oats."

Not waiting for the stable boy's response, he charged into the house in search of Josceline. He couldn't wait to tell her he'd found a solution to the "Bessie".

He'd only taken half a dozen strides when Tedham stopped him in the hall.

"There is a package for you, Mr. Sharrington. Jefferson retrieved it from the post this morning." Tedham pointed to the wood slatted box on the floor of the entrance hall.

"A package?" Christopher furrowed his brow.

"Yes, from London." The butler coughed behind his hand. "Er, water colors, I believe."

What the devil? Water colors? Of course, the supplies he ordered for lessons with Josceline when first he engaged her services.

Christopher grimaced, raking his hands through his hair. How long ago that seemed, when his main concern had been to better his dance skills and ply a brush with water colors in an attempt to mimic a genteel lifestyle. He prodded the box with his toe. How silly it all seemed now, how frivolous.

"Have the box delivered to the nursery, if you please. I do believe my wife shall make good use of it. Is she there?"

"Of course, I shall have the box taken up immediately." Tedham bowed. "Lady Woodsby is in the garden with Philip and Tom. She took them outside for their lessons."

"Then I suppose I shall have to find her there, thank you, Tedham."

* * *

Christopher's eyes widened appreciatively when he spied Josceline's hair glinting with gold and copper highlights in the spring sun. It was a perfect match to the bronze cloak pooling about her on the bench, apparently too heavy for the mild day.

Mentally he chastised himself. Of course she should have new clothes. Perhaps a dressmaker in town would allow her to order several new frocks on the promise of the success of his first voyage.

If there was a first voyage, he reminded himself grimly.

Emerald eyes sparkled at him as he drew nearer.

"Christopher!" she exclaimed. "You have been out, your cheeks are wind burned. Do they sting? If so, I have just the potion." A warm smile crossed her lips.

She was glad to see him. A tide of wellbeing at the realization flooded through him. How nice to have someone fuss on his behalf.

"I took Vesuvius for a gallop. He's been too much in the stable lately, he was getting fat and lazy."

He smiled back. “Are you alone? Tedham thought Philip and Tom were here with you.”

“They are long gone.” She giggled. “Jefferson spotted them running about the garden and hauled them off to look at the new foal. I fear my slate and primer were no match for that.”

“May I?” He pointed to the bench. At her nod, he dropped down beside her, taking her hand in his and giving it a squeeze. “Josceline, I have the solution to the “Bessie”.

“Why, that is wonderful news.” Delight filled her face. “What do you propose?”

“I shall steal her.”

“What!” The delight on her face transformed to disbelief then, when she understood he was serious, to horror.

“Are you mad?” she gasped. “That’s thievery. You shall be clapped in irons or transported or worse. Tell me you are not in earnest.”

“How can it be stealing? She belongs to me,” he said reasonably. It made perfect sense to him. If no one could help him, then he would do it himself.

“A proper gentleman would never consider such a course of action.” She set her lips firmly. “It is an outrageous suggestion.”

She had hinted he was no proper gentleman. The idea stung, for he did consider himself thus.

“Spoken like the proper lady,” he sneered in retaliation. She thought him improper then by his words he would live up to her expectations of him.

His comment hit its mark. She rocked back, face flushed.

"A proper, law abiding lady," she said icily and she pulled free her hand. "If you choose to go through with it, you shall be a proper scoundrel."

Proper scoundrel. The insult brought to mind a footpad garbed in velvets and satins and the ludicrous vision drummed some sense into his head. It was no less than he deserved after he had mocked her station. Contrition filled him and he hastened to make amends.

"Perhaps that is fitting," he said in a conciliatory tone. "However if becoming a proper scoundrel is what is required then that is what I shall become."

"No," she sniffed. "I shan't hear of such nonsense. You must confront Candel again."

"It is of no use. I tried that already. If you recall, he denied me entrance to his home."

"You must try once more." She looked him square in the face as if to say, you must not defy me.

He almost laughed at her expression. She reminded him of a spitting kitten – all bluster and no substance. However, as appealing as she appeared, he found her reasoning lacking.

"Lord Candel?" he scoffed. "He won't listen. The man is a law unto himself."

"Return to the gaming house and confront him there," she pleaded, obviously changing her tack. "Play another match. You bested him once, you can do it again."

"And if I don't?" He crossed his arms. Lud, to approach Candel again would be a waste of time. Christopher's preference was to take matters in his own hands and face the consequences then.

She gave him a disdainful stare, patently unimpressed with his recalcitrance.

"I still have your handkerchief. I can accuse you of highway robbery."

A cloud passed in front of the sun, a sudden slice of gloom. A chill gust of wind lifted her skirts; she avoided his gaze as she pulled the cloak over her.

Accuse him of highway robbery? She wouldn't dare. Or perhaps she would. He regarded her with new found respect – her wits were keen and she was willing to use whatever tactics she had on hand to win her battle.

"You're my wife, you shan't be allowed to testify against me," he retorted.

"Can't I? I'll say you forced me to marry you." She looked down her nose at him, eyes smoldering.

Christopher felt as if he had been punched in the gut at her haughty demeanor. The implication was clear. She was a duke's daughter and he a lowly commoner. Uncertainty nibbled at him and for an instant he remembered the merciless teasing he had endured as a child. How would she regard him when she discovered his dark secret, that he was bastard born to a nobleman who had scorned his mother?

Defeated, he sucked in a long, ragged breath.

"Please, Christopher, I beg of you, find another way." She fell to her knees in front of him and forced a smile. "It's too dangerous," she whispered so softly he could scarce hear her words over the sough of the breeze.

She worried for him. An appealing notion. He looked at her long and hard, losing himself in her tear-lined, emerald gaze before lifting his head to inspect the clouds scudding overhead.

Josceline asked him to pursue a path he knew was doomed to failure. But if it would restore the affection he had glimpsed in her eyes when he had first found her on the bench, then he would do it. If it would build her confidence in him so that if, when, she discovered the truth of his birth, she would disregard it, then he would do it.

"Very well, Josceline. I shall approach the wretch one last time." He pulled her up to sit beside him and dropped a kiss on her nose. "However," he warned, "if he does not accede, then I shall follow my instincts to steal the "Bessie" and deal with the consequences later."

For a long moment, Josceline stared at Christopher, stomach in knots. His mind was made up; her argument had not changed it. True, he had agreed to approach Candel one more time, but if Candel didn't acquiesce, then Christopher would proceed with the audacious idea of taking the "Bessie."

That venture was sure to come to failure and he would end up in jail, sentenced for transportation to the colonies or worse, sentenced to hang. She couldn't let that happen. She couldn't bear to lose him now.

She loved him.

An idea almost as audacious as Christopher's plan but there it was. She loved him.

Now how to stop him from certain failure.

Chapter Twenty Two

Christopher threw down his pen in disgust. Again he'd splotched ink on the paper. He turned the page in the ledger and began again. However, he had only copied over a couple of numbers before they swam before his eyes to be replaced with the vision of a pink cheeked Josceline in the garden earlier this afternoon. Once more he threw down his pen to stare blankly outside at the falling dusk.

He drummed his fingers. The discussion with Josceline had left him in an unsettled state. In his mind, he could see the instant when she had looked down her nose at him and he remembered the welling insecurity. Yet, mere minutes later she, pleading for him to reconsider his plan, had knelt on the ground at his feet as if she were a serving maid and he a mighty lord.

Tears had threatened to spill from her eyes. Perhaps feelings for him stirred within her after all. However, feelings for him weren't enough. He needed her unreserved love. He knew beyond a shadow of a doubt Oliver Candel wouldn't give in and therefore he, Christopher, had no choice but to take the "Bessie" from beneath the man's very nose. An action that, despite his brave words to the contrary, would have him flirting with the law.

It was sure to draw Josceline's ire and would strain even the strongest bonds.

For a second time he remembered her tear filled eyes. Tears signified emotion.

A hopeful surge propelled him to his feet and he leaned forward to splay his hands on the desk. Tanned and calloused from years at sea, they stood out stark against the white pages. The hands of an honest man, a working man. The hands of a man who would protect and honor his wife for the rest of her days.

He began to pace, prowling the library as if in that room he could find the secret to earning her esteem.

Absent minded, he pulled on his watch fob to glance at the time on the ivory inlaid watch he'd bought in Morocco. Half past six. He'd ordered supper for eight o'clock and had requested Josceline to join him. An invitation she hadn't wanted to accept. At first she had frowned, however when pressed she had agreed, albeit reluctantly.

That gave him an hour and a half to devise a plan, a first step, to secure her love and confidence.

* * *

Their conversation in the garden this afternoon still disturbed Josceline – Christopher could see it in the heightened color of her cheeks, hear it in the swish of her skirts when she walked into the dining room, smell it in the intensified scent of violets and sandalwood.

She wore her green frock, the one that turned her hair into deep russet and her eyes into an even deeper shade of emerald. For a second, he let himself simply enjoy the charming vision she made.

Paying him no heed, she sat down and made a show of smiling prettily at the footman who, blushing at her attention, dropped her linen napkin on the floor. In reaching down to fetch it, the unfortunate fellow bumped his head on the table which elicited murmurs of sympathy and a concerned gaze which lead to another round of blushes on the part of the young man.

Christopher gritted his teeth. When the footman, still blushing furiously and shaking like a leaf at Josceline's attentions, knocked over Josceline's empty wine glass, he ordered him away.

"You need not be so harsh with the poor fellow." Josceline said, honey dripping from her words.

"Me, harsh? You were the one putting the poor lad through his paces."

"And are you jealous?"

Yes. Yes, he was. Damnation, how weak that made him.

"No. No, of course not," he blustered. "Merely intrigued by your ploy. Is there something you wish to discuss?"

"I am going with you." She lifted her chin and gave him a defiant gaze.

"I must beg pardon?" Christopher gaped. "With me? Where?"

"When you pay another call on Oliver Candel. I know you have no stomach for it and will not give it your best effort. Therefore," she turned a saccharine gaze on him, "I am going with you."

Was she serious? The idea was shocking, her paying a visit on an unmarried man, even if Christopher did accompany her. What could she hope to gain? Desperately he wracked his brains for a response but she spoke before he could answer.

"Yes, I am serious."

She read his mind; the idea of her doing so staggered him and he continued to stare at her, mouth agape.

"I can help you, you know. I do travel in the same social circles as Candel. I know his father. Lord Thaddeus Candel has had more than enough of Oliver's escapades and, I'm quite certain, will do anything to avoid further scandal. Bristol is quite the end of England and Oliver really has nowhere else to go. So, unless he wishes to find a new life for himself on the continent or in the colonies, I believe he'll be quite happy to avoid any news of this reaching his father."

Christopher cocked his head. "I don't believe you. Was it not only last night you told me you were a social pariah?"

"True. However, I am banking on the fact Oliver doesn't remember that. Let us just say, he could be a fine member of the Hellfire Club.

"The Hellfire Club. Now there is a pack of rogues if ever there was one," he muttered.

A second footman appeared, carrying a soup tureen.

"Why, that smells delicious." Josceline gave the man her brightest smile; the footman almost dropped the tureen. A few drops of soup spilled onto the carpet.

Christopher scowled. She would have all the dishes in ruin and turn the men servants into blathering idiots if she continued on in the manner she was.

"Very well," he sighed heavily, hoping she would notice the mournful expression on his face. "We shall call on Candel together."

"Splendid." She clapped her hands. "I'll have one of the footmen deliver our calling cards on Monday. You do have a calling card, do you not?" she added when she saw his addled look.

"I do," he growled. They had not stepped one foot from the house and already she had planned the appointment.

"Then it is decided." She gestured to the hapless footman still standing with the soup tureen. "Soup, if you please."

And she graced both of them with a charming smile which seemed to say: See how easy I managed to get my way?

Christopher had the sinking feeling this wouldn't be the last time she twisted them all about her little finger. She had neatly taken the wind out of his sails and he was still no further ahead in winning her esteem.

* * *

Josceline pulled out the pins from her hair and shrugged off her stays, loosened by the ever obliging Mrs. Belton, who had bustled off immediately, shaking her head over "the silliness of fashion". Josceline smiled at the memory. Such a dear, warm hearted woman.

She stripped off her shift and donned the flimsy scrap of silk nightgown. It wasn't her warmest, far from it, but an uninspired flannel sack served as her warmest night gown and she meant to be attractive if Christopher decided to visit her. He hadn't done so since their wedding but sooner or later she knew he would demand his conjugal rights.

She sat down to braid her hair, and with the aid of her comb and mirror, sectioned the heavy tresses precisely into three equal swatches.

A knock sounded on the door, a sharp rat-a-tat-tat as if the owner of the unseen fist could bore a hole through the wood.

Christopher.

She dropped her comb. He knocked not the hallway door, but the door between their rooms. He meant to visit with her.

The world tilted crazily, her heart pounded. It was as if he had heard her thoughts about sharing a bed. Feeling suddenly exposed in the scrap of nightgown, she reached for her wrapper.

"Come in." She hated the quaver in her voice.

In the mirror's reflection, she could see the door swing open on silent hinges. Christopher stood there, expression enigmatic. He too, apparently, was ready for bed, for he wore a night shirt. Her eyes darted to his calves. They were shapely, lightly covered in hair.

Her heart jammed itself in her throat. She had never seen a man's bare legs before. Ludicrous thought, they didn't look much different than her own. Bulkier, perhaps, but still the same general shape. She forced her gaze back to his.

"That was quite a display this evening at dinner." His voice, soft yet ominous, caressed her ears and sent shivers down her back.

"A woman has weapons in her arsenal. I merely thought to use them," she replied coolly, relieved to note her voice had steadied. She didn't want him knowing how gauche his presence made her feel, as if she was a silly girl still in the school room learning her first minuet.

She couldn't catch her breath for his eyes were on her, probing, searching, raking her body from top to bottom.

She sat paralyzed as he moved into the room.

"Weapons." He snorted. "Lud, not even Bonaparte's armies could withstand the wiles of a thousand women."

"Oh," she gasped then started to laugh at the mental picture of an army of scantily clad women halting an army of soldiers in its tracks.

Nerve fuelled hysteria sharpened the peals of laughter into shrill barks. Balderdash, he had totally unnerved her. This must stop. She closed her eyes and collected her thoughts.

She didn't know his intentions but if he did mean to bed her, she couldn't stop him. Nor did she want to. The remembrance of the feelings he had aroused in her that night in the library sent more shivers down her spine. With a start, she realized she wanted to relive the sensations.

"Do you care to share the joke?" He strolled over to stand behind her, dropping both his hands on her shoulders.

"Oh," she gasped again when the heat of his hands burned her shoulders through the thin fabrics. She stiffened.

He appeared not to notice. “I should like for you to buy some frocks, or fripperies or whatever it is women need.”

“What?” The change of topic surprised her. One minute he spoke of Bonaparte’s armies; the next he spoke of clothing for her.

“Josceline.” He pulled her back to lean against him, leaning down to rest his head on her shoulder.

Together they stared into the mirror, his dark head nestled snug against her russet one.

She felt him inhale.

“I love the way you smell,” he whispered. “Violets and sandalwood. I want you tonight, Josceline. I want you to share my bed. I want to show you how a man truly loves a woman.”

She gulped.

Christopher grasped her upper arms and tugged her to standing, then turned her about. His head lowered, blotting out the rest of the room, he brushed his lips once against her nose before slanting his mouth to capture hers.

He kissed her.

It wasn’t like his kisses before. This kiss was gentle, tender, even reverent. As if he worshipped her with his lips.

His teeth nipped her lower lip and then his tongue danced against hers.

“Come.” He pulled away his face.

It was a command yet not a command.

“Christopher,” she breathed.

I love you. I’ll come anywhere with you.

She couldn't tell him that yet. Not yet. Not until they recovered the "Bessie" and she gained his approval. Then he would see she truly shared his dream.

He threw aside her wrapper then picked her up and carried her into his room. Candles flickered on the mantel and on the bedside table. His room was dark, masculine, dominated by a luxurious Persian carpet on the highly polished floor on which stood a four poster bed with canopy. A bed truly fit for the master of his own domain.

A mountain of blankets and coverlets draped the end of the bed, exposing clean, crisp sheets. He placed her gently in the middle of the mattress.

"I want to show you how a man should love his wife." He started with her toes, nibbling them and kissing each one. He worked his way up, kissing every inch of her calves, her thighs. He pushed up her nightgown to expose her stomach. It caught on her buttocks but she shifted her bottom so he could shimmy it over her hips. Finally he undid the ties and tugged it off.

"I want to see all of you," he whispered, "all of you, my beautiful, beautiful wife."

The cool air kissed her skin; goose bumps rippled along her arms but she wasn't sure if it came from the air or the sweetness of his words.

"You're cold. Here." He lay down beside her and pulled up the blankets, turning her and pulling her close so that her back was tucked up against his front.

With one arm, he held her close, nuzzling past her hair to kiss her neck. He cupped one breast, teasing the nipple with gentle fingers while his tongue flicked against the smooth skin in the little hollow beneath her ears.

"You smell delicious," he murmured. "Promise me you'll use that scent always."

Was she supposed to answer?

She couldn't. Remembered feelings ricocheted through her body, from her breasts to the woman's place between her legs and back to her breasts. Something hard jammed against her buttocks. His penis. Rock hard. Ready for her.

She shifted away and rolled on her back to look at him. In the dim light, his dark, mysterious eyes glowed with love for her.

He lowered his head and his mouth found the neglected breast. He nipped it, flicking his tongue against it until it pebbled to match its partner.

"Oh," she breathed. "That's so much better."

He smiled down at her then moved to his knees, nudging apart her legs to kneel between them. He loomed above her, a handsome shadow.

"Let me love you," he whispered, leaning down on one elbow. With his free hand, he guided his engorged tip, nestling it securely between her cleft before settling himself between her thighs.

She could tell him now, she thought. She could tell him now she loved him. Then he started to move and her mind emptied of all thoughts.

* * *

Christopher awoke the next morning to find himself lying on his back, one arm around Josceline and her head snuggled up against his shoulder. A feeling of contentment filled him like a jib sail billowing before a fresh breeze.

He glanced down to find himself being sharply regarded.

"You're awake." He dropped a kiss on her head.

"I am," she nodded. "I've been awake for a while, thinking."

"Thinking?"

Thoughts of last night rose in his head and he felt himself grow hard. Making love to her now, this very instant would be a delightful way to start the day. He dropped another kiss on her head.

"It is Sunday today. We shall go to the parish church for service," Josceline said firmly.

"I see." He scowled. His brief thought of pleasurable morning activities tempted him much more but Josceline had already sat up and was casting around for her nightgown. "I must say attending Sunday services is not my cup of tea. Won't it bring unwanted attention to us?"

"Of course. But we must show we have nothing to hide. We've done nothing wrong."

"Very well." He sighed. Lud, Sunday morning church. He couldn't remember the last time he'd attended church.

He wasn't going without at least one last cuddle. He pulled her down beside him again and nudged her head onto his shoulder.

However, it was what Josceline wanted and he had to agree her suggestion made sense. They had done nothing wrong and for them to keep themselves secluded at Midland House would only make them look suspicious.

He rubbed his chin against the top of her head. The way he felt right now, he thought wryly, he would swim to the West Indies if that was what she wished him to do.

Chapter Twenty Three

A misty rain had started by the time they stepped down from the carriage. It turned the Cotswald stone of the church into dark gold on which the ivy stood out in stark green relief, and gave the air the clean, fresh scent of budding life. Josceline took an appreciative sniff then yanked the hood of her cloak over the battered bonnet she wore. By the time they reached the shelter of the doors, a fine silvery sheen covered both her and Christopher.

"Mr. Sharrington, Mrs. Sharrington," nodded the kindly vicar, standing just inside. "Welcome."

"Thank you," murmured Josceline, throwing back her hood to bob a small curtsy. They entered the sanctuary and amidst a sea of swiveling heads, made their way to an empty pew.

Throughout the service, Josceline felt the prick of enquiring gazes. She could only hope it was the surprise of seeing her here with Christopher, and not for the sad state of her bonnet. Paying scant attention to the uninspiring sermon, she mentally prepared herself for after the service. She was fairly certain curious worshippers would approach them then.

The notes of the final hymn died away and Josceline laid her hand on Christopher's elbow, giving him an encouraging smile. His eyes twinkled in return and together, they followed the congregation outside.

It rained still. Josceline wasn't sure if she should be relieved or disappointed that most people hurried off on foot, umbrellas in hand, or into the refuge of waiting carriages.

"How lovely to see you both here." An elderly, small, bird faced woman in an unflattering brown bombazine frock and charcoal pelisse stopped them, apparently unbothered by the constant drizzle. Her wet hair stuck to her head like grey plaster.

"I must beg pardon, to whom do we speak?" Josceline wrinkled her brow. "Have we met?"

"Yes, well, no, not really. I am Lady Lucy Westfall. My husband is Baronet Westfall. He and I were at Oakland Grange last Friday evening but you left before we were able to be introduced. Sadly he has taken a bit of gout and did not accompany me this morning." She unfolded her umbrella and held it out to Christopher. "Perhaps you could hold this up for us. I declare, this thin rain is the worst and soaks through in a matter of a minute or two."

"How nice to make your acquaintance." Christopher stepped forward and bowed before taking the proffered umbrella. "I fear my wife and I are not acquainted with the local society."

"Lady Oakland fancies herself the matriarch of the region but rest assured, not all of us are in awe of her self-imposed status," sniffed Lady Westfall. "Oh look, here comes Mrs. Grenville. She's the wife of the local magistrate." She waved one hand frenetically. "Yoo hoo, Mrs. Grenville, this way."

A tall, thin woman with scraped back features darted over.

Josceline marveled how perfectly the woman held her umbrella above her - rain dripped off the edges in an exact circle yet not a drop touched her clothing.

"Oh my, this rain is dreadful," chirped Mrs. Grenville. Guileless, she inspected Josceline and Christopher from hazel eyes. "What an appalling display at the Oakland's event and a well-deserved set down for Lady Oakland. Pay no mind, she's quite harmless."

"You were there as well?" asked Josceline, astonished. How fortuitous the trip to church seemed at this very moment. It was clear not everyone had succumbed to the ploys of Lady Oakland and Lady Swinton. Indeed, there appeared to be little sympathy for the woman and her ruined fete.

"Oh yes. It is like a penny novel. You escaped the clutches of your father and an unwanted suitor to marry for love. How romantic," sighed Mrs. Grenville, fluttering her hands over her heart. "Robert Burns could not have done better, I swear."

Romantic? Romantic if it were true but Josceline knew better.

"And how horrid of Lord Candel to tease you so," interrupted Lady Westfall, beak-like nose wrinkling in contempt. "The man is an unmitigated rogue and an embarrassment to the Candel Company. The wretch," here Lady Westfall leaned over to whisper conspiratorially, "Leaves their warehouse by noon every day. It's common knowledge he spends his afternoons and nights gaming at the Clifton Hotel."

Beside her, Josceline could feel Christopher's interest had been piqued by the woman's statement for he pulled himself up ramrod straight.

"The Candel Company warehouse? Where might that be?" His voice was casual yet his eyes were steely.

"On Back Bridge Street. It is one the better locations for a warehouse for the river widens a bit there."

"Oh dear" interjected Mrs. Grenville apologetically. "Do excuse me, I must run. Mr. Grenville comes with the carriage." She darted off, her spare, angular frame slicing through the rain.

"Oh yes, you must excuse me as well. The baronet waits for my return." Lady Westfall held out her hand for her umbrella. "If you please."

"Of course." Christopher inclined his head and passed it over.

Lady Westfall nodded her thanks and turned away. She took a step then turned back. "Are you receiving visitors? There has been much to do about the goings on at Midland House."

"We are," Christopher replied.

"With pleasure," Josceline added.

"Look for my card, then." And the woman hurried off, umbrella in hand, leaving Josceline and Christopher in the downpour.

"Ah, curiosity. Apparently it is not limited to cats," Christopher joked.

Josceline couldn't keep the delighted smile from her lips.

“She wishes to call on us. Others will take her lead. All is not lost, Christopher. We may find our investors yet. What’s more, we know where best to find Oliver. In the warehouse of the Candel Company.” She beamed at him. “See? Attending church was a brilliant suggestion.”

Christopher wasn’t quite willing to agree. His idea of how to spend the morning had been as good, if not better. At the thought, he felt heat pool in his loins. Nonetheless, Josceline’s excitement was contagious and Christopher felt an answering enthusiasm well within his chest. He tamped down his rising desire to comment. “Candel’s not the only thing we should find at the warehouse.”

“Yes?” Josceline’s emerald gaze swept over his face.

“The deed to the “Bessie”. It would be kept there, would it not? But,” he grabbed her hand. “We’re both soaked to the skin. I see the carriage waiting for us.”

Briskly, he moved off, towing Josceline behind him.

Despite the grey sky and unending rain, the day seemed suddenly bright and full of promise.

* * *

If there was one thing Lord Oliver Candel hated, it was being made to wait. Particularly after Fitzsimmons, the haberdasher, had informed him his new overcoat would be ready by Monday morning and in fact, the man was still sewing on the buttons when Oliver swung by in his phaeton to pick it up.

He could wait, Oliver decided sourly, but it was sure to cost Fitzsimmons for now he fully intended to haggle over the price. And if the man refused to drop the fee, then he, Lord Oliver Candel, would make sure everyone in this hellish backwater that was Bristol would know of the poor service of the Fitzsimmons establishment.

And so he waited, one satin clad knee draped over the other, staring with distaste at the street outside with its rowdy sailors, grizzled fishermen and farmer's carts. If not for the edict of his father, he would be ensconced somewhere in Pall Mall, watching handsome carriages and their matching teams trot by, genteel ladies strolling arm in arm and finely clad gentlemen out for a brisk stroll.

Oliver meant to return to London, sooner rather than later. In the meantime, he presided over Bristol's society. A poor second but it was better than nothing.

He continued to stare outside while behind him could be heard the snip of the scissors and the frantic whispers of the tailor and his assistant. The sound filled him with satisfaction. Good. The tailor knew with whom he dealt.

Oliver sighed and uncrossed his legs.

Frankly, if he were honest with himself, he would admit it wasn't really Fitzsimmons who had set him on his ear. It was that lackwit, Christopher Sharrington, who annoyed him no end.

Sharrington's insistence on getting the prize won over the gaming table was becoming annoying. If the man had any sense of his own proper place in the world, he would forget about it. The man's impertinence was beyond the pale; his accusations at the Oakland's fete ridiculous.

Some had paid attention that evening, however, for a few men had snubbed him openly over port and cigars. The memory burned. Really, the local gentry were too tiresome.

He, Lord Oliver Candel, was the local representative of the Candel Company. He, Lord Oliver Candel, was a prominent member of Bristol's Society of Merchant Venturers. He, Lord Oliver Candel, was the sole heir to one of Britain's finer families.

Sharrington, that imbecile, that upstart, that man of little consequence, had become a problem. Surely the man had an Achilles heel.

And Oliver would wager his right arm it had something to do with the urchins the man had brazenly shepherded from this very haberdashery.

Candel's eyes narrowed menacingly. Sharrington would soon find out he was not a man to be crossed.

Chapter Twenty-Four

In the carriage on the way home from church, Josceline and Christopher decided the best day to call on Oliver Candel was Wednesday. Mid-week, when memories of the scene at Oakland Grange would still be fresh but not so fresh as to sting overly much.

Josceline knew she needed to look her best for the visit. Lord Candel was a dandy, one for whom fashion played a central role.

She brushed her brown walking dress and dabbed at several muddy spots on the hem. She rinsed out her yellow shawl and carefully hung it to dry outside on the wash line behind the kitchen. Her newest shift she washed in the privacy of her room, letting it dry before the fire there. Her slippers were more of a challenge however she managed to scrape off the mud then re-pinned the satin roses on them to hide the stains.

Finally, Wednesday arrived.

As she dressed that morning, she summoned her courage. True, she had spoken bravely to Christopher but who knew to what lengths Candel would go to best Christopher? A worrisome thought for the man was untrustworthy and selfish.

* * *

The morning fog hung thick. Between that and the muddy road, the carriage was slowed so much the usual hour's ride into Bristol stretched almost into two.

They journeyed in companionable silence.

Josceline sat primly, twisting her handkerchief over and over until it was nothing more than a crumpled little mass. She regarded Christopher covertly from the corner of her eyes. He obviously chafed at the delay. He checked and re-checked his pocket watch constantly then frowned at her when she started tapping her foot.

As they crested the hill and followed the road leading down into the area of Bristol known as Redcliff and the harbor, an interested Josceline leaned forward to peer out the window. This was to be the epicenter of their as yet unnamed shipping enterprise.

The river bed was a jumble of ships, aground on the mud. Masts tilted crazily, flags fluttered in the breeze, and gulls drifted lazily overhead. A chaotic array of buildings and warehouses lined the stone jetties. A narrow sliver of silver threaded its way through the beached ships. The Avon River had shrunk almost to nothing.

"Where is the water?" she exclaimed. "The ships are all lying in the mud."

"The river rises and falls with the tide."

"It does look silly. The ships look like wallowing sows in a pigpen."

Her droll observation drew forward a guffaw.

"Why yes, I suppose so. However, Bristol is in a convenient location and the local merchants make it work. They build their ships stronger so the hulls can withstand the weight when the tide ebbs. There's talk of damming the river to build a floating harbor to accommodate more ships. That notion is why I decided to make this my home. The townspeople are forward thinking for they know if they do not change the harbor, captains will go elsewhere to dock."

They pulled up outside a large warehouse, a two story structure freshly painted and in good repair that stretched back against the cliffs. A large, red lettered sign hung over the large double warehouse doors: "The Candel Company". Off to one side, a smaller door overhung with a red and white striped awning led into what appeared to be an office.

On the quay in front of the Candel warehouse was a haphazard stack of cargo: wooden boxes and crates of varying sizes, leaking barrels, and bales of what appeared to be leather but on closer inspection looked to be dried leaves. Tobacco, Josceline surmised.

A motley crew of men moved the goods inside the warehouse, overseen by an officious looking man with his sleeves rolled up. Intent on his task, he paid them no mind when Christopher and Josceline approached him to ask for Lord Candel. Head down, lips moving silently as he read the bill of lading, he pointed to the office.

They knocked on the door to have it opened by a rotund, bespectacled man who, by virtue of his bulk, blocked their way quite neatly.

"May I help you?" he wheezed. He regarded them over the top of the spectacles perched on the tip of his nose.

"We are here to see Lord Oliver Candel. Is he in?"

Christopher's booming voice sent the clerk stumbling backwards.

"Why, er, why, yes, I do think so."

"Splendid." With a flourish, Christopher handed the clerk his card. "Tell Lord Candel I am here to discuss a matter of extreme interest to the Candel Company. It's regarding a new trade route being opened up."

Josceline darted a quick glance towards him. New trade route? Could it be true or was it merely a ploy to gain audience with Candel?

While the hapless clerk looked down at the card, Christopher laid his hand on Josceline's where it curved around his elbow and maneuvered her so that they both shoved past the man.

"Stop," the clerk shrilled. "Wait here." He glared at them then shuffled off.

The little office seemed suddenly bare without him. And bare it was – a tall stool nestled beneath a massive plank table; floor to ceiling cabinets lined the wall opposite.

Nothing softened the place, Josceline noted. No pictures, no maps, nothing on the walls; the wooden floor uncovered and scarred. Perhaps because it didn't do to show one's success. Or, perhaps the Candel Company didn't wish to make things too comfortable for their associates.

If it were the latter, they had succeeded admirably. Something hard, a pebble or possibly a nail head, pressed through the thin sole of one slipper. She shifted from foot to foot trying to find a comfortable stance.

The seconds crept by and turned into minutes. She gripped her reticule. What if Lord Candel refused to see them?

"I still think it would have been the proper thing to do to send our cards to the Candel Company before our actual arrival," Josceline grumbled. "We are being made to wait."

"He shall receive us," Christopher replied confidently. "He fancies himself a man of business."

His confident air bolstered her courage.

She loosened her grip on the reticule and sniffed the air. The scents were sweet, foreign to her, yet brought to mind sun-soaked fields and fragrant breezes.

"Rum, tobacco, sugar cane." Christopher smiled and his eyes crinkled in that way she loved.

Her knees turned wobbly. Concentrate, she sternly warned herself.

Now is not the time for wobbly knees and dotty thoughts about the handsome man at your side. Your husband.

She sucked in another deep breath and straightened her shoulders, maintaining her ramrod stance until thankfully, another moment later, the clerk returned.

"His lordship will see you." He pointed to a dark hallway leading to the rear. "Through there."

"I thank you, my good man." Christopher pressed a coin into the man's fleshy palm.

With Christopher holding firm on Josceline's elbow, they made their way through the dim hall to find it ended in a closed door. He banged on it with such force the door rattled in its hinges.

"You may enter," Candel's hated voice floated through the air. "But do promise me next time you shall not take out your frustrations on my door."

Christopher unlatched the door and positioned Josceline before him.

"After you," he muttered to her. "He shall be surprised to see you with me. The element of surprise, I think, shall be to our benefit." He winked at her.

Together they stepped into Candel's office.

Surprise rippled through Josceline at the opulent display before them, so different from the stark room they had just left.

A number of thick, jewel toned wool carpets lay on the floor, some overlapping. Rich tapestries, exotic woven hangings and maps swathed these walls – the obvious fruits of the sea trading business. Candles sputtered in several intricately wrought wall sconces. Candel himself sat behind a richly carved, ornate teakwood desk on top of which stood a massive brass candelabra. Even at this hour of the morning, and with every candle ablaze, the room was dark - only two small windows let in the light and they were too high to be very effective.

A lair. That's what it reminded Josceline of – the lair of a dangerous beast. They must be on their guard here.

"Oh my, I see it is the daughter of the much maligned Duke of Cranston come to pay me a visit."

Candel's voice irritated her. Did the man speak in anything other than sneering tones?

"Lord Candel," Josceline replied coolly, inclining her head. She wouldn't allow his insolent manner to irk her.

She moved forward enough to allow Christopher to stand beside her. The light touch of his hand on her lower back soothed her and she welcomed his quiet strength.

"I warn you, Candel." Christopher's voice cut through the room like the keen blade of a saber. "Do not seek to insult my wife or you shall pay the consequences."

"You don't frighten me," Candel said, pointing to Christopher with a languid finger. He lolled back in his chair. "Why are you here? Your ploy about the new trading route was too transparent for words, Sharrington. Don't tell me you mean to again bring up that tiresome nonsense of the wager."

"No, he is not to bring it up for I shall." Josceline's voice was icy. "A true gentleman honors his wager. You, I fear, are no gentleman. However, if you would kindly hand over the deed won fairly by my husband, you may regain your good name."

Candel sat up and slammed his fist on his desk. "I say desist in your accusations."

Josceline shrugged. "I would imagine your father would be interested to hear of your escapades even here, far from London. Was it not he," she added slyly, "who banished you from London? Or at least that is the tittle tattle on Lord Oliver Candel." She glanced up at Christopher, a little smile playing on her lips. "Such an amusing tale, my love, shall I recant it for you?"

"Enough," Candel roared, face crimson red and eyes bulging. He leapt to his feet. "Enough."

"If you hand me the deed to the "Bessie", you shall be rid of us," Christopher interjected calmly. "And your father shall not be the wiser."

"Your threats do not frighten me. Who shall my father believe? His son and heir, or the daughter of a decrepit duke?" He locked his eyes on Josceline's, ignoring Christopher completely.

"Oh," she gasped. His deliberate snub of Christopher stung her. She could only imagine the pain Christopher felt.

"Lady Woodsby," he taunted, "do you wonder why I do not include your husband? I'll tell you why." Propping his fists on his desk, he leaned forward. "I've engaged a Bow Street runner and done a bit of investigating. Enough to know your husband hides something from you. He is not who he seems to be. And those disgusting urchins? Bought to play some part. Sharrington has no son. I don't know the whole of it, but be assured I shall not rest until I do. And I would be glad to share it with you if you would be willing to share with me." He dropped a rude gaze to her bosom in clear implication.

Josceline blushed. The impertinence. A wave of dislike, nay, hate, rolled through her. Now his attack included her as well.

"Candel. The deed. I demand it of you," snarled Christopher.

Candel inspected his finger nails. "Oh, so tiresome. No."

"Come, Candel, the deed is here. Where else would it be. It is a ship, this is your warehouse. It only stands to reason you would keep it here along with all the papers of the ships of the Candel Company."

"Deeds?" Candel's eyes darted behind Josceline back to Christopher then back behind Josceline again. "You shan't find them here."

Christopher dropped his hand from Josceline's back and stood, chest heaving so hard he found it difficult to catch his breath. At this moment, he was powerless against the wretch. Worse, Josceline had seen him fail. Not unexpected but her sweet courage had led him to believe perhaps, perhaps, Candel would acquiesce and hand over the Bessie's papers.

"Are you quite finished? If you don't mind, I have correspondence to tend to." Candel dropped to his chair and shuffled the pile of papers before him. He picked up a quill and, dipping it in the ink well, began to write. All that could be seen was the top of his bent head.

In the ensuing silence, the quill scratched, the papers rustled, his chair creaked as he shifted.

He ignored them totally, fumed Christopher. Shamelessly. With the air of entitlement that comes only from the high born.

Josceline tugged at his sleeve and when he turned to look at her, she inclined her head in the direction of the door. She wanted them to leave. Like cowards.

A spurt of rage lent strength to Christopher and he lunged forward, grabbing Candel by the collar to pull him up. The quill went flying, spattering ink across the desk top and the sheaf of papers fluttered to the ground.

"This isn't over," warned Christopher, jerking Candel's collar. The man's head bobbed back and forth with the force of Christopher's grip.

The man's hate filled gaze flicked over his face. "You do not frighten me, Sharrington," he jeered. "For what is there to fear from a man who hides behind a woman's skirts?"

At this very instant, Christopher felt keenly the knife blade hidden in his boot. It weighed heavily against his ankle.

Nothing would give him greater pleasure than to whip it out and hold it against Candel's neck.

Nothing would give him greater pleasure than to see the thin red line of blood welling over the blade as he began to apply pressure.

Nothing would give him greater pleasure than to hear the man's dying gasps, to see his bulging eyes as the knife cut further into his throat.

But he would not.

Josceline was here with him. A proper lady should not be witness to such vulgar doings. Reluctantly, he dropped his hands and stepped back. Sweat dripped down his forehead; he swiped it away.

"Come," he said curtly, gesturing to Josceline. "There is nothing for us here."

The glance she gave him was searching, penetrating, as if she knew very well what he had been thinking.

He gave her a wry look then took her hand and tucked it into its familiar place on his elbow.

Arm in arm they strolled from the office, to all appearances content and carefree as if the disappointing interview with Oliver Candel had never happened.

As they strolled down the dim hall, one thing niggled at Christopher.

My love. He had distinctly heard her call him my love. Did she mean it? Or had it merely been part of the charade?

* * *

Christopher handed Josceline into the carriage and swung himself in behind her. Before she had a chance to settle herself fully, he wriggled himself in beside her. She was about to chastise him until he laid his arm around her shoulders and pulled her close.

"We failed," she whispered, leaning her head into his welcoming chest. His warmth penetrated her cheek, she smelled his scent of leather and citrus, heard the breath hissing in his lungs. Safe. Safe here, with him. The carriage jostled then they clip clopped away. Away, thankfully, from that wretched man.

"Did we?" Humor tinged his voice and she lifted her head to look at him. His face was bland, indeed, almost content. The horrid interview didn't appear to have disturbed him in the least.

"Did we not? We do not have the deed. You were right when you said Lord Candel would not give it to us."

"True, but now I know where it is. His eyes gave it away. It's in the roll top desk beside the door. Where, I would wager, the rest of the important documents are kept. Besides, we saw the warehouse and the layout of his office. So did we fail? No, I think not. You, kitten, were correct." He tilted her face and kissed the tip of her nose. "It was best to meet him again."

"How do you propose to get it?" she asked, puzzled at his insouciant manner. "He refuses to give it to you."

"Ah, now that is a very good question. To which I have a very good answer." He tapped her lightly on her chin. "With Philip's help."

"Philip's help," she echoed stupidly. Whatever did he mean? She pulled away to sit upright.

"Yes. I shall bring him back here with me at night, when there is no one in the warehouse. He's small enough to fit through one of the office windows. Once he is inside, I shall get him to open the door for me."

"What if the door is locked? What if there is a night watchman? What if he falls from the window and hurts himself? What if he is frightened of the dark?" Questions tumbled pell-mell off her tongue.

He chuckled. "Do you always worry so?"

"That is not worry," she replied loftily. "I am merely airing my concerns."

"Worries, concerns, both seem the same to me." Hecocked an eye brow. "Philip is a strong lad. He is up to the task."

"No." She shook her head so firmly, a few curls bounced free of her knot. "No, not Philip. Me."

Chapter Twenty-Five

Horror washed over Christopher as the meaning of her words sunk in. Josceline would help him? A duke's daughter, a member of the upper class had offered to climb through a warehouse window on his behalf?

The impropriety was enormous. Their worry over the scandal of a governess with no children to tend to was nothing in comparison to someone discovering her creeping into a warehouse in the middle of the night to search for a missing deed.

Anxiety stabbed him in the gut at the thought; he crossed and uncrossed his legs several times before setting both heels firmly on the floor only for the toes on one foot to pump up and down incessantly.

How daft. How brave. How foolhardy. How loyal. How-.

How like the woman he loved. An idea he still had difficulty accepting but there it was – the woman he loved. He could not permit her to expose herself to the risk.

"No," he growled. "I shall not allow it."

"Then I believe we are at a stalemate. For I shall not allow you to use Philip." With her lips set in a mutinous line, her eyes lobbed daggers at him.

Again her demeanor reminded him of a spitting kitten and he choked back the sudden urge to laugh.

"Are you always so stubborn?" he asked mildly.

The coach jostled over a rut in the road and threw her against him. Before he could catch her and pull her close again, she pushed herself away and glared at him.

"I'm not stubborn." She continued to glare at him. "I'm simply being reasonable. Besides, if not for Philip, who else shall help?"

"Why would you put yourself in that danger?"

The question appeared to leave her at a loss for words for she blinked her eyes and opened and closed her mouth several times. Finally, she shrugged.

"Because as your wife, I have as much to gain as do you. You would have me believe we are almost penniless. If that's the case, then what are we to do? In all truth, should both of us happen to find work, it shall not nearly be enough if we wish to keep Midland House. I am familiar with the cost of keeping an estate home and truly, a governess' wage will not suffice."

"Does Midland House mean that much to you?" His voice registered his amazement. "You have only recently become its chatelaine."

How he enjoyed the idea of her as chatelaine over his home, a home which they would lose in a matter of months. A home which she was prepared to fight for. Yet he could never forgive himself if something were to harm her. She spoke again and he left his thoughts behind to concentrate on her words.

"Of course it means that much to me. If for no other reason than we need a roof over our heads." And because, Josceline thought, Midland House is important to you. As is recovering the deed and getting the "Bessie".

Furthermore, the importance to him made it important for her for she wanted him to be happy. A silly notion for she had no idea if his feelings towards her were sincere or not. He had never claimed to love her and though she loved him, she had not yet found the courage to tell him.

Later, she reminded herself, later she would tell him, when the "Bessie" had been recovered.

"When we have the ship," she continued, her words confident, "we can begin our shipping enterprise and keep Midland House."

She clasped her hands in her lap and sat there, calm as anything. She wouldn't take no for an answer. She would find the deed and together they would get the ship. Then Christopher would be avenged and truly happy.

Confidence flowed from her like a cool river flowing through green fields. They would not fail. Then, perhaps, just perhaps, he would tell her he loved her.

Her bold words won over Christopher. He draped an arm over her shoulders and pulled her close again, letting her scent fill his nostrils and nudge away his reservations.

How could he not accept her offer of help? As long as they were careful and chose their time prudently, she should be in and out of the warehouse with none the wiser. Perhaps a midnight visit to the Candel warehouse wouldn't be so dangerous after all.

In the meantime, there were more mundane matters to consider. Like a visit to the *modiste*. It was time to upgrade her woefully inadequate wardrobe.

* * *

Josceline's proposition to help Christopher retrieve the deed didn't seem so wonderful now. Not now, when she actually stood in the narrow, refuse strewn laneway alongside the Candel warehouse.

Facing the quay and the river beyond, she sagged against her mount, waiting for Christopher to finish tying up Vesuvius and come back for her mare. She felt safe enough for the gloom of a Bristol night hid them well from prying eyes that may happen to pass by on the quay. Although, she sincerely doubted anyone else was foolish enough to be about at this hour.

Two days had passed since their unsuccessful visit with Lord Candel. Two days where they had plotted their foray into the warehouse, from the lads' breeches - hidden beneath her cloak - stretching uncomfortably over Josceline's hips to the moth eaten hat borrowed from the stable boy to cover her hair. Two days where they had decided to forego the carriage, opting, in the name of speed and simplicity, to ride individual mounts. Two days where Josceline had witnessed Christopher swing from optimism to despair then back to optimism as he contemplated the task before them.

"You should not help me," he had once growled at her. "It's too dangerous."

"And neither should a child of six years," she retorted pertly. "And danger is only to be feared if you let it." Where she found the resolve to utter those words, she didn't know.

Actually, she did know.

Simmering anger made her bold for Candel's insult of Christopher now included her as well. That and a nagging concern for Christopher and his unfinished business with the wretched Candel.

Frowning, she bit her lip to keep from screaming out her frustration. Where was Christopher? How long did it take to tie up a horse?

A stealthy footstep whispered behind her; a hand dropped on her shoulder. Her heart somersaulted then settled back in its usual steady rhythm when Christopher spoke.

"Keep your thoughts to the matter of hand," he teased gently. "A face full of frowns and scowls doesn't become you."

She slanted a wry glance at him then ignored him to tilt back her head to inspect the windows. Were they really that high? What had made her think she would be able to climb through them? Stifling a groan, she looked back towards him.

He held a finger to his lips and took the reins from her hand, backing her horse away and further towards the far end of the tiny lane. Man and beast disappeared in the gloom.

A few moments later, he materialized from the shadows and stood before her, teeth glinting in the wan light of a sickle moon as a reassuring smile limned his lips.

"Ready?" he whispered, cocking an eyebrow, the motion barely discernable in the shadows covering his face.

She nodded.

"I've found a barrel to stand on," he whispered and stepped away, melting once again into the shadows.

She heard a grunt and a creaking thud, then a rumble and in a matter of seconds, a ghostly Christopher reappeared, rolling a large wooden barrel before him. Bracing himself against the warehouse wall, he righted it, rocking it back and forth until it lined up beneath the window closest to the rear of the warehouse.

He stepped back, dusting off his hands and now she noticed the coil of rope slung over his shoulder.

"That should do," he muttered more to himself than to her, then moved to stand beside her. "Do you have the tinder box?" he whispered in her ear, brushing his lips lightly along her ear lobe before stepping back.

That feathery touch sent shivers up and down her spine, matching the nerves churning in her stomach. Drat the man, he seemed not to realize the importance of keeping to the matter at hand.

"The tinder box?" he repeated, a half smile lifting one corner of his mouth as if he knew full well he had disconcerted her.

Which he had.

She scowled at him, at his poise, his bravado. The two of them stood in a stinking alley about to break into a warehouse yet he seemed so flippant and showed not the slightest concern over what they planned to do.

"The tinder box?" He frowned this time. "Josceline, you must concentrate."

"Then don't kiss my ear," she retorted. She patted the bulge in her pocket. "The tinder box."

"And the knife?"

"Yes, in my boot, where you told me to put it." She leaned over to run her fingers down the shape of the knife.

"And you remember what you're supposed to do?"

"Light a candle, pry open the desk, find the "Bessie's" papers then you shall pull me out with the aid of the rope."

It sounded easy. Too easy. And she didn't even want to think about trying to climb back out through the window. Even with Christopher's help, it would be difficult.

"Very well." He dropped a kiss on her forehead then hopped on the barrel and stood up. He pulled his handkerchief from his pocket and wrapped it around his hand.

Realization dawned on Josceline – he meant to knock out the window with his fist. It would be awkward for him, though, for the window was above his head. Would he be able to or would they need to waste more precious time trying to find something with which to smash the glass?

With lips compressed, Christopher braced himself against the wall with one hand then with the other began to pound on the window overhead until finally, it shattered with a sharp crack. A tinkling shower of glass fell inside the building.

Josceline's breath jammed in her throat. Surely someone had heard. Christopher cocked his head to listen.

Other than the bark of a distant dog, peaceful silence reigned.

Josceline began to breathe again. Christopher gave her a reassuring nod then broke away the rest of the glass until the frame was smooth.

He knelt down and held out a hand. “Come,” he mouthed.

She nodded and climbed up beside him. It was cramped beside him on top of the barrel and it took some maneuvering before she was able to climb onto his shoulders.

Shaking like a leaf, she sat on his shoulders, legs dangling on either side of his head.

He shifted and she lurched sideways. A frantic grab with both hands netted her his forehead and she clung tight.

“Hold on while I stand.” He started to rise, balancing himself with one hand against the wall, pushing off the barrel with the other. She lurched the other way, this time saved by a firm arm wrapped over her knees.

“Lean forward, over my head,” suggested Christopher. “Use one hand to balance against the wall.”

It made sense to her, and she complied. Up, up, up, she went, quaking so hard she was certain she would tumble them both off the barrel. However, Christopher’s strength sustained them, his legs firm stanchions and he easily reached full height.

Now the window was there, just above her head. Close enough for her to loosen her grasp on Christopher’s head and grab the frame. One at a time, she placed her feet on his solid shoulders before pulling herself up.

The window was now at her midriff. She felt his hands around her ankles, steadying her.

"Ready?" His whisper floated past her ears.

No! She thought wildly, teetering on his shoulders, clenching the window frame so tightly her knuckles gleamed in the moonlight.

"Yes," she squeaked and squeaked again when he propelled her upwards. Twisting, she managed to swing one leg up and through so that now she straddled the window.

"Wait for the rope." And he nonchalantly tossed half the rope, still coiled, up to her. She caught it and unwound it enough so she could string it around her chest. He waited while she tied a firm knot before wrapping the other end about his torso, winding it several times beneath his arm pits.

"Now go." He poked up his thumb in an encouraging gesture.

Grasping the upper frame, she managed to swing the other leg through then squirmed around to face downwards. The frame cut sharply into her stomach; a wave of nausea took away her breath.

Josceline looked down at Christopher's upturned face. He had jumped off the barrel and it seemed a fair distance although in reality, it couldn't have been more than six or seven feet.

"Well done," he drawled, again poking up one thumb.

This wasn't really happening, she thought wildly. She really wasn't dangling out a window, half inside and half outside.

She wiggled backwards, the frame scraping her stomach, then her breasts. With shaking hands, she handled the rope, adjusting it beneath her arms before backing in further. She began to slide and scrabbled wildly for the window sill with her hands, dangling for a moment before she let go.

Into the murk she dropped.

Whoosh. The rope cut into her chest, hindering her breath. Or perhaps panic hindered her breath. She hung there, twisting slowly back and forth before finally, she could feel herself being lowered, bit by bit. With one foot, she kicked herself away from the wall, only to swing into it again, bumping her elbows and knees repeatedly.

Her palms, slippery with sweat, burned with the effort of holding on; the rope beneath her armpits sliced into her flesh. Where was the floor?

In the absolute blackness of the office, it was difficult to tell. Desperate, she searched beneath her with one extended foot. Please, she prayed, let me feel the floor. I cannot hold on much longer.

Her toe nudged something solid.

The ground. At last, she stood on the ground. She tugged the rope to let Christopher know she was safely down and felt an answering tug. Weak with relief, she turned to press her back against the wall. Glass crunched beneath her feet as she shifted her weight. Loosening the knot, she shrugged out of the rope and let it fall to the ground. Her heart pounded so fiercely, she was certain it would leap from her throat.

Calm, she told herself. You must keep calm. She inhaled deeply, once, twice, three times while her eyes adjusted to the gloom as black as the ink spilled on her cloak that night in Christopher's library. Something ran across her feet accompanied by a squeak and she shuddered. A rat scenting blood, no doubt.

Then a grim smile creased her lips. How surprised Lord Candel would be to discover the night time visitors to his office.

Seconds ticked by although if it had been ten seconds or ten minutes, she couldn't have said. Continually sucking in deep, ragged breaths, she eventually regained her equilibrium. Her eyes adjusted enough to spot the twisted shape of the candelabra. She tiptoed to it and reached into her pocket for the tinder box.

Her pocket was empty.

She gritted her teeth. Balderdash. The box must have dropped from her pocket when she was crawling through the window. She tiptoed back to the wall beneath the window and dropped to her knees, gingerly patting the ground and the shards of glass. A sense of triumph seared through her when she encountered the sharp edges of the metal box.

Returning to the candelabra, she lit one candle then carried the candelabra over to the roll top desk before lighting the rest. As the candles blazed into full flame, she noted fresh blood smears coating the base of the candelabra. How odd, she thought, from where? A frisson of apprehension whisked down her spine.

Josceline lifted her hands to inspect them and with a jolt, realized her blood smeared the candelabra for several deep cuts crisscrossed her palms. There must have been shards of glass still wedged into the window or perhaps she had cut them while searching for the tinder box.

Stoically, she wiped them on her breeches. She must focus on the matter at hand.

Experimentally, she tried the desk. Locked, of course. She unsheathed the knife from her boot, sliding it carefully between the lock and the frame the way Christopher had instructed her.

It was a tight fight for the blade and it stuck. She shoved again, as hard as she could, grunting with the effort. No luck. She tugged it out.

Defeated, she sank to the ground and propped her back against the desk. She wasn't strong enough to open the desk. Now what to do?

Twist, Christopher had said. Twist the blade.

She tried again, sliding in the blade until it caught then giving it a sharp twist. The handle slipped in her sweaty, bloody hands and she pulled them away to wipe on her breeches again, leaving red brown smears.

The knife hung suspended in mid air. She needed something to wrap around the handle, something to give her leverage.

Holding her breath, Josceline tried all the drawers beneath the roll top portion of the desk. Luck was with her, for none were locked and she discovered a length of ornately patterned silk cloth in the bottom one. She pulled it out and wound it about the handle, ruing over the fine silk being put to such mundane use. Ruing, too, the blood stains left on the delicate fabric by her hands.

With another firm twist, the lock sprang open with a clack. She pushed open the roll top, cringing with every creak and snap as the wooden slats disappeared one by one into their slot. To her ears, the noise was horrendous and sure to draw attention. Christopher had said there didn't appear to be a night watchman but one never knew.

Carefully, she began to paw through the papers stacked in vertical piles, briefly scanning each one. The first stack contained nothing but bills of lading. So she began on the second stack: A deed to a house in Bristol. A deed to a plantation in the West Indies. A deed to the three-mast schooner, "Morningside." A deed to a sloop, "Molly May". May what, she wondered wryly before pulling out the bottom bundle.

And there she found it in a package of several pages tied together with a leather thong - the deed to the "Bessie". She untied it and scanned the top page. A broad grin slipped across her mouth as she flipped through every paper in the package. Carefully rolling them up, she retied the leather thong and tucked it into her shirt.

She slipped the knife back into her boot and closed the desk. It was scarred where her blade had spun out of her hands. Between the broken window and the damaged desk, Oliver would soon discover his papers had been stolen. However, that wouldn't matter for by then she and Christopher would be long gone.

Carefully, she replaced the candelabra before blowing out the candles then she crept to the dangling end of the rope, giving it a tug as Christopher had requested.

There was no answering tug.

Shouts sounded through the door, followed by pounding footsteps. The latch on the office door rattled ferociously, accompanied by severe pounding and a series of muffled curses.

Fear spiked through her and her stomach turned into a tight little knot. Someone knew there was an intruder in Lord Candel's office.

Frantic, Josceline tried tugging on the rope again. The more she tugged, the more it slithered through her hands until finally, the rope snaked down beside her to land in a muddled pile on the floor. She stared at it with disbelieving eyes.

Christopher had disappeared.

Chapter Twenty-Six

Terror struck, Josceline gazed at the pile of rope now lying useless at her feet. Beads of perspiration pricked her scalp; sweat trickled from her arm pits.

She was trapped and sure to be caught.

The thought had no sooner crossed her mind when the door crashed open behind her. Whirling about, she caught sight of a white faced Christopher.

"Josceline!" Christopher shouted, his voice filled with alarm. "Run!"

Panic rooted her to the spot, held her captive. They had been so quiet, so careful, how had they been discovered?

He hurtled across the room towards her, dodging the desk and gripping her shoulders with fierce hands.

"Do you have it?" He demanded, expression fierce.

"Yes." She patted the bulge beneath her shirt.

"That's my girl." He smiled and dropped a resolute kiss on her lips before pulling back. "You must run," he ordered, his eyes firm on hers. "We've been caught out. I'll divert them but promise me you shall ride as if the very hounds of hell follow you."

"But what of you?"

"This is no time for feeble arguments. Do as I say." And he dropped another kiss on her lips before shoving her, hard, towards the door. "I'll see you at Midland House. Wait for me there, you'll be safe until I return."

Stunned at his obvious panic, she took a few stumbling steps, glanced back to see him pull out a pistol from his waistband. The grim look in his eyes convinced her more than anything of the need for escape and she pelted through Candel's office, down the darkened hallway and into the clerk's room.

There she stopped for a moment to collect herself before peeping out the door at the quay beyond, first one way, then another.

In the distance to her left, several dark shapes carrying torches converged then galloped towards the warehouse. A clatter of hooves sounded, angry shouts rent the air, a hound bayed. One of the shouting voices she recognized as Lord Oliver Candel's and revulsion surged through her.

Enough. She had seen enough.

Doubled over, Josceline slipped out the door and turned right to creep across the front of the warehouse before disappearing into the laneway. It stank as much as before and did nothing to lessen the nervous queasiness threatening to engulf her.

Groping along the wall to help her find her way, she shuffled along. Her foot squished into something soft and she pulled it free. The odor of horse manure wafted to her nostrils and inwardly she groaned at the thought of riding home with the noxious mess stuck to her boot.

Silly goose, she chided herself, you have more serious things to fear than that. She scraped off the mess as best she could before creeping on.

A large shadow loomed; a friendly whicker welcomed her. Her mount, Poppy. Josceline buried her face in the horse's neck for an instant then loosened the reins from where they were draped over an abandoned cart. Tugging gently, she led the animal back to the barrel they had used earlier and clambered up onto it then onto the broad back.

With a squeeze of her knees, she urged Poppy on, stopping only long enough where the lane met the quay to determine she could safely ride away from the fast approaching group of riders.

She adjusted the reins gingerly in her cut hands and set her heels to Poppy's sides. The horse sprang forward as if propelled by her rider's fear. Concentrating on her seat, for riding astride was unfamiliar to her, kept her mind occupied for a few moments and kept fear at bay.

The two clattered over the cobblestones, then thumped over the bridge across the Avon River before heading up the hill towards Clifton. Her hat fell off, her thick braid fell down her back, wisps of hair blew across her cheeks. Her eyes watered with the wind and she tried as best she could to ignore the fact she needed to relieve herself.

It wasn't until she had put a fair distance between her and the harbor that Josceline allowed herself to dwell on what she had seen, or rather, not seen in the laneway.

Vesuvius.

Vesuvius, Christopher's stallion had vanished. How was Christopher going to escape?

* * *

He should have listened to his instincts, Christopher thought angrily. He should never have brought Josceline with him to try and find the papers to the "Bessie." He should just have stolen the damn ship and forgotten about the deed.

At least, he consoled himself, Josceline was safe and far from here.

Here being jail, and a more miserable, putrid, disgusting place he could not imagine himself ever being in. No, he corrected himself. The brigs on board a ship were far worse for there a man had to deal with water and waste sloshing about his feet, and weevils in his food.

Christopher grasped the thick iron bars and shook the cell's heavy planked door as hard as he could. How idiotic of him. Meant to keep in thieves, murderers and footpads, the door would most certainly not budge beneath his hands.

Which, of course, it didn't.

He kicked at the solid bottom half, beneath the small window cut out and set with bars. "Guard!" he bellowed.

It elicited no response, only a shower of catcalls and jeers from his fellow inmates.

"Sure and likely the guard will come ta you," teased a youngish man from the cell beside him.

“Oh, ‘e’ll come, all right. When yer ready to face the magistrate.” This from the man in the crowded cell across from him.

“When might that be?” He raked his hands through his hair. He’d already been here three days and had had more than enough.

“I dinna know. Could be days, could be weeks. I think it depends on the number of inmates,” chimed one of his cellmates, a wizened, elderly man by the name of McEllis.

“Damnation.” Christopher leaned his head against the door.

Josceline must be worried sick about him. How could he get word to her? Never mind Josceline, how was he to get out of here?

For it had been his nemesis, Lord Oliver Candel, who had discovered him.

Curse the luck that the cur had chosen that night to make a midnight foray to the warehouse. Curse the stray cat that spooked Vesuvius and sent the stallion charging out of the lane. Curse the luck that put Candel in that spot just at the precise moment the horse bolted clear of it.

Thankfully, Candel had galloped off to find the night watch which had given Christopher time to warn Josceline.

His hands dropped into clenched fists.

He, Christopher Sharrington, had never felt so impotent and useless in his entire life. His plan to retrieve the deed had come to failure.

What would Josceline think of him now?

* * *

"There is a letter for you, Mrs. Sharrington." Tedham paused at the entrance of the drawing room and at her nod, stepped in. He carried a small pewter tray on which lay an envelope rimmed in pale blue.

"Is it from Christopher? Have you heard aught of him?" Josceline almost tripped over the hem of her skirt in her eagerness to rise from the chair. She stretched out trembling hands to receive the missive.

Tedham shook his head. "I do not believe so. The seal is unfamiliar to me."

"Oh," Josceline ripped it open then sighed with disappointment. She sat down again. "It is merely the *modiste* telling me my gowns are ready." She tossed the paper aside. "How frivolous, how silly, when I have more worries over Christopher."

The butler inclined his head. "The master is more than able to look after himself," he reassured her. He folded his hands over his stomach; his eyes were sympathetic. "More than able."

"But I've had no word from him for three days. He just rode away one morning with nary an explanation." Not true, of course, but she couldn't risk letting the butler know of their escapade at Candel's warehouse. Nerves tickled her stomach at the remembrance; her palms still stung from the cuts and scrapes.

She clung to Christopher's final words that he would meet her at Midland House. Wait for him, he had instructed. However, the more the hours sped by, the more she became convinced that Christopher hadn't escaped.

What had happened to him? What to do? Josceline jumped to her feet and began to roam the room, coming to a stop in front of his empty chair.

She couldn't wait any longer, she decided, staring at the imprint of his body outlined in the leather. Christopher may be in real danger. Even if it meant drawing his ire, she must find him.

But how?

The idea struck her as if a blow from a prize fighter. Why, look in the last place she had seen him. The Candel Company warehouse.

Resolve coursed through Josceline and she straightened her shoulders. She had a plan. Plus she had the perfect cover - her errand to pick up her new dresses from the *modiste's* shop.

"Have the carriage brought round, if you please, Tedham," she ordered briskly. "I am off to Bristol."

Chapter Twenty-Seven

The only indication anything had gone amiss at the Candel Company warehouse was the newly repaired door. Josceline didn't recall it being damaged but Christopher must have smashed it when he broke in to rescue her.

The memory of his white face and grim eyes rose in her mind and she had to blink back the tears.

Christopher, my love, my dearest, where are you?

Blinking back more tears, Josceline straightened her back. That was why she was here. To find out what had happened to him. Firmly she pushed open the door to step inside.

The rotund clerk looked up at her from his seat behind the piles of paper on his table.

"You again." He frowned.

"Good afternoon." She nodded pleasantly, deliberately ignoring the man's rude tone.

"Lord Candel is not here," sputtered the clerk. "And I'm afraid I'm not able to help you." He gestured to the papers on his table. "As you can see, I have paperwork to attend to."

Ignoring her, he pointedly dipped his quill into his inkwell and put nib to paper to write.

Nonplussed, Josceline stood and watched him for a minute or so. The office remained quiet, the only sounds were the quill scratching on paper, the occasional clink of the nib in the glass inkwell, and the man's labored breathing. Quite honestly, indecision beset her. She hadn't expected him to welcome her with open arms; yet neither had she expected him to ignore her.

Her blood began to boil at the rude display. Well, if he expected her to leave, he was sadly mistaken. She wasn't going anywhere until she had the answer she sought.

Meanwhile, as long as he ignored her, she would try and see if any evidence remained of their visit here. She peered over his shoulder to look down the hallway but it was difficult to make out anything for the wall sconces were unlit. The door at the end leading to Candel's office was closed.

She glanced back at the clerk's bent head and his bald spot. It gleamed with perspiration – the man was obviously in a funk about something. Her presence, perhaps. Or perhaps it was something else?

"Ahem." Finally she cleared her throat. "Are you able to tell me when the next shipment of tobacco arrives?" An inane question but it was the only thing she could think of to gain the clerk's attention.

"Can't say it is any of your business." With the air of one who has long suffered fools, the clerk put down his quill. "Look, miss, I'm a busy man. The warehouse was broken into. Lord Oliver has ordered me to work night and day until I find what, if anything, is missing. A hellish job, if I may say so," he added, his voice full of self pity. “Years and years of accounts, ship’s logs, and oh, all kinds of paperwork to be reviewed and listed.”

“Oh, how horrid.” She plied him with sympathy. “And how horrid for you.” She wrinkled her brow in what she hoped was a convincingly sympathetic manner.

“Oh yes.” The clerk shook his head; his spectacles slid down his nose and he pushed them back up with one pudgy hand. “I’m afraid all the bills of lading are mixed up. I’m trying to right this mess before the master arrives.”

“Lord Candel will be here shortly?” How fortuitous if it were so. Then she could ask him straight out about Christopher. Hopeful, Josceline fixed her gaze on the clerk.

“Depends on which Lord Candel you mean. Oliver, no. Thaddeus, yes.” He placed his hands on his desk and leaned forward, chest puffed out with self-importance. “The lord hardly ever leaves London but he checked in last night at the Greyhound Inn, he did. Lord Oliver and the night watch caught the rogue who did it and the old man wants to talk to him first hand.”

“You cannot mean -.” She left her voice hanging in an effort to encourage his confidence.

“Yes.” The clerk leaned even closer. “The man is in Newgate gaol and refuses to talk. He claims he’s done nothing wrong.”

Josceline rocked back as if struck. Christopher was in jail. She swallowed hard against the sudden lump in her throat. That explained his disappearance. It also explained why he hadn’t contacted her.

Summoning all her resolve, she flashed the rotund clerk a brilliant smile which had the desired effect. He turned beet red.

"Thank you, you have helped me immensely," she simpered, clasping her hands to her bosom. Surreptitiously she pulled down the neckline of her frock just a fraction. "And if you please, my family would be most unhappy with me if they were to learn I was here. Perhaps my visit could be our little secret?"

"It was nothing," stammered the beguiled clerk, eyes glued to her hands and what they concealed. "Nothing at all, my lady."

"And?" She smiled at him again, batting her eyelashes.

"You were never here, my lady. I didn't see a thing."

It wasn't until she was safely ensconced in the carriage that Josceline succumbed to the luxury of tears. Covering her face with her hands, her shoulders shook with the force of her sobs.

Christopher sat in jail, assuredly at the behest of Lord Oliver Candel. Who knew what Christopher faced now? Would he be exonerated when he came to trial? Or would he be sentenced under what were doubtless trumped up charges?

Tears finally spent, she sat up and dabbed at her eyes with her handkerchief.

Waves of hate for Candel roiled within her breast. It was entirely the man's fault that Christopher was in that situation. If he had just paid his gambling debt, none of this would have happened. The man would be a formidable foe but she vowed he would be made to pay for what he had done.

* * *

Josceline stood in front of Newgate jail, eyeing the intimidating building nervously. Garnished with rows of windows set into solidly built stone, it stretched up high above her. The windows were too tiny, obviously, for any prisoner to squeeze through.

The stench of unwashed bodies and human waste rolled into the street and briefly she lifted a gloved hand to her nose in a futile effort to staunch it.

Swallowing her trepidation, she stalked through the main door and buttonholed the first guard she came across. "I demand you free my husband. It's all been a terrible mistake."

"Mistake? They all say that, dearie." The rumpled guard leered at her, exposing a row of rotted teeth and bathing her with his fetid breath. "But," he leaned closer, holding out a hand and rubbing his thumb over his fingers, "Freddie may be able to help you."

She drew herself back and put on her best aristocratic bearing. She didn't have a penny in her reticule therefore the only way she would get entrance to Christopher was by sheer bluster.

"I am afraid I do not participate in bribery," she snapped, lifting her chin to glare at him down her nose. For good measure, she crossed her arms. "I seek Mr. Christopher Sharrington. Please bring me to him."

"Talk to magistrate Grenville," the guard growled, having lost interest once he realized no money could be had. He pointed towards one of several narrow corridors. "Ye'll find him through there."

At the end of the corridor, Josceline discovered a large, bright chamber filled with a multitude of people. Apparently, she wasn't the only one to have a loved one incarcerated. She joined the line waiting to speak to the bewigged magistrate sitting on a raised dais at the far end. To one side of him sat a clerk; to the other hung a limp Union Jack flag.

The line inched forward slowly and her back ached by the time it her turn arose.

"I am sorry". The magistrate shook his head after she had introduced herself and stated her case. "There is nothing I can do for you. As sympathetic as I am to your husband's plight." He half stood to peer at her over the edge of his desk. "I was there, you know, at the Oakland's. Such a set to. And so inequitable to both you and your husband. Candel should be ashamed of himself." He tsk'd sympathetically then nodded at her once. "However, I will allow you to visit him."

Magistrate Grenville motioned to a nearby guard. "Bring Mr. Sharrington. They can talk there". He pointed to a simple bench at the rear of the room.

"Thank you, magistrate." She curtsied and moved aside to wait.

Her heart squeezed when she saw Christopher walk in. His skin was pallid, his shoulders hunched and he limped slightly. Squinting against the sudden brightness, he searched the room until he spied her.

His beautiful mahogany brown eyes widened; a broad smile creased his stubbled face. His shirt was grimy, his breeches soiled, his boots scuffed, but sheer happiness lined his features at the sight of her. Ignoring the guard, he shuffled over as fast as the iron manacles about his ankles would let him.

"Josceline!" He gathered her close and rested his chin against her forehead. "They told me you were here but I didn't believe them. How did you find me?"

She luxuriated in his closeness for an instant and inhaled the faintest trace of citrus and leather that mingled with the acrid scent of despair. Yanking herself away, she reached up and gently traced his jaw with one finger.

"I paid another visit to the Candel warehouse."

"After you picked that up, I would wager. No one could deny you in that frock." His eyes swept her up and down appreciatively, taking in the yellow and white striped muslin with its matching slip of yellow taffeta and fringed yellow shawl. "I vow, that frock is just as lovely on you as I thought it would be."

How like him to pretend as if all was well when in fact, everything was crashing about their ears. But she loved him all the more for it, loved that he remembered picking out the fabric with her, loved his air of normality.

She smiled in response. "I will tell you it pleased Mademoiselle Francois that I insisted on wearing it right away. Apparently she thought it would do well for her business for a duke's daughter to be seen wearing something new straight from the shop. But enough. We have other, more important things to discuss." She tugged on his hands. "Come."

"Kitten, I would love to but I don't think I'm going anywhere." He glanced down at the shackles about his ankles; his face flushed.

"There, silly." She pointed to the bench beside the far wall. "It's about as private a spot as we can find in here."

They pushed their way through the crowded room to the alcove holding the bench. Josceline sat at one end and faced him. She wanted to throw herself in his arms again but she refused to touch him. If she touched him, she would be lost in a sea of despair and she couldn't bear that right now.

"Sit," she ordered, gesturing to the other end.

Silent, he complied, dropping onto the bench and leaning against the wall behind him. He pulled his feet beneath him, the scrape of his manacles almost lost in the hubbub of the room.

She waited until he had settled himself and turned to look at her before she spoke.

"Christopher," she pleaded. "You must tell me the truth. You must tell me all of it."

"There's nothing to tell." He thrust out his jaw and refused to meet her eyes.

"This is no time to be stubborn, Christopher." She faced him squarely. "What of Candel's accusations? That you are not who you claim to be."

"You would believe him over me?" Her last question wounded him - she could see it in the way he flinched.

"I don't know what or whom to believe anymore. But I shall believe the truth. Your quest for revenge has landed you in jail. So please, I beg of you, what is behind this matter you have with Oliver Candel?"

"No. There's nothing to tell," he repeated, meeting her eyes at last. He clamped his lips until all that was left was a thin line where his mouth should be.

He looked away but Josceline knew his eyes were vacant - he was merely avoiding her gaze. She felt her face grow hot with frustration and she wanted to smack him. Instead, she sat forward and placed her fists on her hips.

"I can't understand your obsession with Lord Candel. The man is a cheat and a liar. Do you think to make yourself better by besting him? In my estimation, that proves nothing for besting a man of little character is besting nothing at all."

He opened his mouth to answer but she held up her hand.

"Does having a title make one a better man? The circumstance of Candel's birth doesn't make his behavior acceptable. Noble blood may run in his veins, I warrant you that, but he's not worthy of it."

Christopher sat forward and leaned his elbows on his knees, burying his face in his hands before turning again to look at her. "What if we forget the whole thing? The "Bessie", Midland House, our shipping enterprise, everything?"

Josceline's mouth dropped open. Christopher's question made no sense.

Had he lost his reason during his sojourn here?

Chapter Twenty-Eight

"To do what?" screeched Josceline.

Christopher shrugged and the manacles on his ankles clanked as he shifted position. "That evening of the Oakland's fete, Lord Oakland called me into his library. He offered to purchase Midland House from us. We could leave, Josceline."

His steady words carried no hint of madness. Reassured, she lowered her voice.

"Are you daft? After all this? After we get you out of jail we are simply going to walk away? No. We will not be bested by Oliver Candel."

Christopher's shoulders slumped. It appeared a thousand thoughts churned through his mind for he rubbed his jaw and raked his hands through his hair repeatedly. At length, he dropped his hands to rest on the bench beside him and twisted his head to place a firm gaze on her.

She held her breath. Was he finally going to tell her the truth? What could be so horrible he had taken inordinate risks to rectify it?

Again he looked away. "I am also the son of Lord Thaddeus Candel." His voice was steady, resolute as if now that he had decided to divulge his secret, he would do it properly. "I am Oliver's half brother. The eldest. I am the rightful heir to the Candel Company. Or would be, if not for a cruel trick of birth. He has everything. I have nothing. I am a bastard, Josceline. You are married to a bastard."

Christopher closed his eyes. He had done it. He had told Josceline the secret of his birth. A secret only he and his mother knew. A secret he had never entrusted to anyone.

A secret that could destroy him and he had let it loose.

The thought of Josceline's hatred now that she knew the truth about him curdled his blood. He couldn't bear to lose her for it would be the loss of the very thing he held most dear - more than Midland House, more than the "Bessie", more than becoming a sea captain of means.

Josceline.

Josceline was the prize. And perhaps by divulging the secret of his birth, he had lost her forever.

Taking a shuddering breath, he forced himself to look at her, to face her squarely and see the disgust he was sure to see in her eyes.

Only it wasn't there. He scoured her features, searching for a clue, any clue, to her feelings. Her face was still then comprehension flared across it, lighting up her gaze.

"Now I understand the animosity you hold for him," she declared triumphantly. "I knew there was more to it than a wager gone awry." She cocked her head as she continued to regard him, the comprehension in her gaze slowly replaced by something else.

Love. Could that be the warmth of love he saw in her eyes?

Hope bubbled through his chest. The noise of the room penetrated through the haze in his mind and the aroma of warm pastries drifted through the air as a maid in a starched white apron walked by carrying a covered basket. His heart began to beat again. For the first time in days, he felt buoyant.

A corner of his mouth lifted, soon joined by the other until a broad smile stretched from ear to ear as he realized no dismay filled Josceline's eyes, no revulsion crossed her face.

Instead, she inched forward across the bench and laid both her hands on his knee. Her face was earnest as she spoke again.

"You have me," she said fiercely. "All is not lost. We shall free you from here and we shall reclaim your ship."

"Why would you help me?" He lifted one of her hands to his lips. "I am an accused man. You could walk away this very instant and no one would cast blame on you for it." Gently, whisper soft, he replaced her hand on his knee. Still she watched him solemnly and he loved her all the more for it, for the sincerity shining in her eyes.

Here was her moment, thought Josceline. He had divulged his greatest secret, could she divulge hers? Would he scorn her for the soiled blood running through her veins? Or would he accept her love unconditionally?

She inhaled deeply, trying to still the nerves jumbling in her stomach.

"Because I love you", she whispered, smoothing back the hair that had fallen over his forehead. "And with love comes loyalty. For without loyalty from our loved ones, who can we rely on?"

"You love me?" His mouth dropped open; happiness cascaded across his features.

"And you've been wrongfully charged. You did nothing wrong, as you said, you only tried to recover what was yours. Christopher, I read the deed. The "Bessie" belongs to Thaddeus, not Oliver. Oliver had no right to gamble with it in the first place."

"No, no." He waggled a finger at her. "Let us talk of what you said just before. That you love me."

Josceline hastened to retract her words at his inscrutable expression. Perhaps she had made a grave mistake in admitting her love.

"Forgive me for the fanciful notion," she said, her voice light. "I know my father is a despicable coward."

"Do you think I care about your father?"

"But he is a drunk and a gambler and a treasonous thief," she cried.

"Who also cares for you in his own manner. So he gambles and drinks – it's no reflection on you. I see merely a sad man." He quirked an eyebrow. "So is it true?"

"It is true. I do love you," she replied staunchly.

"You can't love me," Christopher protested, unable as yet to believe her. "You never wanted to marry the merchant Thomas Burrows because he's a merchant. As I plan to be."

"Why ever would you think that? Mr. Burrows is old and mean and spiteful, that's why I did not wish to marry him. There's no shame in earning one's living." Sincerity shone from her eyes.

Burgeoning love for her loosened his lips at last.

"I love you, Josceline." The words freed him as much as if the manacles had been removed from his ankles. He felt as if a load had been pushed from his shoulders. All would work out now.

"And I you, Christopher."

He pulled her close and tilted up her face.

"This isn't the most romantic place," he said ruefully.

"What comprises the perfect spot to profess one's love? I declare, I don't really know for it seems to me the importance of the words far outweighs the importance of the place."

He kissed her thoroughly, enjoying the flavor of impending freedom.

"So what do we do next?" she asked when he finally, reluctantly, pulled away his lips from hers.

"I want you to go to London, Josceline. I want you to approach Thaddeus and inform him I am here under false charges."

"No." She shook her head.

Christopher's heart sank. She refused to do that for him. So much for her talk of loyalty and love. He looked away, disappointment squeezing his chest.

She tugged on his arm and it was all he could do to force himself to look at her serious face.

"No, I shan't go to London. For Thaddeus is here. In Bristol, the Greyhound Inn. I believe he suspects something is not quite right. Don't forget, Oliver is a wastrel and his father – your father," she corrected herself, “knows that. I shall do as you say. I shall pay a visit on Lord Thaddeus Candel and plead your case.”

“ ‘ere now, that’s more than enough time.” The guard returned and clamped a fist around Christopher’s shoulder.

They clasped hands, holding on until the guard pulled Christopher away. The last glimpse she had was of him craning to look over his shoulder as the guard led him away.

For a moment, she savored the idea of his love and a happy grin lifted her mouth. Tears of joy threatened to spill but she blinked them back. There was still a hurdle to be crossed before Christopher could be free.

She clasped her reticule as if it could save her from drowning in a sea of hesitation and stood up with shaking knees.

Reality hit as she walked out of the dismal jail and into the fresh afternoon air. Her words had been bold, boastful but the awful truth was that Lord Thaddeus Candel was the man who had accused her father of theft, the man who had pushed her father over the precipice into debauchery and drunkenness. For certain, he would have nothing to do with her.

But for Christopher’s sake, for the sake of the man she loved wholeheartedly, she had to try.

* * *

The Greyhound Inn was much as Josceline remembered. Only today, a carriage emblazoned with the Candel coat of arms was put up in the courtyard.

An encouraging sign for it meant Thaddeus was within.

"Wait for me," she ordered the coachman and stepped inside the inn. While her eyes adjusted to the dim interior, she pulled off her lace gloves - another item purchased from Mademoiselle Francois - and folded them inside her reticule. Tucked under her arm was the bound package containing the deed to the "Bessie."

"Lord Thaddeus Candel, if you please," she said to the tired looking innkeeper. Without looking up from the coins he was counting, the innkeeper gestured with his head to the common room. "Through there. Back corner, behind the screen."

"Thank you." Josceline hesitated. Entering a public room unaccompanied dripped of impropriety. She shrugged, immediately discounting the thought. How silly to worry about being proper or not when Christopher was the only thing that mattered.

Ignoring the leers and lewd suggestions of the other, mostly male, occupants of the room and holding her skirts to one side, Josceline threaded her way across the room to the woven screen. Peeking around it, she spied the finely dressed form of Lord Thaddeus Candel. She pulled back to ready herself.

If Thaddeus Candel denied her, if he spread word in London of her escapade here, her already tattered reputation would be reduced to gossamer fragments. She wouldn't be welcome anywhere in London.

And so? She asked herself. What worth was her reputation if she couldn't come to the aid of the man she loved? Christopher desperately needed her help and she would give it, regardless of the consequences.

Josceline peeped around the screen again. Thaddeus' back was to her and as showed by his motions, he ate. Thankfully, he sat alone so he would have no choice but to favor her with his attention.

She peeked at him again, unsure as to how to approach him. How much rancor did the man hold for the actions of her father? Would he listen to her? Would he acknowledge Christopher?

Standing here worrying about it wouldn't help.

Gathering her courage like stalks of wheat into a sheaf, she marched around the screen and into his line of vision.

The elder Lord Candel at first didn't see her for he concentrated on the newspaper spread out on the table beside his plate of meat, bread and potatoes.

She cleared her throat.

Still he didn't lift his head.

"I must beg pardon, Lord Candel, but may I have a word with you?" Her voice squeaked and inwardly she chided herself for it. "May I have a word with you?" she asked again more resolutely.

He continued reading the paper. "May a man finish his meal in peace?" he growled.

"I assure you, my lord, this shan't take but a moment."

He heaved a sigh and pushed away his plate. Carefully, he folded the paper before finally raising his gaze. Puzzlement creased his brow and he pursed his lips. "Do I know you?"

"Yes, Lord Candel." She curtsied. "I am Lady Josceline Woodsby. You knew my father once. Lord Peter Cranston. The Duke of Cranston," she added.

He flushed with remembrance, a red tide that turned his scalp beneath the thinning, graying hair to pink.

"How is your father?" His eyes were wary.

Christopher's eyes, Josceline realized with a start and she sucked in several huge breaths of air before she could answer.

"As well as can be expected, I suppose."

Thaddeus Candel leaned back and pulled the napkin off his lap to pat his mouth. "Let us forget about the niceties. This is hardly the place for a young aristocratic woman. Why are you here, Lady Woodsby?"

He used her full title and it rattled her a bit. She sucked in another huge breath.

"To plead for my husband."

"Why should I care about the welfare of the husband of the daughter of the man who betrayed my trust?" he asked, eyes narrowing.

"Because he is your bastard son," she whispered.

He blanched. "Anyone can claim to be a bastard son and none would be the wiser. What proof have you of that?"

"Would you deny your own flesh and blood through a mishap of birth which is not his fault?" she countered firmly.

"What proof do you have?" he repeated. With studied movements, he folded his napkin and placed it on the table between them.

It formed an obvious barrier.Josceline winced at the implied insult but forged ahead. This man and his airs would not deter her. "Your eldest son faces punishment for a crime he did not commit," she exclaimed. "Have you so little feeling you would see him come to harm?"

"Whether or not the man is innocent is of no consequence to me. I say he is not my son. You say he is yet you have no proof."

She stared at him, frantically trying to find the words to sway the man seated before her but it was no use. Her mind remained blank.

"You're right, I can't prove he is your son." Defeated, her shoulders slumped. Had it all been a lie? Was Christopher really Candel's son or had he played her for a fool, gambling that she, as the daughter of a duke, had some clout and could fight for him?

A wispy curl somehow worked itself free to fall across her eyes and she lifted her left hand to brush it away impatiently.

"Where did you get that?" Thaddeus barked suddenly, his eyes glued to her left hand.

"I must beg pardon?" Was the man mad? She had nothing of value on her.

"Your ring." He pointed a trembling finger at her wedding ring. "I have only ever seen one like it."

"From Christopher. From your son."

He sat down suddenly and scrutinized her more closely. "Where did he get it from," he demanded.

"His mother".

"Could it be," he muttered, staring intently at the ring. "May I?" And he held out a pale, slender hand framed in a froth of lace.

She pulled it off her finger and handed it to him. Her finger felt bare and she missed the weight of it, missed the courage it gave her.

He turned it over and over in his fingers then sagged against the back of his chair. "It's her ring," he whispered, stunned. "It is the ring I gave Madeline."

"Madeline?"

"Christopher's mother."

"How could you abandon them?" The words burst from her mouth and she felt herself grow hot. How rude he must find her. "I am sorry, something that happened so long ago is not of my concern."

He accepted her apology with a nod and began to speak, voice barely above a whisper.

"It was not my wish. I couldn't marry her for it was understood I would marry another for the sake of the Candel name." He stopped and drew in a shuddering breath. "I couldn't offer her marriage and so Madeline refused to be my mistress. I had no idea at the time she carried my child. Years later, when she became ill, she contacted me. She knew she was going to die and she wanted me to provide for Christopher. You can imagine the shock for by then I had a wife and another son. I did the only thing I could – I found him a position with the Navy. And, to my discredit, I forgot about him."

"Now you can put things right. Drop the charges against him so he can be freed from jail," she pleaded.

Without knowing it, she had laced her hands in supplication. She pulled them apart again and balled them into fists. She must convince the man by merit of her argument, not by melodramatic gestures. Thaddeus must take her seriously or Christopher would be lost.

"Christopher is in jail?"

"Oliver claimed he stole the deed to the Bessie and had him jailed. But the Bessie belongs to Christopher," she pleaded. "He won it fairly in a game of chance with Oliver. Oliver refused to honour his debt."

"Oliver." He shook his head. "I don't know whose blood runs in his veins. Rather I do." A spasm of agony stiffened his features. Just as quickly as it came, it disappeared. "Not only will I help you for Christopher's sake, but I will help you for the sake of your father."

"My father? How is my father involved?" Stupefied, she grasped the edge of the table to steady herself; the bound sheaf of papers beneath her arm fell to the ground.

"The claims I made against him were untrue. I misplaced the documents. They were of extreme importance and I didn't have the courage to admit I'd lost them. I fabricated the story against your father to save my own skin. Shortly afterwards your mother died and that, coupled with the blow of my unjust accusations, did him in. I am so sorry."

"Make it right now. Go to him when you return to London. He is a sad man in need of friendship." She picked up the papers at her feet and handed them to Thaddeus. "But please, not until you visit the magistrate and drop the charges against Christopher. Please," she begged, "make things right for him."

He shifted his gaze away from her, eyes empty as if he looked into the past, a past only he could see.

"Never mind what has gone before," she urged. "It cannot be changed. But you can change what is happening right now. You're a lord of the realm. Your word carries weight. Magistrate Grenville is a just man and he will listen."

"I cannot promise success. But I shall try." His eyes watered and he dabbed at them with his handkerchief.

"That is all I can ask, Lord Candel. That you try."

Chapter Twenty-Nine

Christopher lifted his head from where it rested on his knees. Judging by the pale light crowding through the slit of a window, another uncomfortable night had passed and another uncomfortable day was about to begin.

His right leg cramped and he straightened it, giving an inadvertent kick to McEllis sprawled out dead to the world mere inches away. If only he could sleep so soundly in such miserable conditions, Christopher thought grimly.

All he had been able to manage in the time he had been locked up was to nap occasionally sitting up, with his back tucked up against the stone wall. Albeit cold and damp, the wall was the only thing he trusted in here.

"I must beg pardon," he said as McEllis rolled over and tossed a few choice epithets his way.

In the wan light of dawn, Christopher surveyed the cell, crammed full with assorted, snoring shapes and figures, now serving as home. Stinking riff raff the lot of them although he undoubtedly stank with the best of them.

Not for the first time, a peaceful image of Midland House saturated his mind and he embraced it. Embraced too the memories of Josceline: In the garden, sunlight glinting off her glorious russet curls. In the library, her face animated as she taught him how to dance. In his arms, the flush of love staining her cheeks.

He focused on the latter image the longest. For a few moments at least, he would be far from Bristol Newgate.

Too soon, however, the chill of the floor gnawed through his breeches to interrupt his dreams. He shifted from one buttock to the other.

The cell was so crowded, not even an inch of unoccupied floor space remained and this time, he knocked the man beside him in the head. Christopher uttered a hasty apology which only earned him a murderous glare. Christopher responded with a glare of his own, blatantly flexing and un-flexing his fists. The ploy worked for the other man shook his head and went back to sleep.

Sleep. The only thing he could do to forget about the surroundings.

Closing his eyes, Christopher leaned his head back against the wall. This time the mocking face of Oliver Candel danced across his eye lids. Rage, impotent yet pure, surged through Christopher's torso, pushing against his lungs with such force he could scarce breathe. His fingers curved with the need for revenge.

Revenge. That would be the first order of things when he was released. When, he told himself. Not if.

He would surely go mad if he continued to think about the injustice forged upon him by Oliver Candel. Christopher tried to think again of Josceline but questions swarmed through his mind.

Damn it all to Hades, how much longer would he be here? How had Josceline fared? Had she been able to persuade his father to drop the charges?

His father. He snorted. The man had been no father to him.

If nothing else, the thought of his father stopped him from thinking about his half-brother.

Christopher must have dozed off for a rough hand shook his shoulder.

"It's yer lucky day." The burly form of the guard swam into view. "Ye can leave."

A chorus of jeers and shouts met the guard's announcement. Christopher felt a flare of sympathy. The hapless residents had naught else to do but make noise.

"Lucky sod," muttered McEllis, swiping a grimy hand across his jaw.

"Ye must have friends in 'igh places," whined another. "It ain't fair."

"Don't forget us, captain," mocked an unseen voice from the far corner.

"Shut yer yaps, the lot of ye." The guard laid his hand on the club at his waist then gestured to Christopher to stand. "Don't be wasting any more time."

Christopher lurched to his feet and addressed his former cellmates: "The second I leave this room, gentlemen, you can rest assured, I shall think of you every day." And he gave them a mocking bow.

Ignoring the curses showering him, he limped behind the guard. He reached out and tapped the man's shoulders.

"I presume you will remove my shackles?"

"Aye. But not until we reach the magistrate's chamber."

"Then let us make haste, shall we?" Christopher increased his pace, almost shoving the guard aside in his hurry to leave the stench and noise of Newgate behind him.

The magistrate's room was quiet save for the magistrate himself who read, lips moving silently, from a large, leather bound volume. The man glanced up to look at Christopher. A slight smile flowed across his lips then he went back to his book.

As the guard unlocked his shackles, Christopher surveyed the room. The hour was early and save for a distinguished gentleman in a beaver hat sitting on the same bench he and Josceline had sat on yesterday, the chamber was empty.

His heart sank. There was no sign of Josceline. Then how had he been released?

"She's waiting for you in the carriage." The distinguished gentleman got to his feet and strolled over to Christopher.

"I must beg pardon, are we acquainted?" he asked warily. The gentleman was unknown to him although he did wear a faint cloak of familiarity.

"Sadly, no."

"Then who in blazes are you?"

The man nodded. "I would be angry too if I were in your boots." He stretched out a hand. "I am Lord Thaddeus Candel. Your father."

Incredulous, Christopher stared at the proffered hand. He lifted his gaze slowly to look into brown eyes.

His own eyes. He looked down again at the hand still extended towards him. He swallowed hard against the lump expanding in his throat.

How did one greet one's father for the first time? A father he had never met until this very moment, a father who had not recognized him, indeed had banished him to the Royal Navy?

Anger waged a battle with expectation within him. Now what? Would he become part of his father's life? Or would he be shoved away again, an embarrassment to the Candel name by reason of his birth?

He started to quake with the force of it which brought forth a wave of shame at his weakness. He, who had faced enemy cannon and musket fire, had bested the sea during her stormy moods, had fought hand to hand battles on deck with fierce enemies, was at this very moment unsure of himself.

"I'm not going to let it drop until you shake it so unless you wish to sorely tire an old man, I suggest you return the favor."

Christopher extended his hand. It wobbled like a wheel about to fall off a cart and didn't stop wobbling until securely clasped in Thaddeus'.

"You look like your mother," he said mildly. "I loved her, you know. I don't expect you to forgive me but perhaps one day you will understand the choice I made."

Tight-lipped, Christopher looked at the man before him and nodded once, a slight motion that barely lifted his chin.

"This is a small gesture on my part," continued his father, gaze steady on Christopher, "a small attempt to rectify matters between us." He handed over a package bound with a leather thong.

Christopher recognized it; his mouth fell open.

"The deed to the ship your brother cheated you of. She belongs to you well and truly." A wry smile ghosted across his lips. "Both of them, I suppose. The "Bessie" and Josceline. She's a lovely girl and you are indeed a lucky man. She fought for you. Her love for you made her as strong as any soldier."

He lifted his walking stick and tapped it against the brim of his hat. Without a further word, he turned on his heel and strode away, his steps firm and steady against the stone floor. The gait of an important man, a man who knew he wielded power.

Christopher fought the urge to vomit. Hunger, he decided. It wasn't the emotion of the moments boiling in his belly, it was hunger. Choking back the bile, he watched the receding back of his father and felt-.

Nothing. He felt nothing.

Bemused, he shook his head. His father. A strange notion. The man had given him life and a means to earn a living but nothing else. He was a stranger to Christopher.

Still, Thaddeus had come through for him.

Sudden warmth flushed through Christopher and his forehead and groin dampened. He tossed his thoughts to Oliver and waited for the hatred and disdain to surge, waited for the envy to bubble to the surface, waited for the familiar feelings of inadequacy to squash him.

And none of it happened.

Peace descended on him like a shower of gentle spring rain. For once, his father had sided with him. His father had recognized the injustice dealt to Christopher and had done what he could.

With amazement, Christopher realized his half brother didn't matter anymore. The odd sensation made him feel naked and lost without the familiar emotions to cling to.

But now he could find new emotions to fill the void, emotions to build on. He could find stability in the love he felt for Josceline and the love she claimed she felt for him.

They had their ship.

They had Midland House.

They had a future.

He let out a whoop of joy and sprinted for the carriage and Josceline, clutching the deed in his hand.

Chapter Thirty

"I still say you should have rested another day," scolded Josceline. She glowered at Christopher sitting across the table from her in the morning room.

Sunlight filtered through the freshly laundered lace curtains, dappling his face and leaving a pattern on the crisp table linens. It promised to be a fine day and pleasure welled within her – spring had well and truly arrived.

He cocked a familiar eyebrow at her; a small smile hopped around the edges of his mouth. "There's nothing wrong with me, kitten. I've been flat on my back for two days and am bored silly. Besides, it was only four days in jail." He patted his midriff. "I vow, it doesn't hurt a man to lose a pound or two."

"I know just the thing." She leaned over the table to grab Christopher's plate then made her way to the sideboard. Lifting first one silver lid, then another, she finally decided on the thick slices of ham. She piled high his plate with them and threw in a spoonful of scrambled eggs for good measure.

With her back to him, she didn't see the indulgent look on Christopher's face as he watched her, or the growing heat in his eyes as he regarded her pert bottom when she leant over the sideboard.

His face was bland as she turned back to him.

She gave him a suspicious look as if to say: I know very well what you're thinking.

"Here." She plopped the plate down in front of him. "See that you gain them back. I should like my husband to have a little meat on his bones."

She didn't move away, just stood there with her fists on her hips. Christopher glanced up at her and flashed his most winning smile. A lock of hair, mahogany in the morning sun, curved across his forehead and his eyes twinkled with good humor.

He looked precisely like a naughty little boy caught with his hand in the sugared plums. She swallowed her laughter – it would do no good to let the man think he could wheedle her into having his way.

"That will not work, Mr. Sharrington," she said with mock severity although an answering smile tickled the corners of her mouth. She pointed to his plate. "Eat."

He rolled his eyes skyward. "I vow, Josceline, if I had known you were such a termagant, I would have thought twice about engaging you as my governess," he teased.

He pushed away the plate.

She pushed it back.

"Mr. Sharrington," she began again then squealed when he grabbed her around the waist and pulled her down onto his lap.

"Do you suppose if I kiss you thoroughly you will stop nagging me?"

"Really, Mr. Sharrington, where do you get these outlandish notions from?" She lifted her lips. "But if it will make you happy, please do so."

He dropped a quick kiss on her lips. "Count yourself lucky to get off so easily, Mrs. Sharrington," he whispered. "We have an audience."

Josceline giggled. "I suppose Philip and Tom are here?" She slid off his lap and adjusted her yellow and white striped frock.

She had worn it today at Christopher's request – he had told her she reminded him of sunshine that day she had visited him in Bristol Newgate. She turned to the door to find two pairs of blue eyes fastened on her. "You may come in, boys."

The two vaulted into the room at full speed and skidded to a halt in front of the sideboard.

"When are we leaving?" Philip asked, stepping from one foot to the other like a little mechanical soldier. "To see the sailing ship?" He turned to Christopher. "You promised you would take us, you promised."

Christopher laughed and the joyous sound sent thrills down Josceline's back. How he had changed. The haunted, angry look no longer lurked in his eyes and his mouth no longer pinched as if he was always wearing boots two sizes too small.

He hadn't told her yet about his encounter with Lord Thaddeus Candel but she knew he would tell her when he was ready to.

The most important thing, however, was his father giving him the papers to the "Bessie." How Christopher had cradled that package in one bent elbow all the way home; with the other arm, he had pulled her close, holding her so tightly to him he was worse than any corset she had ever worn. And she had loved every second of it.

Tom tugged on her sleeve. "Are you coming with us, Lady Josceline?" His little face beneath the tousled blonde curls was solemn. "I should really like you to come."

"Of course, Tom. I shan't let you fellows have all the fun."

Tedham poked his head in the door. "The carriage is ready, Mr. Sharrington." He held aloft a basket covered with a linen cloth. "Mrs. Belton sent this. She said two growing boys shall be hungry in no time."

"Splendid," Christopher nodded. "Shall we?" He got to his feet and pointed to the door.

"So thoughtful, please give her our thanks," Josceline murmured as she trailed behind them.

They piled into the carriage, with Philip and Tom insisting on sitting beside Josceline on the rear squabs.

"Mind you sit still and don't bother Lady Josceline," Christopher ordered. "If you don't, you shan't have pudding for lunch."

"We'll be good, we promise." Philip took command. "Tom, you must not sit too close to Lady Josceline or she shall break."

"Good heavens, I shan't break that easily." And she gathered the two of them close to her, wrapping her yellow shawl about them like a mother goose shepherding her goslings.

Christopher could scarce fathom the unfamiliar swell of love threatening to overcome him at the sight.

His eyes prickled with emotion and he had to blink several times before leaning back to regard the trio.

They regarded him back with equal intensity.

"Is aught amiss?" Josceline's brow wrinkled with concern.

"Nothing. Nothing at all." He leaned across to smooth away the furrows between her eyebrows then dropped his finger to trace the outline of her lips. She kissed the tip of it lightly before he pulled it away. He lifted that finger to his own mouth to kiss and blew it back at her.

"Ooooh." Philip grimaced. "Don't kiss. It's disgusting."

"Disgusting," echoed Tom.

"Not to worry, we'll behave," replied Christopher, ruffling a hand through Philip's hair. "Now let's play a game, shall we? Let us count all the horses we see between here and Bristol."

With the boy's attention diverted outside, he winked at Josceline. She responded with a mock frown then burst into laughter, blushing prettily at his steady regard.

He had every intention, he decided, of gazing at her the entire trip. That would make the journey to the harbor pass very pleasantly.

* * *

The "Bessie" floated tranquilly at her berth in the harbor. The tide was in; the gang plank lowered, ready for their visit.

"Mind you do not run on the gang plank," cautioned Christopher with a stern look to Philip and Tom. "We don't want you ending up in the river and floating out to sea. And mind, too, not to run on the deck. It could be slippery."

He waited a moment until the boys reached the ship proper before guiding Josceline ahead of him with a light hand on the small of her back.

"She's beautiful. Or as beautiful as I imagine a ship could be," breathed Josceline from her vantage point on deck between the first and second masts. She rotated slowly, blatantly taking in every detail.

Christopher could have swept her in his arms then and there for the interest she showed. Instead, he too, swept a prideful gaze over the vessel.

Three square rigged masts pierced the clouds skittering overhead; the furled sails looked like so many white sausages linked up on the cross bars. Wings of rigging fell from the mast tips and a waist high, solid planked railing enclosed the deck. Brass fittings glinted in the sun; coils of ropes lay neatly piled and two longboats flanked the main mast. The bowsprit pointed regally forward, held up by the carved figure of a woman, her smile forever frozen in wood.

"Bessie?" Josceline asked, pointing to the carved head just visible above the railing.

"Aye." Christopher nodded. The deck of fresh wood, not grey for it was not yet weathered, stood firm beneath his boots.

Pride swelled his chest and he looked to the stern. The ship's wheel stood alone in majestic splendor on the poop deck; his palms itched to grasp the oiled spokes, itched to feel the drag of the water as he pulled, itched to feel her respond. He was about to tug Josceline over to the wheel and show her how it worked but a sardonic voice stopped him.

He stiffened as if his spine had become a mast itself.

A cloud shifted and hid the sun; a sudden gust of wind ripped across the deck, mussing even further the already mussed hair of Philip and Tom.

Slowly, he turned his head.

To spy the foppish figure of Oliver Candel on the quay at the base of the gang plank.

"What are you about, Sharrington?" drawled Candel. "Come to inspect my property? And once you're finished," he added, bottom lip curled, "I should ask you to remove yourselves."

Christopher took one step forward. "I should ask the same of you. Remove yourself," he replied, face devoid of emotion. Inside, anger churned, turning his guts into a sour mass. He had thought Oliver vanquished. Had Thaddeus not told Oliver he had given the deed to Christopher?

Without invitation, Oliver minced his way up the plank and stalked to where Christopher and Josceline stood together. He raised a pomander, a clove-studded orange, to his nose in obvious insult. On tiptoe, he peered over Christopher's shoulder onto the poop deck. "Where's Captain Smythe?"

"I am the captain here now." Christopher spit out the words with contempt and fought the urge to knock the orange from Oliver's hand. Fought, too, the urge to unsheathe his knife from where it rested in its familiar spot inside his boot. "The "Bessie" belongs to me. If you don't believe me, here are the required papers." He unrolled them and pointed out his name. "I assume you can read?" he taunted. The roaring in his ears subsided somewhat when he saw Oliver blanch.

Oliver yanked the deed from Christopher's hand and scanned it then tossed the papers to Christopher's feet. "A forgery, I am certain. Don't think you shall get away with this, Sharrington," he hissed. "A word or two to my father and he'll reclaim this for the Candel Company. And toss you back in jail where you will soon hang for the thief you are."

"Your threats mean nothing to me, Oliver. The ship is rightfully mine as it always was. Your father saw to it that it would be so."

"What!" sputtered Oliver, "my father? You lie. My father knows nothing of this."

It was time to remove the smug expression on Oliver's face. How Christopher had waited, hoped, plotted for this moment.

"My father too," he said quietly, a steely edge to his words. "We share the same father. You cheated your own brother. You had your own brother clapped in irons. It was my father, our father who put things to rights."

Oliver reeled back, nostrils flared. "You're no brother to me," he sneered. "I renounce you as my brother." His voice rose. "I want nothing to do with you."

Christopher shrugged. "That suits me. You are a coward and a wastrel and I wish no kinship with you either."

"I'm not finished with you, Sharrington. No one gets the better of Oliver Candel."

"It appears I have," Christopher replied coolly. "Now." He stabbed Oliver's chest with one stiff finger. "Get." Stab. "Off." Stab. "My." Stab. "Ship."

Oliver blinked, disbelief filling his eyes. "Your ship," he repeated. Disdain flashed across his face. "You are welcome to it. The "Bessie" is shoddy workmanship at its best. The Candel Company is well rid of her."

Beside him, Josceline gasped. "We are well rid of you, Lord Candel," she said, voice taut. "Get off our ship."

"Hiding behind skirts again, are we, Sharrington?" Candel shook his head mockingly.

"Think what you will. We are finished here." Christopher felt Josceline move forward; he placed a warning hand on her arm. Together they held their ground.

"Indeed we are." Candel's face hardened. "Oh, such a dreary waste of time this has been." He turned on his heel and sauntered away. Attack me, his receding form seemed to say. Attack me and we shall see who comes out the better.

Christopher watched him leave, mouth quirked in annoyance. Lud, with any luck, he wouldn't cross paths with the man again. He chose not to think of him as his brother – they may share blood but it ended there. He wanted naught else from Lord Oliver Candel.

"I should like nothing better than to throw that odious man into the river," Josceline said indignantly.

Christopher chuckled at the vehemence in Josceline's voice. He pulled her in front of him so her back faced him and wrapped his arms around her midriff to rest his chin on the top of her head. "We're well rid of him. Nothing else matters."

"Hmmph." Her chest heaved with every breath.

"Nothing else matters," he repeated softly, rubbing his chin against her hair. "Only you and I and Sharrington Shipping."

"What did you call it?"

"Sharrington Shipping. Do you like it?"

"Of course." Josceline pulled away and whirled about to face him. "But I should like better a proper kiss from a proper scoundrel," she declared, mischief dancing in her eyes.

Christopher grinned, eye brow quirked in just that way she adored.

"Just a quick one to keep you happy," he suggested, face full of unspoken emotion. "We know how Philip and Tom detest kisses."

His eyes were warm and sweet, the color of hot chocolate. Josceline's heart lurched as he leaned towards her. Her head spun as his lips brushed against hers.

He nibbled on her lower lip, sucking it into his mouth. She felt him moan, a low rumble only she could sense. Her breasts tingled and she leaned into him, relishing the feel of his mouth on hers.

Regretfully, she pulled away. "Careful, the boys shall see us."

"If I recall, the kiss was your idea." He cocked his head to one side. "But I daresay you're in luck. The last I saw, they were climbing on the ship's wheel. They're doubtless too busy to give us a second thought."

"You're very patient with them." She loved him all the more for it. Her mother once told her the true value of a man was shown in how he treated children. And he treated the two boys very well even though no one would have thought ill of him for sending them back to St. Peter's once their usefulness to him was over.

He shrugged but didn't loosen his grip on her. "Because I know what it feels like to be alone."

His head lowered once more and once more she tasted him on her lips. She delighted in the flavor, licking with her tongue to taste even more.

Another thought intruded and Josceline pulled away again to cup her hands about his jaw. "What shall happen to them now?"

He sank his chin in her cupped hands. "I thought to give them the chance to sail with Sharrington Shipping. In a few years they are old enough to be cabin boys. They could work their way up much as I did."

"I can't bear them to leave. They were our little heroes."

He grasped her hands in his and stepped back to gaze at her fully. "They can stay on at Midland House as well," he replied quickly as if he didn't want her to have even a second of disappointment.

"Yes, we could engage a school master so they could finish their education," she mused. "That should lead them to law or the clergy or teaching."

"I cannot deny you anything, my love. If that is your wish, then it shall be so."

"Am I really?" she whispered, leaning her face into his chest. "Am I really your love?"

He tilted up her chin and stared in her eyes, his gaze so piercing that she literally felt it in her heart.

"You are my love," he whispered huskily. "Forever my love. My partner. My wife."

"And you are mine, Christopher," she answered joyfully. "Forever my love. My partner. My husband."

Thus they stood, gaze entwined with gaze, until footsteps scampered across the deck. Josceline stepped back to find two sets of blue eyes fastened on them; she giggled at their grave regard. "May I ask what is of such concern to you both?"

"We're hungry, may we go look in Mrs. Belton's basket? She told us she was going to send cake." Philip's voice was shrill with excitement.

"Cake," echoed Tom. "I should like some cake."

"Off you go then," laughed Christopher, holding out one hand to Josceline.

She tucked her hand securely into the warmth of his and hands clasped, they followed the two excited little boys into a future filled with promise for them all.

Epilogue
One year later

Christopher knew he would find Josceline in the garden. He rounded the gnarled plum and spotted her immediately, sitting on her favorite bench, eyes closed and face lifted to the sun, cloak pooled around her hips.

He stopped for a few moments to watch her sleep. The sun slipped in and out of the clouds like a round card being pulled in and out of an envelope, turning her hair from burnished copper to dull russet and back to burnished copper.

"I heard you," she said at length, sitting up. She wrinkled her nose at him. "You weren't quiet in the slightest." Then she giggled. "Rather, I would say you were very noisy."

He sauntered over and sank to his knees in front of her. "Not as noisy as Philip and Tom, I wager."

She giggled again. "I didn't know how noisy boys could be. They're in the stable. And as much as it pains me to admit it, yes, you're not nearly as noisy as those two."

Placing her hands beside her, she shifted her growing bulk, pushing away her cloak in the process.

"You're not cold?" He patted her very round belly.

"Cold," she hooted, green eyes sparkling. "I'm not cold. I have my own brazier. Ooof." She leaned back on one arm and straightened out a leg. "He's busy today."

"He? And why not a she?" He grinned and shoved back the lock of hair draped over his forehead.

"Because he never sleeps." Her expression turned serious. "How did you fare today in Bristol?"

Quiet excitement pulsed through him, matching the steady beat of his heart. How to tell her without disturbing her or the child she carried? He sat back on his heels and plucked a blade of new grass, jamming it into his mouth. He chewed on it for a minute or two, watching the hawks circling high overhead before he answered.

"She's almost home, Josceline. The "Bessie" is almost home."

Josceline sat up straighter. "When?" Anticipation colored her words; her lip twitched.

"She's been spotted by one of the other merchant ships. She made good time across the Atlantic and barring a storm, she'll be home safe and sound in three weeks."

A smile curved her lips and she reached forward to take his hand. "Wonderful. Two successful voyages in one year."

"Aye. It means our initial investors can be repaid. We shall be free of debt. We shall be able to buy our own cargo and go it alone from here on."

"And the Merchant Venturers?"

"The abolitionists grow stronger and I predict the slave trade is soon to be a thing of the past. Because of that, the Venturers are losing their importance. Now that Sharrington Shipping has demonstrated success, they're willing to include me even though I refuse to carry slaves." He rubbed his jaw. "To tell the truth, Josceline, we've made it so far without them. And once the floating harbor is built, there will be more room for ships and shipping traffic."

"So we follow our own path."

"Aye." His eyes crinkled. "A path of our own making."

Her gaze raked his face. "Are you sad you're not the "Bessie's" captain?"

"Never for a moment. I wouldn't miss this." He laid his hands reverently on her stomach and smiled up at her. "Besides, I have grown accustomed to the life of a married gentleman." Josceline returned his smile.

"I've been busy today." She held out a little cloth bundle tied up with a narrow blue velvet ribbon. "For you."

"For me?" His brow wrinkled as he took it; he held it between thumb and forefinger and looked at it with suspicion. "I vow, this looks like no gift I have ever received."

"No, I don't think it is."

Josceline held her breath while he pulled on the velvet bow. Would he pleased? Or would he be insulted?

The ribbon dropped off and the cloth bundle fell open leaving a bemused Christopher holding onto the corner of a handkerchief.

Why in blazes had she given him a handkerchief? Fitzsimmons the haberdasher had given him more than enough to last him for years.

He inspected it more closely to find the handkerchief freshly laundered and pressed. Then he unfolded it to see his name embroidered on it.

Realization cascaded through him.

It was the handkerchief he had given to a young woman in a carriage on a cold, dark winter night long ago. And she had returned it with all evidence of their initial encounter washed away.

Any lingering doubts he had harbored over their marriage and of his worthiness to her disappeared like spindrift flung from a bow.

He tipped back his head and laughed for sheer joy then held the handkerchief up to his nose to inhale her scent, the scent of violets and sandalwood.

"Do you like it?" she whispered, eyes tender upon him. "I forgot all about it but found it when the maids were cleaning the room for Elizabeth's visit."

His eyes grew moist. "It's the best gift ever. It's love and trust and loyalty all bundled up into one," he said huskily. "Just like you, kitten. Just like you."

The End

Author's Note

All characters are fictional although I do mention Mary Wollstonecroft, a proponent for women's education, and the English artist Thomas Girton.

St. Peter's Hospital, the Greyhound Inn, Broadmead, Redcliff, Clifton, Broad Street, Back Bridge Street are all actual places. Bath Road, where Christopher and Josceline first meet, was notorious for highwaymen so Josceline's accusations would have been correct.

I have a personal connection to Bristol – my brother's wife and my critique partner are both Bristolians. It seemed like a good setting for a book, particularly in light of Christopher's nautical background.

Bristol has always been a thriving port and because of its location on the west coast, its importance increased with the growth of the colonies in the West Indies and North America. However, its position inland on the Avon River meant the harbor was severely affected by tides. As a result, the river could be too crowded with ships trying to reach or leave Bristol. Regularly, tides were not high enough (neap tides) and ships could be stranded for weeks in the harbor itself or at the mouth of the Avon River. Also, at low tide all the ships in the harbor went aground and fire was a very real risk. To that end, a floating harbor was proposed to alleviate these concerns. It was completed in 1809.

Christopher chose not to carry slaves on the "Bessie." During the 18th century, however, Bristol was heavily involved in the slave trade. Goods such as woolen cloth, brass and iron were bartered in Africa in exchange for slaves who were then transported to the West Indies or North America. They were sold for tobacco, sugar, rum and cotton which were then transported back to Bristol. The route formed a triangle. The slave trade was abolished in 1807.

Christopher mentions several times the Society of Merchant Venturers. It was incorporated in 1552 to protect the interests of the merchants of Bristol, and effectively controlled the port.

About the Author

From Vikings to viscounts, join the adventure, live the romance.

Living by the motto "You don't know unless you try", A.M.Westerling started writing historical romance because she couldn't find the kinds of stories she enjoyed. After all, she thought, who doesn't enjoy a tasty helping of dashing heroes and spunky heroines, seasoned with a liberal sprinkle of passion and adventure?

Westerling, a former engineer, is a member of the Romance Writers of America and active in her local chapter. As well as writing, she enjoys cooking, gardening, camping, yoga, and watching pro sports.

Visit her at:
http://www.amwesterling.com
www.facebook.com/A.M.Westerling
www.Twitter.com/AMWesterling

Note from the Publisher

Thank you for purchasing and reading this Books We Love Book. We hope you have enjoyed your reading experience. Books We Love and the author would very much appreciate you returning to the online retailer where you purchased this book and leaving a review for the author. *Best Regards and Happy Reading, Jamie and Jude*

21681773R00184

Made in the USA
Charleston, SC
26 August 2013